To En

BIKE SHED

BULLY HUNTERS

NATHANIEL TOMLINSON

Published by Nathaniel Tomlinson

Printed by Book Printing UK www.bookprintinguk.com
Remus House, Coltsfoot Drive, Peterborough, PE2 9BF

Printed in Great Britain

ISBN 978-0-9935153-0-9

This book is dedicated to my life, my wife…my personal Bully Hunter.

Aisha **ELISE** Tomlinson (Formerly **WALKER**)

Prologue

As the rain pummelled the ground, the hooded figure stood there, not moving, just waiting for the bell to ring. He tightened his grip on the belt wrapped around his fist, took a few deep breaths, and looked at the clock across the street above the town square building.

It was 15:03. There were two minutes left. The hooded boy reached into his pocket and felt the sand inside. One minute left. He looked at the belt, positioning the buckle over his knuckles, and waited. Finally, the bell rang, leaving an empty silence in its wake. He could feel his heart rate increase. His muscles tightened, and his breathing became more laboured.

The doors opened, releasing the school kids, who poured out, like rats from a sinking ship. The hooded boy walked forward, disappearing into the swarm of children.

'Get out of my way you little prat!' resounded the thunderous voice of James Grainger, as he exited the school.

James was twelve, but he had the build and voice of a twenty two year old. His face was covered in stubble, and his fists were the size of melons. He was known across three boroughs, from

Hillingdon to Brent, as was his brother before him, and his Dad before that. A rumour had circulated that James' grandfather had kept James' father out of school until he was seven, then enrolled him into nursery, to ensure that he would always be bigger than everyone else; an attempt to stop him from getting bullied. It seemed that James' father had done the same to him.

The crowd parted as James pushed a boy onto the floor, who slid at least five metres before finally coming to a stop. James looked around at all the kids watching.

'What you all looking at? Move, before I move you!'

The crowd jumped as if they'd all been shocked by the same current, and continued on their way. The only person still motionless was the hooded boy, who now appeared to be fairly small, compared to some of the children that passed him. He looked like a rock parting a river, as the children shuffled around him. The hooded boy stared straight at James, taking deep, controlled breaths, whilst clutching onto the belt.

'Didn't you hear what I said? Move!' ordered James, confused by the fact that he had to repeat his instruction. James had never had to say anything twice, even to a teacher.

'Maybe he's deaf James?' said one of James' lackeys. 'Yeah, maybe you should punch some hearing into his head.'

'Would you like that? You want this fist inside your skull?'

James edged towards the figure.

The hooded boy reached into his pocket, grabbed a handful of sand, looked up at James.... and smiled.

Autumn Term

1

Jermaine Pearson

The first day of secondary school was a lot less stressful for Jermaine than most of the other children in year seven, as he'd grown accustomed to being the new kid at school. He had been to five different primary schools between Year 3 and 4 alone, as his mum constantly moved him, his brother and his two sisters, for multiple reasons, mainly in an attempt to stay one step ahead of the debt collectors.

This, not surprisingly, caused Jermaine to be a bit of a lone soul, as well as 'odd', as the other kids liked to put it. He could speak to people when he needed to, but tended to be more of an observer. Funnily enough, his favourite characters in the Marvel comics were always the Watchers in the 'What if' issues he'd found in a box his dad had left behind when he moved away.

Jermaine walked through the front gates, whilst scratching his head through the small afro he had grown over the summer holidays. His mum couldn't afford to send him to the barbershop that month. There were not many months when she could. He adjusted the bag on his back, looked around, then pulled up his trousers, which were still too big for him, mainly because they were not bought to fit him; they weren't bought for him at all. Jermaine was the third child of four. He had an older brother and sister who were both in college, as well as a younger sister in year 5. As his older brother was 18 years old, this made his clothes perfect for hand-me-downs.

Jermaine had been subjected to this his entire life. In Year 4, Jermaine had torn the sole of his shoes, whilst playing football. His mum gave him his brother's old Adidas trainers, which were two sizes too big for Jermaine. When he contested wearing them, his mum had said,

'Wha ya mean you don warnt it? Tek wha ya given bwoi, ya shud be grateful ya hav anyting to put pun ya foot an don walk like them yute them in Africa who wud kill fe them shoe der!'

Jermaine decided not to argue with her, as he could just about make out what she had said. He had always found it hard to understand what his mum was saying when she was angry, and reverted back into patois. He could get a slight grasp of what most Jamaicans were saying, but found that they all spoke too quickly for him.

Even though his family were from Jamaica, Jermaine had never been there. He wasn't a fan of traditional Jamaican food either; he'd always preferred fish and chips. He also never really enjoyed the summer, he felt it was too hot; his favourite seasons were autumn and spring, as he could walk in the rain, which he had a strange fondness of doing. His mother had always called him a "real English bwoi", as if it was a negative thing, but Jermaine was quite proud of this fact.

Walking through the school, towards his form class, Jermaine looked at all the children towering above him. The abundance of adults walking around the school, and the general sound created from the sheer mass of people, all heading to their separate destinations was overwhelming. Jermaine felt lost within the crowd, but took comfort in the feeling of the weight of the books in his rucksack. The thought that he had a book for each subject in his bag, especially the thick textbooks, made him feel content. He loved to read.

Although he had a sporadic start to life, this didn't seem to effect Jermaine's education, or general fondness for learning. Any time he was out of school, he would watch the educational programs that came on, early in the morning, on the Discovery channel, which is probably why he was so good at science. He also read as many books as he could get his hands on, which wasn't hard, as he would borrow them from the school libraries, and always leave before he could give them back.

Whilst walking past a group of older boys, standing near a toilet door beside the boys' gym; their hoods covering their eyes, Jermaine remembered the horror stories he had heard about secondary school from the kids in his last Year 6 class. He had anticipated there being a few teething problems when he first arrived, and therefore decided that, in order for him to learn the skills to make it through secondary school, he would need to ask his older brother to give him some essential tips about secondary life.

The night before his first day, Jermaine approached his brother. He never really listened to anything Anton told him, as he wasn't the 'sharpest tool in the shed', as his mum had always put it, but he couldn't deny that Anton did have a decent grasp on how to carry himself on the streets, which he guessed could also be translated into school.

'No worries. I can tell you the rules to surviving secondary bruv,' started Anton, a look of severity on his face, 'first things first; you find the biggest guy in there and start a fight with him. Even if you get your butt handed to you on a plate, you'll be sending a message to everyone that you aren't scared of anything!'

Jermaine looked at his brother and thought that he'd ignore this bit of advice, not because he couldn't fight; with an older brother who hoped to be heavyweight champion of the world one day,

Jermaine knew how to throw a punch. He definitely knew how to take one. Jermaine just didn't see the necessity in getting into a fight with anyone. He probably wouldn't be at the school for very long, and no one ever really paid much attention to him in the first place.

'Next thing you need to know,' continued Anton, 'Learn the layout of the playground. There are certain places you can go, and certain places you can't.'

Anton placed a finger against the corner of his mouth, believing this made him look more thoughtful. It didn't. He pondered for a moment.

'Hmm, I don't know much about St Peter's... actually, there is one thing I've heard, and that's to stay away from the bike shed. Not a good place to be walking around, some...unsavoury characters near there, if you know what I mean. I'd just steer clear.'

Anton concluded by saying, 'the final thing is, you don't tell the teachers anything, and I mean *anything*! I don't care if there's a boy trying to set fire to your trousers every day, you keep that to yourself and deal with it. If you can't deal with it, you come to me. I know a thing or two about dealing with the odd bully,' Anton said, throwing a few jabs into the air, in an attempt to demonstrate his fighting ability.

'Thanks Anton, pearls of wisdom there, we should ask the school to put that on a plaque at the front entrance.'

Anton waited a second, with a confused look on his face, as if he was working out if Jermaine was being sarcastic. After a few moments of deep concentration, Anton jabbed Jermaine clean in the chest.

'Whatever, don't know why I'm telling you any of this anyway, you're gonna be worm food till you get some real muscles on those bones,' said Anton, as he flexed his biceps, smirked, and walked towards the door. 'I'm gonna play some COD when I get back from the gym, so your scrawny butt better be off the PlayStation before then.'

Jermaine was actually an average sized, eleven-year-old boy. Anton always treated him as if he was a weed; to Anton most people were weeds. Anton would constantly advise Jermaine to lift weights with him, but Jermaine would always find a way to avoid it. He did go jogging around the park, and participate in Anton's press up and sit up routines however, as he found them to be quite fun.

*

The first week of secondary school went just as Jermaine had expected it to go. He didn't get into any groups, he didn't really want or know how to. He kept himself to himself, went to lessons, and tended to stand on the side-lines, watching the other kids.

Through his expansive experience of change, compounded with the advice from Anton, Jermaine knew that the key to dealing with this new school was to establish as high a level of familiarity with his new surroundings as he possibly could.

On the first day, each Year 7 class were given a tour of the school. Most of the pupils used this time to chat, reinforcing their newly found friendship groups. Jermaine however, paid attention to the location of everything his form tutor mentioned.

Once the tour had finished, Jermaine had a clear image of the school etched into his mind. He used the playground as a centre point, as that was where the kids entered the school in the mornings. At the far end of the playground were the DT rooms, which he looked forward to entering. The thought of using a saw and drill seemed exciting. Above the DT rooms was the lunch hall. Jermaine considered eating in there on the first day, then swiftly changed his mind.

Beyond the DT rooms stood the languages block, which overlooked the football pitch and basketball courts, if you could call them that. Jermaine didn't think that a hoop attached to a wall constituted as a basketball court. Finally, there was the cage, aptly named, as it was a small rectangle surrounded by a fence. The purpose of this cage was unclear, but it had been adopted as a secondary football pitch, with less rules.

To the right of the playground were the Maths and Science blocks. Jermaine's form class was on the second floor of the Maths block. Jermaine thought that he was quite lucky to be placed there, as the journey to the playground was so short.

Beyond these blocks, on its own, stood the Humanities building. For some reason, this building was detached from everywhere else, as if it were less important, or not regarded as part of the school. Parallel to the Humanities building, and positioned at the opposite end of the sports grounds, were the P.E gyms. There was one for the girls and one for the boys. Past the gyms laid the green expanse of the fields.

Looking at the layout of the school, Jermaine could see which subjects were considered to be more important. The Science, Maths and Language blocks were at least double the size of the ICT and Media block, which only took up a small area, that looked freshly attached to the side of the Science block.

Taking the advice of Anton, Jermaine created a mental map of the territories of the playground. He noticed that the cage belonged to the Year 9 boys. The occasional Year 7 would make the mistake of strolling in there, expecting to play football, and would find themselves as a target for a game of nutmeg rush. The bottom of the stairs, which were beside the lunch hall, were the property of the Year 10 girls, who didn't much like people walking through their conversations, making getting to the playground after lunch a hassle for anyone but the Year 10s or above. The benches between the sports grounds and the field were completely off limits to anyone in school uniform, as they were the hangout spot of the sixth formers.

One of the places that Jermaine had seen, but didn't spend much time observing, was the bike shed Anton had warned him about. As he walked in through the gate, Jermaine would see it everyday. Being situated right next to the gate, it was quite hard for him to ignore. It looked more like a bike rank than a shed, as it had loads of hoops, which people could lock their bikes onto, but no wood enclosing it, as you would expect to see when you heard the word 'shed'. It did, however, have a wooden back and a glass covering over it. Jermaine figured that 'Bike Shed' was just a turn of phrase that had stuck, so he used it.

Every now and again, Jermaine would see a pair of Year 8s and 9s disappear behind the bike shed, and then reappear a few minutes later, looking shaken but strangely reassured. Jermaine noticed that these kids weren't always wearing St Peter's school uniform, which he found bizarre. The teachers, however, did not seem to pay any attention to this. Jermaine considered that this was probably due to the fact that they didn't want the hassle of writing up an incident sheet for catching children who weren't supposed to be in the school. He assumed his brother had got the wrong end of the stick, regarding the shed, and thought nothing more about it.

2

Sean Buckley

As the second week of school came to an end, Jermaine hadn't made any real acquaintances and began to get very bored during break and lunchtime. This was until the following Monday. Whilst seated on a wall, outside the boy's gym, he noticed a boy that he had never seen before. This boy was one of those children you really expected to get picked on, just by the look of him. He was a small, ginger haired boy, who looked as if he hadn't grown at all since Year 4. He wore glasses, which were too big for his face, trousers too short for his legs, and unfortunately for him, the only thing that let you know he had begun to hit puberty, was his affliction of acne.

For some reason, Jermaine couldn't help but watch this boy for the remainder of that week. He made an educated guess that this boy was also in Year 7. Jermaine had observed many Year 7s, who it seemed; either didn't have an older sibling to show them the ropes, or just paid no attention to their surroundings. This boy, however, seemed to be worse at life in secondary school than any other person

Jermaine had seen. He watched him make mistake, after mistake, after mistake.

On the first lunch period of Jermaine's surveillance, he spotted the boy going into the cage, and then exit, covered in footprints. He observed the boy walk past the Year 10 girls, at the bottom of the stairs beside the lunch hall, and have to walk around the rest of the day with multiple pieces of half-chewed chewing gum in his hair. Most surprisingly, Jermaine even watched him walk past the 'Spitters'; a group of boys who collected straws from the local take-away restaurant and spat rolled up, saliva covered, pieces of the wrappers at anyone who happened to walk past the DT rooms. Even the most unaware of pupils knew to stay clear of them. The boy spent the last few minutes of that lunch break picking wet pieces of paper out of his blazer, whilst trying to get the gum out of his hair.

The week continued like this. To Jermaine, it was like seeing a train wreck. He didn't enjoy what he saw, but it was so mesmerising, that he couldn't fight the urge to watch. Even though Jermaine felt sorry for the boy, he told himself that there was no point in helping him; he probably wasn't going to be around long enough to be a friend to him, he didn't even know how to be a friend, so why tease him with the prospect?

The following Monday, Jermaine was sat on the same wall by the boy's gym, which he frequented, when he spotted the boy again.

He was walking across the playground, a wary look on his face. He looked straight at Jermaine, who looked away and continued eating his sandwich.

From the corner of his eye, Jermaine watched the boy. When he'd walked a few steps away Jermaine looked directly at him. At that moment, he realised that the boy was about to make the number one, cardinal sin a Year 7 could make; he was walking over to one of the free benches beside the field and was about to take a seat. Jermaine wasn't aware what he was doing...until he was doing it. He had kicked himself off the wall, and was charging towards the boy. He pushed himself as hard as he could to reach him before he became a pink smudge on the floor, and a fleeting part of Jermaine's memory. Whether it was out of the goodness of his heart, his loneliness, which he hadn't quite admitted to himself yet, or that part of people that can't see a whimpering dog without wanting to give it a home and some food, Jermaine needed to help the kid.

The Year 7 boy was about to place his bum on the last seat in his life, when Jermaine grabbed him by the arm, and pulled him away from the bench. The boy squirmed as Jermaine pulled him away from his inevitable doom. Once a few steps away, he let him go.

'Ow! You hurt my arm!' cried the boy, with a deep Irish accent, not realizing how close to a constant stream of hospital food he was.

Jermaine looked across at the sixth formers, who were intently watching the boys, as they walked away from the benches.

'You seriously don't want to sit there. You need to pay more attention around here. This place is a living death trap, and you seem to be walking into all of them willingly,' said Jermaine, trying to flatten out his sandwich so he could finish his lunch.

'What's wrong with this place, I can't even sit on a bench?' The Year 7 looked back at the sixth formers. As he turned around, he noticed Jermaine was already walking away, 'Hey?'

'Look,' Jermaine turned, looked at the boy, and said sternly, 'don't get the wrong idea; we're not friends now, I just couldn't watch you take a beating, that's all.'

'Well, you're the only person who's actually done something nice for me here. Everyone else has tried to either embarrass, or beat the snot out of me,' said the boy, as he shuffled awkwardly on his feet, 'my name's Sean, Sean Buckley. What's your name?'

Jermaine looked at Sean, rolled his eyes, and continued to walk away.

'Well, you seem to know the rules of this place. Why don't you just, at least, show me the ropes? If you don't, you may as well let me go and take a seat on that bench and be done with it now!'

Looking at the bald patches in Sean's hair, from where he had to get the gum cut out, Jermaine knew he was right. At this rate, he wasn't going to last the rest of the week. The bell for the end of lunch rang. Jermaine began to walk away, and looked over his shoulder at Sean.

'Tomorrow at break, meet me by the water fountain; just don't walk down the stairs near the hall again. You haven't got any hair left for the girls to put gum in.' Jermaine wondered what he was getting himself into.

*

The next day started for Jermaine as it always did. He woke up earlier than the rest of his family, so he could get into the shower first. He then had his bi–weekly argument with his sister Simone, who started college early on Tuesday and Thursday, but never woke up early enough to beat him into the bathroom. Jermaine left the house with a piece of half toasted bread, covered in peanut butter, and began his journey to school.

When Jermaine arrived at school, he went to registration, and sat in his seat. He had chosen a seat in the same position, in every classroom he went into. He had made sure that on the first lesson of each class, he would get there early, in order to strategically place himself. He always sat in the second row, to the far right. His logic was based on the knowledge that most teachers were right handed, which meant that they would stand with their left arm towards the board, so that they could reach in and use it. This enabled him to stay as far away from the teacher as possible, without looking as if he wanted to. This, amazingly, reduced the amount of times he was asked any questions in front of the class. He could probably answer most of them, without any issue, he just didn't like talking in front of a group.

First and second period had passed, and then, with five minutes till break, Jermaine remembered what had happened the day before. He wasn't actually against helping Sean, he was just against talking to anyone he didn't have to. He'd established his own little world, within which he could conduct his day-to-day tasks, without any problems. Whenever he included other people, problems always revealed themselves to him.

At break, he stood across the playground, watching Sean standing by the water fountain for a couple of minutes. He considered the fact that he could easily avoid Sean for the rest of the time he was in the school, leaving the boy to learn things the hard way, just like all the other Year 7s. The only thing that made him begin walking towards the fountain was something that his Dad had said to him; one of the few things he remembered his Dad saying to him:

'A man is only as good as his word Jermaine. If you tell someone you'll do something, whether it's something you still want to do or

not, you follow through with it. Many people believe we are measured by the things we have, or the people we know, but it's not the things we have, it's the things we do that defines us.'

Once he reached the water fountain, Jermaine looked sternly into Sean's eyes and declared to him, 'There are rules to surviving in secondary school. Firstly, and most importantly, you need to pay attention to your surroundings, know where you can go and where you can't. That's what I'm looking to help you with today. Make sure you pay close attention to what I say, and show you, as I don't intend to give you this advice more than once.'

Sean looked intently at Jermaine, a strange look of admiration in his eyes, as if he was looking at the idol he'd been searching for, his entire eleven years of life.

'Secondly,' continued Jermaine, 'never tell a teacher if someone is troubling you. I don't care if the kid is trying to set light to your trousers in Science every day, you keep that to yourself and find your own way of sorting out the issue.' Looking at Sean, Jermaine thought this was probably bad advice to give to the little kid. He didn't know if he had an older brother who could help him with his problems. He scratched his head and said, 'actually, you might want to forget that one. I think you may need help from the teachers.'

Jermaine thought back to his conversation with Anton. He decided not to waste time mentioning his brilliant idea about fighting the biggest kid in school; Sean probably couldn't take on the smallest. He also decided not to talk about the bike shed, it seemed like an irrelevant bit of information to him. The bell for the end of break chimed, and Sean looked noticeably disappointed.

'Are you school dinners or packed lunch?' asked Jermaine.

'School dinners.'

'Hmm, I'd advise you to avoid the hall if possible, place is like a zoo. I'll meet you outside the hall at 12:45. If you're late, I'm leaving.'

'Ok, I'll be there,' said Sean, with an acre wide smile across his face, making him look like an even larger target than before, 'Thank you… I still don't know your name.'

'It's irrelevant. Just make sure you're there,' Jermaine said, as he turned and walked into the crowd of children.

*

Jermaine stood at the hall doors, looking into the chaos that was 'school dinners'. He was entitled to a free meal, as his mum was on benefits, but decided not to take it, for two main reasons: one, he didn't like taking anything he hadn't earned himself somehow, and two, the hall was a death trap. Kids had food stolen from them, if there were any nice things like cake with icing and sprinkles. Seats were taken by brute force if there were none available. As all the teachers were eating their own lunch in the staff room, the small amount of order that did exist in the school, was completely null and void.

As he was about to walk away from the door he noticed one set of sixth formers sitting at a table, at the end of the hall, on the stage. There was a pair of slim twins, who by the size of their legs, looked to be quite tall. They had long blonde hair, making it hard for Jermaine to distinguish whether they were male or female. There was also an extremely pretty, but very serious looking girl with a short bob that looked to have been shaved on one side. Jermaine noticed what looked like dark makeup on the left side of her face, but he couldn't be sure at the distance he was from her. Next to her was a large boy, with a full head of curly hair, wearing glasses, stuffing his face with a slice of pizza.

Finally, in the centre of the group was a boy standing up, surveying the hall. He looked like a Year 7 or 8 pupil, pretending to be in sixth form. He was no more than a few inches taller than Jermaine, according to his estimation, with what looked like a scar on his left cheek, and a scary looking scowl on his face. After a few moments, Jermaine realised that this boy was staring straight at him.

For some reason, a strange sense of fear travelled through him. Something about the look in his eyes, a sense of self-confidence, made Jermaine feel very uncomfortable. Abruptly, he averted his gaze and stepped away from the door.

3

Toilet Troubles

Jermaine waited until he saw the minute hand on the clock above the doors land on 46, and then turned to leave, when he heard someone burst out of the doors of the hall. He turned to see Sean standing there, sweat dripping down his forehead, crumbs covering his face.

'We haven't got much time, and there's a lot to see,' said Jermaine, fighting a wry smile from his face.

The two boys travelled from one side of the school to the other. Jermaine pointed out all the major details to keep Sean out of harm's way, throwing in the odd comment like, 'Here's a good spot to watch the Year 11 girls playing netball, if you're into that sort of thing,' and 'If you ever want to leave school to go to the shops, there's a hole in the fence over there, just don't get caught.'

Sean was writing as much of the information he could into a notebook, which he had produced out of his back pocket, so he wouldn't forget anything.

Jermaine pretty much covered the whole school in his crash course, and had arrived back at the gym, where the tour began, when Sean asked if he was permitted a toilet break. Jermaine agreed to this, considering that Sean had been subtly jumping on the spot for the last ten minutes.

After waiting for Sean for a few minutes, Jermaine noticed people rushing towards the toilets that Sean had just left towards. A feeling in his stomach made him feel like something was wrong. He ran to the toilet, and saw Sean standing up against a wall with three Year 10 boys surrounding him.

'Didn't I say jump?' demanded one of the boys. He was the biggest of the three, with a Mohican haircut and an ear spacer in his left ear. Sean whimpered against the wall and jumped. Jermaine charged over and pushed himself between the boys and Sean.

'Leave him alone,' Jermaine demanded.

'Who are you talking to? Who do you think you are telling me what to do?' replied the Mohican boy, prodding Jermaine in his shoulder.

Jermaine looked at his shoulder, then back at the boy. 'I'm not trying to tell you what to do.'

'Well then stay out of it! That boy stepped on my trainers. Do you know how much these cost? He's gonna have to pay me back for them,' the Mohican boy explained.

'I'm sure it was just an accident, which he's really sorry about,' Jermaine looked at Sean when he said this, trying to let him know he should be apologising.

'Ye...yeah, v...very sorry!' stammered Sean

'You see? Just cut him some slack.'

As Jermaine said this, the small crowd had begun to grow into a larger one, every person wanting to see what the commotion was about. Jermaine was kicking himself for not paying closer attention. Since the first day of school, he knew to stay clear of the toilets beside the gym. The boys there seemed highly-strung, ready to release their hormonal anger at the first opportunity. The Year 10 boys looked at each other and then laughed.

'Go on Dean, cut him some slack,' the fattest of the Year 10 boys said in a sarcastic tone, to the Year 10 with the Mohican, 'why don't we cut *everyone* some slack, why don't we just let everyone step on our feet?'

'Look, you little toad, these cost me money, and now they're ruined, so he pays,' Dean replied, this time prodding Jermaine even harder on his shoulder.

Looking at his shoulder again, Jermaine made a fist with his right hand.

'Touch me again and you'll regret it for a week,' he responded through gritted teeth.

The crowd began to grow larger as this conversation continued. In the back of the crowd, the small sixth former from the lunch hall walked past, along with the two tall twins. He saw the commotion and noticed Jermaine in front of Sean, with his fist clenched, and a look of rage building up on his face. He stopped, and leaned against the wall to watch, with a twin on either side of him. A girl, standing immediately in front of the sixth former, noticed he was there and moved out of the way. She then touched a boy in front of her, and whispered something into his ear. He then turned with a look of horror in his eyes, and stepped to one side, touching the boy in front of him. This continued until the small boy had a tunnel leading from him, to the altercation between Jermaine and the Year 10s.

Dean looked at his two friends, and they all laughed uncontrollably for a while. Dean then reached out and pushed Jermaine on the shoulder, saying, 'Mr tough guy, what are you going to...ughhh!!'

Jermaine swung a right hook right into Dean's left oblique; then followed it with three more in quick succession. Dean keeled over, out of breath, shock covering his face. Jermaine grabbed Sean by the scruff of his collar, threw him into the crowd and shouted, 'RUN!' He then turned back around, to face the other two Year 10 boys who were still staring at Dean on the floor, completely gob smacked at what had just happened.

Dean looked up at them, tears gathering in his eyes. The two boys returned their attention to Jermaine, who was standing in a fighting pose, his back planted firmly against the wall, left foot planted firmly on the ground in front him. The fatter Year 10 boy charged at Jermaine, and received a punch to the stomach, which didn't seem to faze him. He wrapped his arms around Jermaine, and pulled him away from the wall.

The other Year 10, who wore a cap on over his hood, threw punch, after punch into Jermaine's back. Jermaine couldn't free himself from the bear hug he was in, so he lifted his right foot into the air, slamming it down onto the fat Year 10 boys left foot.

The fat boy lifted his foot, letting out a yelp; this also caused him to loosen his grip slightly. This proved to be enough for Jermaine to get his arms free. He grabbed the fat boy by the sides, wrapped his left leg around the boy's right one, and threw himself forward with all the force he had, throwing them both to the ground. The soft stomach of the Year 10 cushioned Jermaine's fall.

Starting to recover, Dean stood up. Both he and the cap-hood wearing Year 10, began to rain kicks down on Jermaine. The only thing Jermaine could do was try to avoid them hitting him in the face and his privates. Jermaine curled up into a foetal position as the capped Year 10 threw a kick at his stomach. He then, in a last act of desperation, grabbed hold of the boy's leg, and sunk his teeth into the boy's calf, as deep as he could. The boy let out a scream that caused the crowd to burst into a paroxysm of laughter.

A second later the crowd started to run like insects from underneath a rock. The deep voice of a teacher could be heard amongst the commotion.

'What's going on here? Break it up! You! Get away from him this instant!' ordered Mr Matthews.

Mr Matthews grabbed both Dean and the cap wearing Year 10, pinning them up against the wall. He reached down and picked Jermaine up off the floor, dusting off his clothes as he did it. Jermaine let out a wince as the teacher touched one of the many places he was sore after the beating. As he looked around, Jermaine saw that there were only a few stragglers left from the crowd that had formed, all looking as if they were minding their own business. The only person paying any attention to him was the short sixth former, who was staring straight at him. He wasn't blinking or moving a muscle, just staring, like a statue, or a soldier.

The image of the sixth former resembled that of a king, the twins on either side of him, as if they were his knights. The severity of the sixth former's stare reinstated the fear Jermaine had felt outside the lunch hall. A desire to sink his head into the earth came over him as he walked past the sixth former. He lowered his head in order to avoid the gaze as much as he possibly could.

4

Calling Card

Mr Matthews escorted Jermaine, and the Year 10s, to the office of the deputy head teacher, Miss Faring. Jermaine sat outside and heard the barrage of shouting, always followed by a quiet, 'Yes Miss'. He sat there, looking at the fish tank, wondering how it sounded to them through the water, and how many times he was going to be seeing them this year.

Jermaine was never a boy to cause trouble, but for some reason or another, he would always end up in a fight. The prominent cause tended to either be because he was the new kid, or because he was helping out some poor sod that couldn't defend him or herself.

As Jermaine was contemplating his sad existence; feeling extremely sorry for himself, Sean popped his head around the corner. He looked at Jermaine, who, in return, scowled at him. Sean then retreated back around the corner. After a minute or two, Sean walked up and sat next to Jermaine with his head held low.

'I'm sorry you had to get into trouble because of me. I didn't mean for that to happen. I know I'm useless, always have been,' said Sean, with tears falling from his face.

Jermaine was still sore and could feel his anger bubbling inside him, but as he looked at the wet spots on Sean's trousers, from where the tears had landed, he began to feel sorry for him. He knew it wasn't Sean's fault. He even considered the fact that he hadn't actually asked Jermaine to defend him.

'Tomorrow, if I don't get suspended, I'll finish showing you the ropes. Just keep your head down until then,' Jermaine said, resting his hand on Sean's back.

Sean looked up at Jermaine, his face wet with tears. He smiled, stood up and walked to the door. He looked back at Jermaine. 'Thank you,' he said, and then walked away.

The door to Miss Faring's office opened after a few minutes. Dean and the other two Year 10 boys exited, glanced at Jermaine, and walked away. All except the capped boy, who hobbled, as his leg was still hurting from the bite he'd received.

'Mr Pearson, could you come in here please,' called the voice of Miss Faring, from inside her office.

Jermaine stood up. Looking at the fish, he wished he could switch positions with them for the next half hour. Then he thought about what his mum was going to say, and changed his mind. The rest of his life would be a better length of time.

'Jermaine Pearson, it's not very often I get a Year 7 in my office before Christmas. Are you hurt?'

'No, I'll be fine, thank you,' answered Jermaine, trying to hide the pain throbbing in his left leg.

'Now, Dean, Paul and Kel are repeat offenders here in this school, so they've been suspended for a week each. I don't know you as of yet Jermaine, so I'm going to give you the benefit of a doubt that you didn't start this. You won't be suspended, but there will be an e-mail sent to your mother, as well as a letter,'

These were the words Jermaine was dreading. A letter home was as bad as a suspension in his house. The rest of the conversation was the usual warnings, and 'I'll be watching you' comments he received after getting in trouble.

Jermaine left the office, and walked down the hall to his final period. He didn't pay much attention to the PSHE lesson, as the letter was playing on his mind. He went through all the different possibilities to rectify the situation he was now in. None of the ideas he had were any good. He knew that schools expected a return slip, to ensure parents received the letters and they didn't just end up in the bin.

After the lesson, Jermaine made his way to his form class. He spotted a Year 8 boy stood beside the door to the classroom, looking around at the faces of the children, and as Jermaine walked past him, he held out his hand with a card in it.

'This is for you, you'd better take it,' said the boy, forcing the card into Jermaine's hand.

Jermaine looked at the card that had the letters 'BSBH' in bold on the front. On the back was a message that read, '*Tomorrow, break, behind the shed.*' He looked back towards the boy, but the kid had disappeared amongst the other people in the corridor. Jermaine sat through registration, looking at the card, wondering what it could mean, as the bell rang.

5

Face-To-Face

Earlier than usual, Jermaine left his house, closing his front door quietly behind him, in an attempt to avoid waking anyone up. He thought it best to keep as low a profile as possible after the previous night. His mum had received the letter, which had been sent that evening by e-mail. Jermaine then received a lecture from: his mum, his older brother (which he thought was seriously hypocritical, as he was always getting into trouble when he was at school) his sister, his uncle (who called to have a quick word) and even his grandparents, who called to speak to him over the phone...from Jamaica. They all seemed extremely disappointed in him.

Jermaine kept quiet throughout the two and a half hours of advice and tales of past mistakes. He didn't do the usual thing of saying it wouldn't happen again; he did that all the time, and it always happened again.

Once he arrived at school, Jermaine walked past the bike shed that now, strangely, had a whole new look to it. There seemed to be a new, ominous aura surrounding it. *'Why didn't I feel this before?'*, he wondered, as he walked further into the school.

Normally, Jermaine arrived at school for 8:15am, which is quite early for most children, but not the teachers. He would usually see them rushing around with photocopying, and setting up for their first lessons with a steaming flask of coffee in their hands, as they prepared themselves for the onslaught to come. He arrived at school for 7:35am that day, and noticed only a single car in the car park. The school was like a ghost town, the most peaceful he'd ever seen it. He walked into the playground and sat at one of the benches near the DT rooms, as the Spitters wouldn't have arrived so early.

Jermaine reached into his bag and pulled out a copy of *Soul Music* by Terry Pratchett, and began to read it. He loved Terry Pratchett books, as they allowed him to escape the world he was in, but in a humorous way, rather than the nerdy process of other fantasy writers. The Death trilogy was his favourite; he'd borrowed them from a library in Ealing once, before moving to Brent, so figured he may as well keep them. No one else would appreciate the books more than he did anyway.

As Jermaine sat there reading, he failed to notice that a girl had sat down a few minutes later, on the bench next to the one he was sat on. Jermaine looked up from his book to see the time on the wall above the gate when he first saw her. He wasn't interested in girls in a romantic fashion. He appreciated the pretty face of a female, and understood what a girlfriend was, he just didn't understand why someone would want to spend all their time with a girl.

Staring at her, Jermaine noted that this girl was quite attractive to look at. Her skin was a little darker than his, and was clearer than crystal, with a strange glow to it. Her hair looked black, but when she moved, the sun revealed a slightly brown tint to it. It flowed down, past her shoulders, but was as thick as a lion's mane. She sat reading a novel, whilst eating an apple. As Jermaine stared at her, the girl looked up, and gave him a puzzled look. She gathered her things, stood up, and stormed past Jermaine,

'Weirdo!' she said, as she disappeared around a corner.

Jermaine felt embarrassed. He couldn't actually say why he was staring at her in the first place. He brushed off the feeling of stupidity, and continued reading his book.

*

The school was now bustling, like it usually did. Kids were walking, shouting, and screaming, even though the person they were speaking to was usually right next to them. Jermaine had moved from the benches, once he had spotted one of the Spitters walking towards him, stuffing a large handful of straws into his bag.

As Jermaine walked towards his form class, he heard a voice calling him,

'Mr Pearson, could you come here please?' called Miss Faring

'Yes Miss,' responded Jermaine, walking towards her, with his head held low.

'I just wanted to remind you that I'll be keeping an eye out for you, as well as an ear to the ground, listening for any information coming down the line about your actions.

'I have informed the teachers to keep an eye out for you also, so keep your behaviour in check.' Miss Faring held an eyebrow raised, turned on one foot and walked away.

*

The first two lessons of the day were Chemistry; Jermaine loved all science subjects. When he was in primary, he always thought they would be full of animal dissections, and bubbling flasks, which exploded after you added a new chemical to it. The reality was much different. The closest he had come to dissecting an animal, was looking at the specimens that Mr Constantine, his Biology teacher, had in the jars on the shelves. The closest he had come to using a Bunsen burner was when he watched Mr Richards, his Chemistry teacher, turn one on. Jermaine realised that all those American shows had lied to him.

Regardless of this fact, Jermaine still really enjoyed his lessons. He learned nearly the entire periodic table, and the ways the elements combined together to create different materials, which were useful in everyday life. This specific lesson, however, Jermaine couldn't concentrate, as he was constantly watching the time, paying attention to every minute movement that the minute hand made, thinking about what he would do when break eventually arrived.

Jermaine played with the card in his hand under the table, flicking the corners underneath his nails. He still didn't understand why he was feeling so anxious about this. What could possibly happen? He tried to logically think all the possibilities through:

1: The card could have come from Dean and the other Year 10s, as an attempt to ambush him. An opportunity to take revenge for them getting suspended? Jermaine eventually dismissed this idea. After the reprimand they received from Miss Faring, they probably wouldn't want to get into any more trouble. He also realised that they wouldn't be able to get into the school, as the fat Year 10 boy wouldn't be able to squeeze through the gap in the fence, near the field.

2: It could be a random set up prank from some kids that he didn't know about? This was a strong possibility, but why would anyone pick him out from the abundance of children in the school.

He knew he didn't stand out. He had got in that fight to bring attention to himself, but wouldn't fighting off three year 10 boys, on his own, deter anyone from purposely upsetting him?

3: A girl had a crush on him, and had someone deliver an invitation, to get him there for a private rendezvous.

All three of these reasons didn't validate Jermaine being scared. He looked at the card in his hand, and decided to forget about it for now. There was no reason for him to waste his time thinking about it. He could easily just avoid the bike shed, staying away from it, like his brother had suggested.

'Jermaine, would you care to help alleviate my pain here, and tell the class the answer?' asked Mr Richards.

Jermaine put the card into his pocket, and looked at the board. The question written asked, '*what products are formed when a metal oxide reacts with an acid?*' Jermaine confidently answered, 'Salt and water.'

'Thank you Jermaine,' said Mr Richards.

*

The bell chimed; Jermaine stood up and began to leave the classroom. He decided to forget about the Shed, and get on with his life. As he exited the room, he threw the card into the bin, and walked through the door, feeling as if a weight had been lifted off of his shoulders.

'Hey, Jermaine!' called Craig Phillips, one of the boys in Jermaine's Chemistry lesson. 'You accidently threw this in the bin. You don't want to lose *this*! How on Earth did you get it anyway?'

Craig was a fairly tall boy for a Year 7. He didn't have any distinct features as such, apart from his bright blonde hair. This would have made him a target for jokes, if it weren't for the fact that he was one of the lucky kids in Year 7, who had an older brother in the school at the same time as him. This offered many benefits, one of which was an assured basic level of protection from the years above. It also put him in the know about what went on in the school.

'It wasn't an accident. What's the big deal, it's just a stupid crush card or some crap,' replied Jermaine, confused that Craig was talking to him at all.

Craig had never seemed to notice Jermaine before now, he definitely never spoke to him.

'Wait, you're not gonna go? Do you know what this is?' Craig had a complete look of surprise illuminating his face.

'Not sure, and I don't really care to be honest.'

'My brother's been praying since he was in Year 8 to get one of these!' Craig exclaimed, examining the card with awe.

'Well, give him that one then.' Jermaine, put his bag on his back and walked away.

*

Throughout the break, Jermaine stayed near the field, which was on the opposite side of the school from the bike shed. He didn't have the same sensation of fear as earlier. He was beginning to get curious after his conversation with Craig, but Jermaine had always believed in the saying, *'curiosity killed the cat'*, and so he dismissed the feeling.

Break ended, followed by a double Art lesson for Jermaine. He went to his class without the thought of the shed even passing his mind. Jermaine's Art teacher, named Mrs Hodges, had a tendency to allow her students to talk, walk around, and generally do as they pleased, as long as it concerned the work, or helped build an atmosphere more conducive to creativity.

Many children used this time as an opportunity to do what they wanted, Jermaine, however, continued working. When it came to art, Jermaine always opted for a Japanese style of drawing. He loved the big eyes, and the exaggerated features. He and Anton used to stay up later than they should have, watching a range of Manga films, as well as tons of Anime programmes. Anton had told Jermaine once that it was their father who introduced them to the animation originally.

Even though Jermaine had sporadic memories of his past, many aspects of it had been lost, as if they had been locked away. His dad, unfortunately, was one of those memories. He could recollect very random situations, such as walking with his dad in the snow, and the odd conversation, but other than that, he was just a ghost of Jermaine's lost past. On the contrary, Anton remembered everything about their father, and attempted, from time to time, to enlighten Jermaine of these things. They never elicited any sincere responses from Jermaine.

Whilst doodling, Jermaine had, unknowingly, created an anime style drawing of the girl he had seen that morning. She seemed to fill the void of thinking space left behind after the shed escaped his mind.

'That's beautiful Jermaine!' commented Mrs Hodges.

'I think it looks amateur,' Jermaine closed his book, in an attempt to stop the teacher from making any further comments or doing what she tended to do with any work she thought was good.

'Why don't we ask the rest of the class then shall we?' insisted Mrs Hodges, as she lifted the book from under Jermaine's elbows and opened it up to show the room. 'Class, Jermaine has drawn a beautiful picture of a young lady. Isn't it wonderful what you can create if you truly try?'

'That meant to be your girlfriend Jermaine?' teased one of the girls in the class.

'Let's be mature about this shall we?' said Mrs Hodges as the bell rang for lunch.

Mrs Hodges closed Jermaine's book and handed it to him.

The class filed out of the room, chuckling as they walked past Jermaine, cooing at him and making kissing sounds. This only lasted a short while, and stopped as soon as Jermaine gave them a serious glare. It seemed that the memory of what had happened with the Year 10 boys was still fresh in everybody's minds.

*

During lunch, Jermaine sat on his usual spot, eating his sandwich.

'You didn't come to meet me. I thought you got suspended,' spoke a voice from behind Jermaine. He turned to see Sean stood behind him.

Jermaine had completely forgotten his deal to finish his crash course with Sean the following day.

'Sorry,' Jermaine said, with a distinct lack of sincerity in his voice, 'had a few things on my plate to deal with. I'll finish showing you how things work on Monday.'

'Couldn't we finish today? I haven't had any issues since I've been following your instructions.'

Jermaine looked back at Sean with a stern look.

'I mean, Monday's fine. Umm, could I stay here for lunch?'

'If you want to, it's a free country, or so they say,' responded Jermaine.

'So, what happened to you then? Did your parents get an e-mail from the school?' enquired Sean.

'Uh huh. Can we not talk about that, had enough conversations about it to last me a lifetime,' requested Jermaine.

Sean nodded and quietly walked over to a free space on the wall. Jermaine noticed how Sean held onto the wall, and jumped up onto it, with relative ease, which Jermaine thought strange. Looking at Sean's physique, Jermaine expected a jump like that to be more challenging than it was. Sean then reached into his bag, and pulled out a sandwich, packet of crisps, along with a carton of juice.

Noticing this, Jermaine concealed a smile by taking a bite out of his sandwich. The two of them sat there, eating, whilst looking at the field, when Jermaine suddenly spotted the look of fear on a boy's face. The boy was looking in their direction, but Jermaine could tell he wasn't looking at them. The boy quickly averted his gaze; Jermaine then felt a strange chill run down his spine.

'You stood me up,' came a monotone voice, from behind the two boys.

Jermaine's heart began to race. He clenched a fist, which began to shake slightly with every surge of blood pumping through his veins. He slowly turned and looked into the eyes of the ominous looking sixth former. He could hardly breathe.

The sixth former reached into his pocket, whilst constantly keeping eye contact with Jermaine, completely ignoring Sean.

'I know you haven't got any siblings in this school, so I'm going to give you the benefit of a doubt that you didn't know what the invitation was for, and especially who it came from,' said the sixth former, who had taken a packet of pumpkin seeds out of his pocket and began to eat them, 'for this reason, I'm going to let this pass as a misunderstanding. I've rearranged our meeting to Monday break time'

The sixth former looked more menacing up close than from a distance. The scar on his left cheek looked like it must have been caused by a painful experience. It started from the edge of his left eye, and ended just below his cheekbone. His eyes had a dead and calculating look in them; Jermaine compared them to a shark's eye, which he had seen on a nature program one morning while he was in-between schools.

'I can't tell you what to do Jermaine, but I would advise that you do not miss this one, as I doubt I will be as forgiving in the future as I have been today.' The sixth former turned, still eating his pumpkin seeds.

Watching the sixth former, as he left, Jermaine observed that all the children in the playground acted as if he didn't exist. It was the strangest thing he had seen in his eleven years of living. The children would look at him and instantly divert their eyes away from the boy, automatically making a path for him. The sixth former walked in a completely straight line, not moving to avoid anyone, as there was never anyone in his path.

Jermaine had seen kids who had been dismissed before, as they weren't important. He saw the sixth formers do it to the Year 11s, the Year 11s do it to the Year 10s, and the same happen all the way through the school. This was something completely different. This sixth former carried a sense of purpose about him, and inspired fear in all of the children.

Who was he, and why had he taken such an interest in Jermaine? Jermaine turned around; his heart rate began to slow to a more regular pace.

'So, your name's Jermaine?' asked Sean, receiving no response from Jermaine.

6

Chris Carcer

In comparison to his face-to-face with the sixth former, the rest of that Friday was uneventful for Jermaine. He finished his lunch with Sean, went to P.E, then started leaving for home. As he left the school, he walked past the bike shed, increasing his pace slightly.

In the back of his mind, Jermaine believed that arriving home would make everything feel better. He imagined walking into his bedroom, lying on his bed and forgetting all about his experience with the sixth former; things didn't quite work out that way. Once he had arrived home, everything seemed muted to him. The television shows he normally watched were no longer interesting. His books served as no distraction, and video games created a frustrating boredom rather than entertainment. All Jermaine could think about were those eyes; that cold, calculating stare, burrowing a hole straight through him.

*

On Saturday evening, Jermaine sat on his bed, staring at the ceiling, still trying to think of a way to get out of the situation he'd found himself in. He knew he couldn't just avoid the meeting; the sixth former had made that clear enough. The only option was to either tell his mother, or tell a teacher, and what would he tell them? Nothing had happened, and even if it did, he wasn't supposed to tell adults about his problems, according to Anton anyway. Both of his options seemed out of the question. Jermaine hit the same brick wall he had been faced with for the past 24 hours. He just couldn't see a way out.

A knock at his bedroom door shook Jermaine free of his tortuous thinking. The door opened and Anton was stood there, taking up the entire doorway, as if he were a replacement for the door itself.

'Mum said to say dinner will be ready in 10 minutes,' he announced, whilst squinting his eyes. Jermaine knew this look; Anton was attempting to figure something out. He walked into the room and stopped a step away from Jermaine's bed.

'Mum is also concerned at the fact that you have been up here for pretty much the entire day. She thinks there might be something wrong...is there?'

Jermaine had to literally bite his tongue to stop himself from telling Anton everything. He usually noticed Anton's size, but at this moment, he looked like a guardian angel, sent purely to free Jermaine from all his worries.

'I'm fine, just a lot of homework to deal with,' Jermaine lied.

'Fine, just come downstairs for dinner, I'm tired of hearing mum going on about you.' Anton started walking out of the room.

'Why did you tell me to stay away from the bike shed?' blurted Jermaine, without intention. The words had seemed to force their way out of his mouth, smashing his teeth out of the way.

Anton stopped at the door and closed it, leaving him alone inside the room with Jermaine.

'What happened with the bike shed?' asked Anton, without tuning to face his brother.

The proverbial 'cat' was out of the bag now, so Jermaine decided to tell Anton everything. He told Anton about Sean and his crash course. He spoke about the fight with the Year 10 boys and then the sixth former. He told Anton of the card, Craig's reaction towards it, and finally about the sixth former approaching him on the Friday.

Throughout the story Anton never made a sound, he listened intently, wearing a poker-faced expression, never looking away from Jermaine at any point. Regardless of this fact, telling Anton everything made Jermaine feel a lot better than he had expected.

'You're lucky that he only gave you a warning and didn't break anything.' Anton's response shocked Jermaine. He expected something more...comforting.

'So you know him?' asked Jermaine anxiously.

'I've never personally met him, no...but I know of him. Nearly everyone knows of him. He's extremely dangerous Jermaine.' Anton had a deadly serious look on his face, one that Jermaine had only ever seen once before, when he had accidentally torn Anton's signed photo of David Haye.

'Who is he? What does he want with me?' enquired Jermaine. He really wanted to hold onto his brother and beg him to protect him, but he knew Anton wouldn't respond to such an obvious sign of weakness too well.

'Everything I know about him is a third or fourth hand account. His name's Chris Carcer apparently, said to be quite a serious character. I've heard stories about him fighting people I wouldn't personally want to spar with. He apparently hangs around with this group of kids, in a cabin behind a bike shed in St Peters.

'His little gang call themselves something, can't remember exactly, all I know for sure is if they come looking for you, hope it's for a good reason. Psychos, the lot of 'em.'

When Anton had finished speaking, Jermaine felt worse than he did when he was just thinking to himself.

'So, what should I do about the meeting with him on Monday?

Should I just tell a teacher?' Jermaine hoped Anton would take back his statement about talking to teachers.

'From what I hear, that wouldn't help you; it would just make them angrier. Your best bet is to do as he's asked and go meet him. They probably only need information from you, or something. If they wanted to hurt you, you'd be hurt by now.'

'So, I just have to take whatever is coming to me, is that what you're saying? You're not even going to try and help me?' responded Jermaine, with a tinge of anger in his voice.

'Boys! Your dinner a get cold! Get down 'ere now!' hollered their mother.

Anton stood up, approached the door, turned his head, and said, 'If I could do something, I'd do it, but I doubt I could take them all on by myself, and I don't suppose you'd be capable of backing me up now would you?' Anton then walked through the door and began to descend the stairs.

Jermaine noticed the anger in his brother's voice. It took a few moments, but he eventually understood that, for the first time he'd ever seen, Anton was actually afraid. Jermaine remembered seeing Anton frustrated over girls at school, upset about losing a sparring match at the gym, or even worried about what their mum would say when she returned home and realised something had been broken, but he had never seen him scared.

He knew his brother had valid points. There were at least more of them than there was of him. If they were as dangerous as Anton suggested, then he wouldn't be able to deal with them alone.

What could they want with him? Maybe it was information about the Year 10s that he had fought with? Could it be that they were working with the Year 10 boys, and he'd embarrassed them all, so they wanted revenge? Whatever it was, he couldn't figure it out without going to the meeting. Jermaine decided to go downstairs to eat his dinner, as his mother being angry with him was a scarier thought than anything he could consider the sixth formers doing to him.

7

Behind The Shed

Monday revealed itself, and Jermaine felt exhausted. He hadn't slept very well the night before. He kept waking up in the middle of the night, due to a reoccurring dream he was having. In this dream, Jermaine would walk behind the bike shed, and there would be nothing there. As he turned to leave, a pair of eyes would be floating in front of him, burning a hole into his soul, breaking him down from the inside, out.

Jermaine would swat at the eyes, but then another pair would materialise, and then another, and another, until he was completely surrounded. The eyes would continue staring deeper and deeper into his very essence, until a rumbling sound, similar to that of a thunderclap, could be heard from above. As Jermaine would look up, the letters B.S.B.H would come hurtling down from the sky, flattening him.

There were slight variations to this process, but he would always see the eyes and the letters. On his way to school, all Jermaine could think about was what the letters stood for.

Jermaine arrived at his school and saw the bike shed in front of him. It stood there, taunting him. It hung over him like a black omen. As he walked past the bike shed, he envisioned the letters BSBH. Suddenly, something clicked, 'Bike Shed!' Jermaine shouted triumphantly. 'BS stands for bike shed!' All the children in the school stopped and looked at Jermaine, with confusion on their faces. Embarrassed, Jermaine lowered his head and walked towards his form class.

'Well, what does the BH stand for?'

*

As the sound of the bell for break rang, Jermaine felt nauseous. Throughout the day, he had come to a stage of acceptance that he would just have to face whatever was waiting for him behind the bike shed. He couldn't decipher what the BH stood for, no matter how hard he tried.

As he walked towards the bike shed, he had the feeling that the entire school was watching him, as if they were all in on something he didn't understand. Conversations would stop as he walked past, people would be whispering and staring at him. The logical side of his brain knew that this was all in his head, but at that present time, he couldn't help feeling that way.

'Jermaine! Hey, Jermaine!' came the voice of Sean from the other side of the playground as he ran towards Jermaine.

'What is it Sean? I haven't got time to show you around remember?'

'I know. I'm coming with you,' responded Sean, surprisingly not out of breath, even though he had just sprinted across the playground.

'What? No you're not. I've got enough problems figuring out how I'll protect myself, if things get dangerous. I don't need to be thinking about you also.'

Sean looked at Jermaine with an expression of severity that Jermaine had never seen on his face. 'I didn't ask you if I could come, I *told* you I'm coming, that's what friends do, we support each other.'

Jermaine felt a chill go down his spine. He'd had acquaintances before, but he had never been called a 'friend' by anybody, mainly because he never stayed in a school long enough to forge any friendships.

'O...ok, just don't blame me if you get a beating,' Jermaine replied, realising that having Sean there wouldn't help in the slightest, regardless, the thought of having a friendly face around did make him feel exceedingly better.

The two boys walked up to the bike shed. Jermaine clenched his fist and looked over to Sean. Surprisingly, there wasn't even the slightest sign of fear on his face. The boys walked around the side of the shed to an opening, which led into, what looked like an alley. There was a glass covering, which went from the outside wall of the school, all the way over the bike shed, creating a covering for this alleyway. At the end of the alley stood the entrance to a port-a-cabin. Jermaine had noticed the side of this room when he was in the playground before, and always found it strange that there was no entrance into it. Now he knew why. In front of the cabin was a small picnic bench.

A few steps under the glass covering, the two twins stood, one leaning against the back of the bike shed, the other against the exterior school wall. At the picnic bench sat the large sixth former with the curly head of hair, eating some biscuits out of a packet. Opposite him, with her back to the boys, sat the female sixth former. The two seemed to be engaged in some form of card game.

Finally, sat on the step of the port-a-cabin, was the small, scary sixth former, Chris Carcer.

Jermaine began walking past the twins with his head lowered, as they watched him intently. As Sean started to follow closely behind Jermaine, the twins connected their feet, creating a barrier, preventing him from passing. Sean looked at both of them, and ducked, in an attempt to go underneath, but the twins lowered their legs, thwarting his plan.

'Um...Jermaine,' called Sean, with half a whisper in his voice.

Jermaine turned, saw the feet barring Sean's entry and looked back at Chris.

'Why aren't they letting him in?' Jermaine asked.

'The invitation was for you, not him. He's not welcome here,' replied Chris; the same deadeye expression he always seemed to carry on his face.

'He's with me.' Jermaine's heart rate was increasing with every second that passed.

'What's your point?'

'If...if he's left out there alone he won't survive till the end of break.' Although Jermaine sincerely believed this, the thought of being alone behind this bike shed with all these sixth formers scared him more than he was willing to admit.

Chris smiled a sinister smile, raised his hand and the twins released their feet, allowing Sean to reunite with his companion. The two exchanged a glance and then proceeded closer to Chris.

As the two boys reached the picnic table, the female sixth former placed her cards down, saying 'Royal flush. Do the honours loser,' and pushed the cards towards the fat sixth former. She then turned her head, gave Jermaine and Sean a single glance, and then looked at Chris.

'Is this them? You can't be serious?' she asked, screwing her face into a surprised expression. At this distance, Jermaine realised that the mark he had noticed on her face from a distance, was actually a birthmark of some kind, not make up, as he had previously assumed. This fact came after noticing just how attractive this girl actually was.

The fat sixth former looked at the two boys, and offered them a biscuit. They both shook their heads, saying, 'No thank you,' in unison. The sixth former then took the two final biscuits out of his packet, crushed the empty wrapper in his hand, and began to eat them, whilst returning his attention to the cards, which he began to shuffle.

The two boys watched the sixth former shuffling the cards for a moment, amazed by the speed his fingers and hands were moving, when Jermaine suddenly thought to himself, *'what does she mean "them"? Doesn't she means him?'*

'Were we that much different when we were in Year 7? Didn't everyone assume we were too weak and feeble to achieve anything?' replied Chris, whilst keeping eye contact with Jermaine.

The female sixth former exhaled and looked back across the table. 'Hurry up and deal!'

Chris stood up, and then walked over to the two boys. Jermaine observed that every step he took felt like a step that would be written in history. The way he moved, as if every action was purposeful. He didn't aimlessly swing his arms, didn't exert any more energy then was needed to complete each action. He never averted his gaze. He had a sort of, destiny surrounding him.

'Do you know why you are here?' enquired Chris

'I've been thinking; it must have something to do with me having a fight with the Year 10 boys.'

'People have fights in school all the time, and they don't get invitations to come here.'

Jermaine stared into Chris' eyes, frantically going through all of the other possibilities, systematically dismissing them based on the ridiculousness of each.

'I'll give you a clue, it has something to do with him,' stated Chris, pointing a finger at Sean.

Jermaine looked at Sean, and then back at Chris. He couldn't comprehend what he could mean. How could it be due to Sean?

'There are many reasons why people fight in this world,' continued Chris, 'for some, it's used as a means of gaining respect. Others fight to defend themselves. There are times when people fight to get revenge, and a select few that fight, purely to exert their power over others with brute force.'

In a blink of an eye, Chris reached out and grabbed Sean by the neck, and then began to squeeze. Jermaine looked at Sean's face, which began to resemble a beetroot and immediately lunged towards

Chris. In the next second, he found himself gasping for air, trying to pry Chris' other hand from around his own throat.

'Then there are those who fight to defend others. You, Jermaine, are quite obviously, the latter.'

Chris then released both boys and turned his attention back to Sean.

'I apologise if I was too rough Sean.'

'I'm fine Chris, it's ok.'

The name *'Chris'* resonated deep within Jermaine as he turned to look at Sean.

'How do you know his name?' Jermaine questioned, filled with confusion.

'Sean is also a prospective member of our group,' replied Chris, 'he's been working with me since he started at this school. He's helped me with some recruitment issues.'

Jermaine didn't absorb anything Chris had said past the words *'member of our group'*. He couldn't help notice that Sean had transformed into an almost new person. His posture had strangely straightened, his facial expression had become more intense, and he now carried a new aura of confidence.

Jermaine began asking himself how he had missed this before. He prided himself on his ability to see things. He was an observer, a watcher, but this had completely eluded him. Then he remembered, the moment before they came to the bike shed, he caught a glimpse of this new Sean then.

'I've been watching you since you started Jermaine. I've noticed your innate ability to observe your surroundings, and your ability to adapt. You've shown intelligence, a desire to learn, and also a strong integrity of character.

'The only thing I didn't know was whether you had the correct characteristics to join our group. That's where Sean came in. I needed to know if you would protect someone, purely from the desire to not see them hurt.'

Jermaine turned his attention away from Sean and looked back at Chris.

'I don't understand, how did Sean become a part of your group? Actually, what is this 'group' in the first place?'

Chris smiled and answered, 'I first met Sean a year ago, when he was in Year 6. A group of boys, who happened to be one of our marks, had chosen him as a target of punishment. One day it all became a little too much for little Sean here, and he decided to fight back. Luckily for him, that was the day we had decided to deal with those boys, and I stopped Sean from attaining any serious injuries.

'After that, I decided to train Sean in our ways. I taught him how to defend himself. When he reached the end of Year 6, he made the decision to join us here, at St Peters.

'To answer your second question; what should a kid do if they have someone who's constantly hurting them? Tell a teacher? Tell their parents? That makes the most sense, right? Now, say they take that route and nothing happens, the issue continues, what do they do then? What if the bully is from a different school, how do they fix that? Unfortunately, some kids don't have the guts of Sean and yourself. Some kids can't bring themselves to stand up to such bullies. That's why we exist. We will take them down. We will show them that there is a force that will make them answer for their actions. We will be the fists of the weak, the protector of those who can't protect themselves.'

Jermaine began to feel a shiver travel down his spine, and the hairs on the back of his neck stand on end. A feeling of admiration was building up within him. At that moment he looked around and noticed that the entire group was now paying full attention to Chris. He looked at their faces and could see the same feeling in their eyes.

The respect they had for Chris was overwhelming, contagious.

Chris walked over to Jermaine, stood a few inches from his face and said, 'We are the Bully Hunters.'

8

Initiation

'Bully Hunters? So what, you guys hunt bullies?' questioned Jermaine, with the assumption that someone was playing a joke on him somehow.

'Yes,' came the straight-laced answer from Chris.

'And...you want *me* to join your group to help you...hunt bullies?'

'I thought that much was clear by now.'

'Why would I want to do that? I don't have a desire to look for fights; I just stuck up for Sean because he looked so weak. Don't want to see anyone beaten up in front of me, if I could help it.'

'That's why we chose you. Many people wouldn't throw themselves in harm's way to protect somebody, other than family, or a close friend, but that wasn't what motivated you. It wasn't a desire to do the right thing, it was an innate drive to do what you supposed necessary,' responded Chris, who then turned and began to walk back to his seat.

'I'm not a superhero. I can defend myself, but fighting bullies? They're usually bigger than me, they tend to move in packs, and are more than likely stronger than I am. How am *I* supposed to protect people?' questioned Jermaine.

The female sixth former lowered her cards, and without turning her head said, 'The ability to fight can be taught to anyone, it's purely muscle memory. What can't be taught is the fighting spirit, the desire to stand up and be counted. That has to be deep within the person's character to begin with,' and then raised her cards and continued playing.

Jermaine felt overwhelmed. None of the possible scenarios for going behind the bike shed had led him to believe that he would be put in this situation.

'So, what will it be?' asked Chris, now sat back on the step of the port-a-cabin.

'I...I don't know, I just, I don't know,' answered Jermaine, his mind racing as he tried to compute all the information he had just heard.

The bell for third period rang. The sixth formers stood, and began to leave from behind the shed.

'We'll give you until lunch to make your mind up. If we see you here at 13:00, then we will begin your training, if not, the offer will be rescinded, and you will never hear from us again.'

Chris then walked past Jermaine, and disappeared around the corner.

All the sixth formers had left, leaving only Jermaine and Sean behind the bike shed. Jermaine turned to leave.

'Hey,' called Sean, as he reached out for Jermaine's arm. Jermaine pulled away violently and scowled at Sean.

'You lied to me. You could have told me what was going on, that you worked for them, but you didn't.'

'I was doing my job; Chris wanted to know that you were the right person. I would have told you, but I had to keep you in the dark,' responded Sean, earnestly.

'Well, it's not like I was your friend anyway, and I don't think I ever will be now. I can't trust you, so I don't want to speak to you,' retorted Jermaine, and walked away, leaving Sean standing behind the shed, with his head lowered to the ground.

*

Jermaine sat in his seat for Geography, but could only think about the bike shed. He considered what was actually being offered to him. The idea of consistently fighting bullies didn't much appeal to him. He had never wanted to have any of the fights he had ever been in.

He had to agree that he had felt a necessity to protect Sean from harm, and that this wasn't the first time he had protected one of the 'not so cool' kids from the 'cool kids'. He did despise bullying, in all forms and the thought of stopping that happening to anyone filled him with a strange sense of happiness.

The final fact that Jermaine couldn't deny was a feeling of excitement. The concept of belonging to a group made him feel elated beyond words. Throughout his time moving from school to school, he had made acquaintances, but those relationships were always fairly fleeting. This, however, felt solid. Regardless of how strange, scary, or dangerous the sixth formers seemed to Jermaine, they wanted him to be one of them, a part of their group.

Jermaine completed the work set and sat staring out of the window. *'What would it be like hunting bullies?'* he thought to himself. He began to have a strange image of himself, stalking through the woods wearing a hunting vest, army fatigues, steel toe capped boots, carrying a bow, arrows and a hunting rifle. He envisioned a group of boys, in a clearing, grazing on some grass, as he lined up his sights on them. Jermaine sat, smiling to himself.

'I'm glad that you find the variations between terrains so amusing, Mr Pearson,' said Mr Balding, Jermaine's Geography teacher.

Jermaine instantly removed his smile. Mr Balding was a small, meek teacher, but Jermaine found him scary, for some incomprehensible reason. Every child showed him more respect than any other teacher, although, none of the children knew why. The fact that he was very kind, was the reason most children deferred to, but Jermaine felt it was something else.

The bell for lunch rang. As Jermaine collected his things, he realised that he had made up his mind.

*

As he finished his sandwich, folded the foil and placed it back in his bag, Jermaine looked up at the clock inside the gym with a bubbling sensation in his stomach. He had never been so nervous in his entire life. He had felt scared the first time he was heading behind the shed, but this was different. This time, it seemed like he was making a life changing decision.

Once Jermaine walked behind the bike shed, he saw the sixth formers sat at the picnic table, talking. He walked over to Chris, who was sat with a book in his hands.

'So, what do I need to do?' Jermaine asked him.

Chris smiled, and the two twins stood up behind him.

One of the twins said, 'There are a few requirements to be a part of this group. You'll have to train yourself in fitness, strength, combat and intelligence. We don't want a mindless grunt who goes around bashing anyone on the head because they believe them be a bully.'

The other twin looked over at his brother, and shook his head.

'What he forgot to say was his name is Maxwell. My name is Alex.' Jermaine could only distinguish the twins between each other because they both wore different coloured hair bands on their foreheads. 'The big guy over there is Jared,' Alex identified, pointing at the fat sixth former, sat on the bench.

Alex placed his hand on the female sixth former's shoulder. She, almost instantly, smacked his hand away.

'This lovely young lady is Camille, and the serious one, sat there reading, as you already know, is called Chris.'

Jermaine looked around at the faces. Knowing the names of each member of the group definitely reduced the amount of apprehension he felt being around them.

'To begin with,' added Maxwell, 'you'll be physically tested by Jared. He will see just how useful you really are in a fight.'

Standing up, Jared was easily double the height of Jermaine. He was at least three times Jermaine's weight.

'Against him? That's like putting a chimpanzee up against a gorilla!' Jermaine protested.

Jared looked down at Jermaine. 'Follow me,' Jared's low-pitched voice boomed.

Jermaine begrudgingly followed Jared out from behind the bike shed, through the school and onto the field. Each step he took made him question whether he had made the right decision. Jared stopped by a bush, reached down, and lifted a large, leaf-covered branch, out of the way.

Jermaine had been on the field a number of times; he'd actually walked past this specific bush, but nothing would have made him think that there was a hidden path through the non-descript greenery.

Jared ushered Jermaine through the bush, and down the path. Once they were both through the entrance, Jared replaced the branch, concealing it again. Jermaine walked onto the grass in front of him and looked around. It was as if he had entered a secret world. Past the bush was a clearing, surrounded on all sides by tall bushes and trees. In the centre of the clearing was a small blue building. There were training mats, which looked like the ones they used during P.E on the floor outside the building, and above the door of the building were the letters BH, in bold black lettering.

Jared walked up beside Jermaine.

'What is this place?' Jermaine questioned Jared.

'It's our personal training building. Our founder acquired it for us.'

'Founder?' Jermaine said quietly, contemplating this piece of information.

'Your sparring partner is inside,' said Jared.

'So, I'm not fighting you? Thank God.' Relief flooded through Jermaine.

The two boys walked into the building. The door opened into a gym room. There were punching bags on one side of the room, kettle bells and weights on another, and in the centre of the room were some mats. Stood in the centre of those mats was Sean, stretching.

'Wait, Sean? This isn't going to be fair...for him I mean,' said Jermaine, confidence oozing out of his pores.

'Well, only one way to truly find out,' responded Jared, who then nodded at Sean.

Jermaine took off his shoes and socks, placed them together near a wall, and walked onto the mat.

'Ok, the bout is won when the opposition taps out, gives up or is knocked unconscious. I want no low blows, no eye gauging, and please remember, this is a sparring match, so I don't want to be sending either of you to a hospital.'

Jermaine looked at Sean, who looked completely composed. Sean kept his eyes on Jared, as he stood with the discipline and posture of a soldier awaiting orders.

'Any questions? No? Good, now take your places.'

The two boys approached each other in the centre of the mat.

'So, are we going to be using headgear, gloves? *Any* form of protection?' asked Jermaine.

'If we're training to fight in the real world, then it makes sense to train as realistically as possible,' responded Sean.

Jermaine looked at Sean with agitation.

'Ready?' called Jared

Sean raised his fists into a boxing stance. Jermaine looked at him, standing nearly a foot smaller than he was and smiled.

'I'll try and go easy Jermaine,' said Sean

The audacity of this statement sent Jermaine's blood boiling. He had intended to go easy on Sean, but now decided to teach him a lesson in humility.

'Fight!' shouted Jared.

Jermaine threw the first punch but connected with nothing more than air. When he looked around, Sean was on his right hand side, bouncing from left to right with the same composed look on his face.

Making another approach, slightly slower this time, Jermaine threw a jab, which connected with Sean's guard, followed instantly with a right hook, but again, felt nothing but air. He looked up, and Sean was gone again. As Jermaine turned, he saw Sean on his right, charging towards him, with his fists covering his face.

Suddenly, Jermaine began to feel a surge of fear grip hold of him. In haste, he raised his hands to protect his face. The impact Jermaine felt in his stomach confused him. He knew he was fighting Sean, but couldn't accept that the blow he just received was a punch from him. It was as strong as, if not stronger, than his brother's.

Instantly after the body blow, Jermaine felt another punch connect with his left side. The force of the blow sent him to his knees. If it had not been for his experience in taking blows from his brother, Jermaine was sure that he would have probably been winded from the punch. He looked up, and saw Sean bouncing from side to side again. Jermaine could hardly believe that this was actually Sean he was fighting.

Jermaine slowly stood up, and adopted a fighting pose.

Unlike before, Jermaine moved in more carefully, keeping his guard up. He threw a few jabs with his left, which connected. He then took a step forward and tried another jab - hook combination, but again, Sean ducked the hook, grabbed Jermaine by his right arm, and pushed his shoulder into Jermaine's side. He then threw Jermaine over his head, onto the mat.

Jared winced at the sound of Jermaine's back connecting with the ground. Jermaine turned over, and watched the sweat, which fell from his head, land on the mat. More than the pain from the collision, Jermaine was overcome with a feeling of embarrassment. He realised that he had little chance of winning the match, but decided that he would, at least, land one decent blow on Sean before the fight was over.

Sean stood up in front of Jermaine, his face still composed, his breathing regulated to a calm pace. Jermaine rose up, lifted his fists and began to slowly step forward. Again, he threw jab after jab. Jermaine then reached in for a hook, causing Sean to evade again. This time, however, Jermaine switched his footing, leant back onto his left foot, and raised a left uppercut, connecting cleanly with Sean's left cheek, sending him reeling backwards.

Spotting an opportunity, Jermaine charged in, throwing hook after hook, but Sean blocked each punch. Jermaine threw another left hook, but this time, he didn't connect with anything. The force he'd used to throw the punch caused him to slightly lose balance. In that split second, Jermaine felt Sean's arm wrap around his neck, and his foot sweep him off the mat. Jermaine hit the floor, and before he realised what had happened, he felt Sean climb onto his back, grab his left arm, and pull it backwards into a lock.

'You're not going to get out of this, just tap out,' advised Sean.

Jermaine struggled, but it only made the arm lock more uncomfortable.

'Stop moving, you're just making it worse.'

'Shut up!' gasped Jermaine, still struggling.

'If you don't tap out, I'm going to have to break your arm,' said Sean, tightening the arm lock.

Jermaine felt the pain from his arm travel down his body, and into his gut. He continued to try and escape the hold, but couldn't. He felt that his arm was about to break at any moment, so with reluctance, he tapped the ground

Sean immediately released Jermaine's arm, and stood up. Exhausted, Jermaine turned over, and sat on the mat, whilst holding onto his shoulder. He looked up at Sean, standing a few steps away from him. It was definitely Sean he was looking at. He still had the same miniscule body frame, the same acne covered skin, as well as the patches in his hair, but something made him seem like an entirely new person.

Sean reached down and placed his hand under Jermaine's right shoulder, helping him up to his feet. Jermaine, filled with embarrassment, noticed Jared walking towards him, but didn't lift his head. Jared placed his hand onto Jermaine's left shoulder, 'Don't worry, the pain will subside.'

Jermaine walked towards the wall of the gym, slowly placed his feet back into his shoes, and began to leave. He glanced up and noticed Sean walking beside him, with a concerned look on his face.

'I'm fine, so stop looking at me like that,' said Jermaine, not wanting any pity from him.

'Well, I'm still following you back into the school,' responded Sean, rubbing his left cheek.

The two boys walked towards the exit.

'Training begins tomorrow Jermaine, lunch time, behind the shed,' called the voice of Jared, as the two boys exited the gym.

Whilst walking back towards the school, Jermaine stopped, and started stretching his arm, trying to relieve the pain.

'Why is he inviting me back to train when I did so badly? You pretty much owned me in there,' asked Jermaine.

'You've got the wrong idea, Chris has been training me for over a year, the fact that you managed to even land a single blow on me is surprising,' answered Sean.

Jermaine looked at Sean with a stern and confused expression.

'So, I was always meant to lose the match?'

'The fight wasn't meant to see if you could win, but how resourceful and determined you are in a situation you couldn't possibly succeed in. If you hadn't have tapped out, that would have been bad.'

'It felt like you were going to snap my arm out of the socket.'

'If you didn't tap out, I would have,' grinned Sean.

*

The remainder of the day drifted by quickly for Jermaine. The pain in his shoulder subsided by the time he left to go home, although it still hurt him to lift his hand higher than his shoulder.

He travelled home, constantly trying to slowly raise his arm, stopping when the pain became too unbearable. Once he arrived home, he managed to raise his arm as high as his cheek before he had to stop. He took his evening shower, went downstairs and ate some food, which was left over from dinner the day before. He then went up to his bedroom, and as soon as his head hit the pillow, fell into a deep sleep.

9

Training Begins

The next morning, Jermaine awoke feeling like a double decker bus had hit him. He felt sore in areas he was sure hadn't even been hit. He crawled out of bed, walked out of his room, and approached the bathroom. He couldn't hear the shower running, but the door was locked. His sister was already inside. Jermaine walked back into his bedroom, looked at the clock and realised he'd slept through his alarm. It was 08:02. The sight of this made Jermaine panic. He hated being late for anything. Due to situations out of his control, Jermaine's attendance record was appalling, but he always prided himself on perfect punctuality.

He ran back to the bathroom and banged on the door.

'Simone, I need to get ready for school. You're not even using the shower!'

'You snooze, you lose, literally,' replied Simone, with a snigger in her voice.

'Fine, I'll just tell mum about your plans on the 15th, I'm sure she'll ask you to come out to have a conversation with you,' threatened Jermaine.

The lock on the bathroom came undone almost instantly, and Simone stormed out of the bathroom, pushed Jermaine up against the wall, pushing her face an inch away from his.

'How do you...I..I don't know what you're talking about, just use the stupid bathroom.'

Simone then stormed into her bedroom, closing the door behind her. Jermaine was surprised that it actually worked. He'd overheard her mention the 15th to someone on the phone a few days before, didn't know the month or what it related to, but thought he'd give it a try.

*

By the time he arrived at school, Jermaine's first lesson had already begun. As he rushed through the playground, he passed the bike shed, but his feelings towards it had changed again. The fear he previously felt had all but completely changed into a mixed feeling of excitement and dread. Jermaine jogged into the Science block and walked through the door of his lesson.

'You're late Mr Pearson, have you got a late slip to give me?' asked Mr Constantine, looking over his glasses. From seeing other kids who had turned up to the lesson late, Jermaine knew that the teacher despised tardiness.

Mr Constantine was exactly what you would expect a Science teacher to look like. He was bald, wore glasses, had a small stature and spoke with a very quiet voice. He was Jermaine's favourite teacher, as he would always give him more challenging work than the other students, and seemed to have the same love of Science as Jermaine did.

'Yes sir, sorry for being late, I slept through my alarm this morning,' replied Jermaine, rushing to his seat.

'I would expect better from you Jermaine. Make this be the first and last time.'

'Yes sir, it won't happen again.' Jermaine felt a wave of embarrassment flow over him.

Mr Constantine turned and continued with his lesson on molecules, as Jermaine began to take out his books and pencil case. In the corner of his eye, Jermaine saw Craig place his books on the table next to his, and take a seat on the stool next to him.

'So, I hear you had quite an eventful day yesterday,' remarked Craig, whilst writing the information from the board into his book.

Jermaine ignored the comment from Craig. He hadn't been told to not mention the Bully Hunters to anyone, but he figured he shouldn't, just in case.

'Well, what did you think of Chris? Bit of an odd one isn't he?' asked Craig.

At the sound of the name 'Chris', Jermaine hesitated. He felt the urge to ask Craig what he knew about Chris, but he thought better of it. He considered the fact that Craig could also be working for the Bully Hunters, and that this was a test to see how well he would keep his mouth shut about the group.

'Those guys are above the law in this school. Rumours say that there's a teacher who runs the show. Not so sure about all that, but it makes sense. Explains how they get away with so much. Not talking much today then? Fair enough. You ever hear about Chris and James Grainger?' asked Craig.

'Craig, would you stop talking and get on with your work,' demanded Mr Constantine.

Craig turned away from Jermaine, lowered his head into his book and continued with his work. Once Mr Constantine's attention had passed on to another set of children, Craig leaned over to Jermaine's ear.

'I'll tell you later then,' Craig whispered, and then went back to his work.

Jermaine looked up and noticed Mr Constantine looking at him in the corner of his eye, put his head down, and continued with his work.

85

*

The lesson ended. Jermaine packed his books into his bag, stood up, and began to leave the room.

'So, where are you off to for break? Bike shed?' questioned Craig.

Jermaine looked at Craig, looked away, and continued walking.

'You can't play dumb forever you know? Ok, where was I? Oh yeah, James Grainger. This beast of a boy was in Year 7 at the time, same year as Chris. Throughout his years, Grainger had become the most infamous bully on this side of the city. He'd terrorised every year group in every school within a five-mile radius.

'He had started to bring his conquering warpath towards St Peters, and apparently, this urged Chris and his friends to act,' explained Craig.

Jermaine had to consciously fight the urge to stop and give Craig his full attention. He did, however, start to slow down once he had reached the playground, so that he could listen to everything Craig had to say. Craig noticed the change in pace and smiled.

'Chris went to Grainger's school, armed with nothing more than a belt, a pocket full of sand, and a continent's worth of courage.

'From this point the tales differ. Some say that Chris took down the entire sect of bullies on his own, others say that James Grainger gave up and begged for forgiveness the moment he saw Chris. I don't know what happened for sure, apart from the fact that Chris went to the school, came back with a scar on his face, and James Grainger's reign of terror ended that day,' concluded Craig.

As Jermaine walked and thought about Chris fighting off a group of bullies, he saw Sean in the corner of his eyes, sitting on a bench alone. The way he looked reminded Jermaine why he had jumped to his rescue in the beginning. He had a helpless small animal look to him. The pain in Jermaine's ribs helped to remind him how dangerous little animals can actually be.

Although the feeling of being betrayed was still fresh, Jermaine couldn't deny that Sean was the closest thing he had to a friend in the school. Yes, he'd lied to him, nearly got him suspended, and had beaten the snot out of him, but from what Jermaine had heard throughout his travels through schools, that was apparently what friends did.

Not only was he the only person Jermaine really knew, but he was also the only person he felt safe discussing the Bully Hunters with.

'The story I believe is that…' began Craig

'Sorry, I've got to go. Interesting chat,' interrupted Jermaine, as he headed towards Sean.

'Ok, it's not like I was half way through a sentence or anything. I'll fill you in on a few more things next time we speak,' called Craig.

Jermaine stopped in front of Sean, who raised his head from his book, and looked Jermaine in his eyes.

'What are you doing sat here on your own? I thought you'd be behind the bike shed or something,' asked Jermaine

'I should be asking you the same question in that case. I'm in the same position as you; I just got recruited a bit earlier. The first time I ever went behind the shed was with you. I only ever followed a training programme that Chris laid out for me. I'm as much an outsider of that group as you are. Also, they're quite scary, especially Camille,'

'Yeah, she is unnerving isn't she? I would say that Chris' eyes are, more than likely, the main thing that has given me nightmares since the day I saw them,' admitted Jermaine.

'It's like they see through you,' said both boys at the same time.

They both laughed and then sat in silence for a couple of moments. The bell, signifying the end of break, rang. Jermaine stood up.

'Don't worry about training today. From my experience with Chris, they come across very serious, but they won't let anything severe ever happen to you...if they can avoid it.'

'Yeah, I'll keep that in mind. You still having packed lunches?'

asked Jermaine.

'Yeah, until I can sit on the top table like the other Sixth Formers, I think having a packed lunch is the safest option.'

'Well, I'm going to be eating my lunch in the usual place outside the gym...if you want to join me, it's a free country,' proposed Jermaine, slightly embarrassed.

'Yeah. Thanks. I'll be there.'

'See you then,' said Jermaine, as he turned and walked away.

*

Jermaine and Sean sat on the wall next to the boy's gym, eating their sandwiches. Jermaine couldn't fully relax, even though Sean had told him repeatedly not to worry so much about the training. Jermaine kept imagining all the possible horrible trials he might have to endure as an initiation.

The boys finished eating and Jermaine felt his stomach begin to turn. They slowly walked through the school towards the bike shed.

Once they were a few steps away, Jermaine's palms became sweaty. The two boys then turned the corner to see Jared sat at the picnic table, eating a packet of Wotsits, whilst reading a book.

Jermaine looked around, but couldn't see any of the other hunters.

'Why are you standing all the way over there? Come here,'

ordered Jared.

Jermaine and Sean walked over to the table, Jermaine straightening his posture, as if he were a soldier.

'So, you're all prepared for your first day of training?' asked Jared, putting a wotsit in his mouth to conceal his grin.

'Yes sir,' answered Jermaine. He didn't know why he'd answered like that, just seemed like the appropriate response.

'Good,' said Jared, as he stood up from his seat, brushed the crumbs off his hands, and reached under the table. 'Prepare yourself.'

As Jared walked over to him, Jermaine closed his eyes and tensed his body, awaiting a blow of some kind. A second later, he felt Jared thrust something into his chest. Apprehensively, Jermaine opened his eyes, looked down, and saw a stack of books.

Jermaine took hold of the books, and then looked up at Jared's face in confusion.

'Wha..?' began Jermaine.

'There is more to being a fighter than just being able to throw a punch. You're physically capable, as you have shown. Giving up when you did shows that you have a decent level of judgement. You're strong Jermaine, but tell me, what is the point in being as strong as an ox if you're as ignorant as one?' enquired Jared, staring intensely into Jermaine's eyes.

Jermaine looked at the spines of the books in his hands. He had never heard of these books before. There were names, such as: *'The Art of War', 'Nineteen Eighty-four', 'The Silence of Animals'*. Each of these books looked daunting to him. He could digest a novel in no time, but even the language he skimmed from the blurbs confused him.

'I expect you to have read one of these books by this time next week. I will be expecting a book report, so make sure you fully understand what it is you're reading,' explained Jared as he turned around, returning to his seat to continue reading *'Fahrenheit 451'*.

Making space in his bag, which was already quite packed with text and exercise books, Jermaine placed his new reading list into his bag, which now felt as if it was about to burst. He looked at Sean, and then back at Jared. Lowering his novel, Jared looked up at the two boys, who were stood awaiting further instructions.

'The rest of the team are at the training grounds. Make your way there, Chris is waiting for you.'

Jermaine nodded, and without protest, began to leave. Jared looked at Sean, and smirked at Jermaine's strange adoption of a military soldier. Sean returned the gesture, before he followed behind Jermaine.

'Jermaine, before you go, you were late today. I understand that you haven't got a great attendance record, which we hope, is probably something out of your control, but you have always had a good level of punctuality. We'll take today as just a blip,' said Jared, reverting his attention back to his book.

*

The two Year 7 boys walked a few steps away from the shed.

'Word of advice, don't get yourself into any issues inside or outside of school; they don't accept that sort of thing. You could get kicked out of the group without a second thought,' said Sean.

'What do you mean trouble? You mean that 'late' comment he just made?'

'Lateness, missed homework, behavioural issues, unsanctioned fighting...'

'*Unsanctioned* fighting? Isn't that the whole purpose of this group, to fight people?' asked Jermaine, confused by the statement.

'No, we protect the weak. If we can do that whilst avoiding a fight, then we will. Violence is used as a last resort. If a situation can be resolved with words, then we take that approach. Of course, there are those odd occasions where words won't have an effect,' responded Sean, 'but you can't just go around beating people up because you feel like it. You need to have a valid reason to fight someone. Can't be a renegade.'

'So, has someone ever been kicked out of the group for that?'

queried Jermaine.

'Possibly, I'm not sure. Just don't break the rules.'

Jermaine considered this for a moment before another thought crept into his mind. How did Jared even know he was late to school? Even more curious, how did he know about Jermaine's attendance and punctuality levels. He considered that confidential information like that couldn't just be common knowledge.

*

Jermaine and Sean arrived at the bush that concealed the entrance to the training grounds. They removed the branches, revealing the mud path, and replaced them once they had stepped through.

As they walked towards the training building, they saw the two twins, who seemed to be having a sparring match. Telling them apart from each other was almost an impossibility for Jermaine, as they were not wearing their head bands.

The speed they were moving seemed unnatural to Jermaine. Once he'd seen one punch being deflected, another counter blow had already been thrown. Even keeping up with the battle visually was tiring.

Realising Sean had already walked ahead of him, Jermaine started heading towards the building. He followed behind Sean, still observing the sparring match as he went.

As they approached the building, Chris walked out, shortly followed by Camille.

'So, you received your first books?' Chris asked.

Jermaine considered the weight on his back. 'Yes sir, I have the books.'

'I appreciate the enthusiasm, but you can drop the sir,' Chris requested, as he walked past the boys, 'Jermaine, when you were fighting the Year 10 boys, how do you think you faired?'

Jermaine thought about this for a moment, following behind Chris. 'I think I did ok, considering there were three of them against just me.'

'If my counting was correct, you were fighting for no more than two minutes, and by the end of it, you seemed to be spent. You laid on the ground, defenceless, hoping that they didn't cause too much damage to you.

'If Mr Matthews hadn't shown up, I wouldn't have liked to see what you would have looked like the next day,' responded Chris, with a serious tone.

'Those three boys are nothing. They have no discipline, no real conditioning. In a fight with a real opponent, they would crumble and result to begging for forgiveness.

'I received feedback from Jared regarding your sparring match with Sean. He told me that you have spirit, but that you lack any true technique or training. I think his exact words to describe your fighting style were, "Wild street brawler".'

Jermaine looked down in embarrassment. He always thought he was a good fighter. He felt like a little child being told that all he believed to be true about the world was actually false.

'Sean,' began Chris, 'I want you to start from the beginning with Jermaine. Teach him the stamina routines I taught you. Everyday I want the two of you to do circuits until further notice. When I feel you're ready, strength training will begin for both of you, but only then.'

'Ok, no problem,' replied Sean.

Chris looked at the two boys as they stared back at him.

'Well, don't put off until tomorrow, what you can do today,' said Chris, as he held his hand out towards a set of empty mats. Sean nodded and began to walk towards the mats. Jermaine followed behind him. He felt like there were a thousand ants in his stomach, crawling around, in search for jam. It was a mixed feeling of anxiety and excitement at the prospect of his training finally beginning.

*

The feeling of apprehension was quickly replaced with the feeling of exhaustion. The circuit was more intense than anything Jermaine had experienced working out with Anton. After 7 minutes, his shirt was completely drenched in sweat, and his legs felt as if they were going to collapse from under him.

'Ok, your body should be warm now, so we can begin,' said Sean, to the horror of Jermaine.

'Begin? What was… all that… then?' Jermaine panted.

'Just a warm up, don't want to pull a muscle or anything.'

Sean began with thirty seconds of burpees, moved on to thirty seconds of shuttle runs, through to thirty seconds of jack push ups, finally concluding with thirty seconds of rock climbers, before having a thirty second break. Once the break was over, Sean began the circuit again.

*

After he fell to his knees, Jermaine gasped for air. Sean walked over to the hut, took a bottle of water out of a cooler, and handed it to Jermaine.

'Did well… for your first… circuit. Lasted… longer than expected,' panted Sean.

'I...feel...like...I'm...dying!' Jermaine struggled to speak. He could feel his chest burning every time his lungs filled with oxygen.

'Well, we'll be doing circuits everyday at lunch and then running for an hour after school. Each circuit will be different, in order to target different muscle groups,' Sean explained, helping Jermaine to his feet, 'Don't worry, you'll be in shape in no time. It won't feel as bad in a couple of weeks.'

'Couple of weeks? ...I'm not sure... I'll survive that long,' said Jermaine, bent over, taking deep breaths.

10

Plans

A tall boy slid along a wall. He peeked around a corner, and saw that a teacher was laying into one of the students, who it seemed, had not brought in his homework again.

The boy quickly ran past the room, turned at the corner, went down the stairs, and stopped at an inconspicuous, wooden door. He suspiciously looked around, ensuring nobody was in sight and then knocked the door in a specific rhythm. Tap, tap...tap, tap, tap..tap...tap, tap.....tap.

Nothing happened. As the boy reached up to knock again, he heard a latch release, and the door opened. The boy saw a table with six boys and five girls, sat around it. He walked in, and the door closed behind him.

'Take a seat Mark, you're late,' said the voice of the boy who was stood by the door.

'It's not my fault, Mrs Benit wouldn't let me go to the toilet, even though I told her my stomach was hurting. Old bat. Either way, I'm here now,' said Mark.

Mark walked over to the table, pulled out a chair and sat down. He looked around the table but didn't recognise many of the faces. He did know a few, such as Wayne, renowned to be the strongest boy in the school, Sarah, the 'queen of the mean girls', as everyone called her, and Gregory, who had opened the door; he was in Year 9 along with Mark.

One of the boys Mark didn't know stood up. He wore glasses, which seemed slightly too small for his face.

'I know you all don't know me. I don't attend Preton High, but I came here today, along with my colleague here, in order for this meeting to take place,' the boy said, pointing to the large boy sat next to him, who looked more like a man than a kid. 'We went to a lot of trouble to get in here without being spotted, as I'm sure did our guests from John Charles High, Wembley State, and even those of you who attend Preton. We appreciate that you would have had to work hard yourselves to get out of your lessons to meet us.

'Although we come from different schools and don't know each other, there is one thing that combines us all. The Bully Hunters.'

All the children around the table murmured and looked at each other in agreement.

'In some way, they have interfered with us *all*. They make rules for us to abide by, then check up on us, as if we are their constituents.

They threaten us with violence, if we choose not to abide by their rules of conduct, and they have the audacity to call *us* bullies?' continued the boy with the small glasses.

The group raised their voices in agreement, except the large boy, who had a ghastly scar on his left cheek. He just sat there, listening silently.

'The world has always functioned on one basic rule; the weak are controlled by the strong. They seem to be trying to upset that basic balance, and we can't accept that. We have to defend the natural order of things,' the small-glasses-boy declared, a fire burning within his eyes.

A pink haired girl from John Charles High School started laughing.

'Did I say something amusing? Please, let us all in on the joke,' the boy said, with a slightly irritated tone.

'Just think this is a joke. You expect us to be able to do anything to those guys. They're *psychopaths*. I think we all know that we don't stand a chance against them,' said the pink haired girl.

'What makes them so dangerous?' asked the large boy with the scar on his face.

'What? Is that a serious question?' responded Mark.

'Yes, what makes them so dangerous? There's only five of them, they're no older than we are, and they're just humans like the rest of us...so what makes them so dangerous?' reiterated the large boy again.

'They have beaten every single one of us into submission. That little one, Chris I think they call him, he took out four sixth formers at John Charles when he was only in Year 9,' answered the pink haired girl.

The group looked around at each other, and began murmuring again.

'They're machines. They train non-stop. Come rain or shine, they train. They are not naturally stronger than we are, but they have more heart, more drive than we do. That's what makes them dangerous,' said the large boy.

The group went silent.

'We became too content with our position. We believed that we were in control because we were bigger and stronger than the others. We allowed ourselves to become weak. I allowed myself to be beaten once because I underestimated my opponent. I didn't think that someone smaller than me would challenge me as much as Chris did, and I failed.

'I look in the mirror every morning and see this scar, which reminds me of my arrogance. It was my mistake that made them dangerous,' said the large boy, as he stroked his finger down the scar on the left side of his face.

'What are you getting at here?' asked one of the boys around the table.

'I propose we beat them at their own game. We unite, train; prepare ourselves for the downfall of the Bully Hunters. We recruit everyone who has ever been hurt by the hands of the Hunters. Bring the pain back to them. I've been dreaming of this for five years,' the scarred boy declared.

'Well, why didn't you just go and deal with them before now? It sounds like you have a plan, and if you're saying you underestimated them, dealing with them now should be easy, right?' asked Mark.

'I could get a few friends together, and most likely beat them in a straightforward fight, but that wouldn't reverse the situation we now find ourselves in. They have become a beacon of hope for the weaklings.

'Haven't you noticed how the weak are now defending themselves where they can? The Bully Hunters have shown them that they can fight. We can't just beat them anymore; we'd only be making martyrs of them. No, we have to destroy *everything* they stand for before we break them physically. We would have to show that they are not these unstoppable machines that they have built themselves up to be. We need to make sure nobody thinks of standing up to us again. The strong *must* remain strong,' declared the scarred boy.

One of the boys from Wembley State, who wore a scarf wrapped around his face, raised his hands.

'Can I ask an important question? Why do we care what happens anymore? Some of us are sixth formers. We're leaving school at the end of the year anyway. What difference does it make to us what happens in these schools?' he questioned.

'Have you not all been embarrassed, reduced to just another face amongst the crowds, by the Hunters? We were known, respected, feared, treated like kings and queens before they came along. Don't you want things to go back to the way they were? If not, do you not at least desire vengeance for what they did to you?' answered the scarred boy.

The group looked around and began nodding their heads in agreement with these statements.

The large scarred boy stood up, his sheer size intimidating, and inspiring at the same time. 'I can grant you that revenge, make sure people remember who we are before we leave. The Hunters took my legacy away from me when it was just getting started, and I don't intend to lie down and just accept it. Stand with me and we can destroy the Hunters!' he confirmed.

The group stood one by one, until none were seated. The boy wearing the small glasses stood beside the scarred boy.

'Who are you anyway?' asked one of the girls around the table, talking to the large boy, stroking his scar.

'My name is James, James Grainger. It's nice to meet you all.'

11

Integrated

The sun was beginning to set, turning the day to dusk. With sweat pouring down his face and steam rising from his head, Jermaine reached down, picked up his bottle and took a gulp of water. He looked around at the frost covering the grass surrounding him.

'You're lasting... as long as me... now,' said Sean, between deep breaths.

'I think... you're delusional... I feel like... I'm at death's door.' Jermaine walked over to the steps of the training building and sat down. He didn't feel as much pain in his muscles as he used to. The two months of non-stop circuits had built up his resilience to the pain of lactic acid. Sean walked over to the steps and sat next to him.

'I think we deserve a break now,' said Sean, his head held back. Both boys sat, looking at the clouds.

'Look at you two micro machines,' intruded the patronising voice of Camille.

Jermaine and Sean had not noticed her walk up. They lowered

their heads, to be met with a condescending smirk on her face.

'We just finished a high intensity workout, without taking any unallocated breaks,' responded Jermaine.

'Really! My gosh! You guys must be ready to take on anybody now? All the bullies in the world will shiver at the mere mention of your names,' Camille said, the statement laced with sarcasm.

'Just ignore her,' Sean advised Jermaine.

'Hey! Have some respect when referring to superiors,' ordered Camille, with a stern tone of voice, and a serious scowl on her face.

Jermaine looked into Camille's eyes and began to feel uncomfortable. Sean stood up, and straightened his posture.

'Sorry Camille, I didn't mean any disrespect, I got a little carried away and...'

'Don't be such a girl, I'm only messing with you,' Camille pushed Sean in his face, back down to a seated position, 'You, stand up and follow me,' she said, pointing at Jermaine.

Jermaine looked at Sean, who shrugged. He looked back at Camille, who was walking towards one of the training mats. He stood up, shook his legs, to get the blood flowing again, and started to follow her.

Once she reached the mat, Camille took off her shoes, and stepped into the centre of it. Jermaine, following Camille's lead, also removed his shoes, and then joined her on the mat.

'Ok, now, try and move me,' requested Camille.

Jermaine looked back at Sean on the steps, who again shrugged. Jermaine slowly walked closer to Camille, as she adjusted her footing. Unsure of whether this was a sincere request, or another of Camille's poor-taste jokes. He slowly reached out, and placed his hands onto Camille's arms.

'Come on, I haven't got the whole evening,' Camille looked at Jermaine, and tensed her muscles. Jermaine could feel her arms harden until they felt like two blocks of stone in his hands.

He tightened his grip, and began to push with everything he had in him, but Camille didn't move an inch. Jermaine stopped after a few tiring seconds of pushing, and started again, to only have the same outcome. It felt as if he was pushing against a statue, which had been nailed solidly to the ground.

Jermaine stopped again and took a few seconds to catch his breath. He then looked up and saw the small frame stood in front of him. Why wasn't she moving?

'I'm too tired from the workout, I don't have enough energy left,' stated Jermaine, thinking that could be the only explanation.

'Try again.'

Again Jermaine reached out and grabbed Camille's arms. He began pushing, using all the energy he had left.

'I can't move you,' he said, feeling defeated.

'Ok then, my turn,' Camille stated, as she grabbed hold of Jermaine's arms, placed her left foot in front of her right, and pushed, lifting him cleanly off the ground. Jermaine landed over a metre away, holding his back from the pain of the landing.

Camille walked over to her shoes, slipped them back on, and strolled over to Jermaine.

'Well, all that exercise hasn't done you that much of a benefit has it? Stamina is useless without strength,' declared Camille. She then looked back at Sean and smiled a maniacal grin.

'Anyway, we need to see you both tomorrow morning at 7:30, behind the bike shed. Be prepared,' Camille then turned, and walked through the bush, leaving the training grounds behind her.

Sean walked over to Jermaine and helped him to his feet.

'She's a monster.' Jermaine complained, as he got to his feet.

'Yeah, a seriously strong one. Anyway, It's getting dark now, we should start making our way home,' said Sean.

Jermaine felt a chasm in his stomach, 'Yeah, I need to get some food in me.'

*

Once he arrived home, Jermaine headed straight into the kitchen, made himself a peanut butter and jam sandwich, and went up into his bedroom to begin his homework. This had been his routine for the past two months. The amount of homework he received had been on a steady incline throughout the winter season. Along with the additional reading, piled on top by Jared, which had to have a report completed fortnightly, meant that Jermaine had little or no time for many leisurely activities.

Jermaine sat on his bed, completing his English homework, when he heard a knock at his bedroom door.

'Come in.'

The door opened, revealing Anton. He took two steps into the room, and looked at all the books on the bed surrounding Jermaine.

'Wanna come and play some Fifa or COD?' he asked, still surveying the miniature library Jermaine had accumulated.

'Can't bro, have too much work to do. It's due tomorrow, so I need to get through it,' replied Jermaine, not looking up from his exercise book.

Anton sat on the end of the bed. He reached down and picked up one of the books, which were laid out next to Jermaine.

' *Demon's Sermon on Martial Arts*'? Why are you reading this?'

'It's a good book, you should have a read some time,' muttered Jermaine, still working.

'I've heard some things about you hanging around those bike shed kids,' said Anton, as he placed the book back down on the bed, 'you need to be careful around them J, they're a lot older than you. They're really dangerous, and have some serious enemies, who will hurt anyone associated with them,' sincere concern littered his voice.

'I'll be fine Anton, I'm not getting myself into any trouble. Hold on, what do you mean you "heard" that I've been hanging around them?' Jermaine queried.

'I know people, and news travels fast Jermaine, especially when it has something to do with the most dangerous kids in the city.'

Anton stood, and started walking over to the door. 'Just remember what I've said, be careful,' he warned, pointing his finger at Jermaine. He then walked out of the room, closing the door behind him.

Jermaine continued with his work, but the words Anton had said kept on ringing through his mind. Did everyone know that he was working with the Bully Hunters? Jermaine had never really considered the fact that everyone may know who he was now. To his surprise, it didn't matter to him. He didn't enjoy attention normally, and would have done anything to avoid being in the spotlight, but now, he just didn't care.

*

Jermaine laid in bed reading, when he heard his mum's voice

calling him and his brother down for dinner. He finished the sentence he was reading, placed the book face down, to preserve the page he was on, and headed down the stairs.

Once he reached the base of the stairs, he could sense the satisfying smell of ackee and saltfish, which he knew always came accompanied with dumplings. He hurried into the kitchen.

'Here, take it in and sit down,' ordered Jermaine's mum.

Jermaine took the plate, placed it on a tray, and carried it into the front room. He took a seat on the sofa, next to his younger sister, who had already begun eating her food. The size of the house meant that the family would have to eat each meal this way. As he sat down, his elbow bumped into Leanne's tray.

'Watch what you're doing you clown! Are you trying to knock my food out of my hand?' she asked, irritably.

'If I wanted to knock something out of your hands, then there'd be nothing in your hands right now,' replied Jermaine calmly, as he took a fork of his food, and stuffed it into his mouth.

'Stop arguing,' hissed their mother, 'Where's your brother? Anton, come and get your food now bwoi!' she bellowed.

Moving the dumplings out of the way, Jermaine continued eating his ackee and saltfish. His eagle-eyed mother noticed this.

'Why aren't you eating your dumplings? I made them sweet, just like you always want them,' Jermaine's mum asked.

'Too many carbs mum, have to watch my intake.'

'Too much what?' replied his mother.

'Oooh, is someone losing weight for a girlfriend?' teased Leanne.

Jermaine gave his sister a harsh look, before placing another fork of the ackee and saltfish into his mouth. At that moment, Anton walked into the room, with his food on a tray.

'If only! He couldn't get a girlfriend if he tried, with that scrawny body of his. You want to be eating more food rather than less,' stated Anton, taking a seat, followed by a large bite out of one of the dumplings.

'Look, if you're not gonna eat mi dumplings, just put them back inna the bowl, I don't want my food going to waste,' snapped their mother, as she turned her attention back to the food on her plate.

Jermaine finished the ackee and saltfish, brought his plate to the kitchen, then reluctantly returned two of the three dumplings into the bowl, but ate one. It was his favourite meal, so he couldn't help himself.

He crept upstairs into his bedroom, and returned to reading his book.

12

Do Over

The next morning, Jermaine arrived at school earlier than intended. As he walked through the playground, he noticed someone sat on the bench outside the DT rooms. He was pleased to see that it was the same girl from a couple of months ago.

Although he hadn't been actively looking for the girl since their first encounter, he had secretly hoped to bump into her alone again. Jermaine had seen her around the school at random moments, but he had no way of finding out exactly who she was without asking around. That wasn't an option as it would have either got back to her somehow, or resulted in a rumour that he liked her being spread around; both of which were not something he wanted to happen.

Worms writhing around in his gut, Jermaine nervously walked over to the bench and sat on the opposite end to the girl. The girl, whose attention was completely directed towards her book, didn't seem to take any notice of his approach. She kept her head slightly lowered, her eyes panning from left to right, absorbing the words on the pages.

Jermaine sat on the bench for a moment, collecting his thoughts. He didn't want to look at her, in case she saw him staring and called him a weirdo again. After a minute or so, he glanced in her direction. He noticed that the book she was reading had been on his private Bike Shed curriculum.

'Brave New World. Really good book. Very, ummm, thought provoking?' Jermaine wasn't sure why he ended that statement like a question.

Startled, the girl raised her head and looked at Jermaine. A slight glimpse of recognition appeared on her face. 'Oh, staring boy. You've read it? I didn't think anyone else our age would be interested in this kind of book.'

'Yeah, it was a good read. I quite enjoy reading those dystopian novels. Have you ever read Fahrenheit 451? If you're into dystopian settings, you'll really enjoy that one,' replied Jermaine, with his heart lodged firmly in his throat. He made a snap decision to ignore the reference to his staring. He didn't know why he felt so nervous around this girl. His palms were sweating, and his breathing became erratic. Speaking between each breath was a challenge.

The girl produced a half smile, only raising one side of her mouth. 'You don't look the type to be interested in those kind of stories.'

'Well, you shouldn't judge a book by its cover,' said Jermaine, instantly regretting the poor attempt at a joke.

The girl continued half-smiling. 'Well, in future, I won't.' She then returned her attention to the book in her hand.

'So, ummm, w-why are you here so early today?' asked Jermaine.

'I could ask you the same couldn't I?' replied the girl, not averting her gaze from her book.

'Oh, yeah, fair enough.'

'I like the peace and quiet of the mornings. Not something you usually get in this school.' The girl kept her attention on her book.

'Yeah, not an aspect of this school that I would suggest be put into the prospectus. So, you just enjoy the alone time then?' asked Jermaine, feeling slightly more comfortable as the conversation continued.

'Not really, it just gives me time to get some reading done, without anyone disturbing me,' she replied, looking up at Jermaine.

The feeling of nervousness gushed back into Jermaine, like a wave filling a ditch with fluid, as he realised what she was hinting at. He stood up and began to walk away.

'Where are you going?' asked the girl.

'Just giving you some peace and quiet to read your book,' said Jermaine with a slight tinge of irritation in his voice.

The girl raised her head from her book, a full smile now on her face. Jermaine found it almost impossible not to stare at her perfect smile. All her teeth were perfectly in line with one another, not a millimetre between any of them, as if they were a shield, protecting her tongue from any danger. She had lines, which appeared on either side of her mouth, accentuating her smile further. Jermaine felt an urge to keep seeing that smile as long as he could.

'You never told me your name,' said the girl.

'I could say the same to you,' replied Jermaine, quite pleased with his display of wit.

'Fair enough. It's Elise,'

'Jermaine, nice to meet you.' He turned, and walked towards the bike shed, feeling surprisingly happier than before he had spoken to Elise.

13

Excursion

A few minutes later, Jermaine arrived at the bike shed to see everyone already there, apart from Jared. He walked over and stood beside Sean, whose face seemed to be beaming with excitement. Jermaine then began to scan the faces of the rest of the group.

'You're late,' came the booming voice of Jared from behind Jermaine. 'Today is your big day. We have a hunt for you and Sean.'

Jermaine looked at Sean again. He now understood why he looked so excited. Over the past couple of months, Sean hadn't stopped mentioning the fact that he'd never been on a hunt. He trained harder than Jermaine, read more than Jermaine, had been trained for longer than Jermaine, but had still never had the chance to hunt. Jermaine understood why Sean was excited, but he couldn't feel anything, except the nervous knot in his stomach.

Jared walked over to the two boys and handed Jermaine an envelope.

'Well, open it then,' demanded Sean, who seemed to be fighting the urge to jump up and down on the spot.

Jermaine opened the envelope, which contained a set of photos, along with a few sheets of paper. Jermaine pulled out the photos, and began passing them along to Sean once he'd had a thorough look. The photos consisted of a group of boys, who were either throwing children around, walking in a pack, or just generally making life difficult for kids around them.

'It's an easy job, a group of Year 8 boys, five to be precise. The tall one appears to be the leader, according to our information. They attend Park High, just a few minutes down the road. Shouldn't take more than ten minutes to walk there, then another ten minutes to do the job. If all goes to plan, you should be back no later than second period, maybe even first,' explained Jared, taking a very stern and professional tone, which he used when he was dealing with a serious matter.

'Remember what we taught you. Try to deal with the situation with as little conflict as possible, but if it does come down to a full-blown fight, be swift and precise with your actions. Aim to hurt and incapacitate, but no serious injuries. A broken bone or two is acceptable, but a bruised body and ego is much more preferable,' Jared explained.

Chris stood up and walked over to the boys, 'Try your best not to get caught. If you do make a mistake and get stopped by either a teacher or the police, for any reason, mention nothing about the group. It was down to a personal vendetta between the two of you and the boys. It will be easier that way.'

'What about registration? What if we don't make it back for first period?' questioned Jermaine, as his excitement was overthrown by his logic.

'You'll be signed in for both regardless. Just concentrate on making this job go smoothly,' answered Chris.

Jermaine wondered how they would achieve that. Did they have body doubles to sit in for him and Sean?

'Remember boys, this is your time to shine,' said Jared, with a smile on his face, 'All the information for your contact is inside the envelope. He'll be waiting for you by the main gates. Have fun.'

*

As they walked up to the gates of Park High, Jermaine and Sean felt the excitement in every fibre of their bodies. They looked around at the other children walking past them. Jermaine studied the faces of the kids around him, recognising that they all had the same confused, lost, and lethargic expressions of all the kids in his school. The only thing that made Jermaine know he wasn't standing outside of St Peters, was the difference in the colour of the ties.

As Sean and Jermaine passed by them, the pupils of Park High seemed to notice that difference also. Anyone who came close to them would look at their ties, then up at their faces, and then give them a wide berth.

A boy, who was taller than Jermaine, stopped in front of him, and began to laugh to himself.

'They're playing some kind of joke on me right? You can't be the guys,' he said, looking around as if he'd spot a camera, or another set of boys hiding behind a tree.

'You're David I presume?' Sean dismissed the boy's surprise.

'When I asked for this situation to be resolved, I expected someone, even slightly threatening to turn up, not a couple of kids younger than me,' David complained.

Sean stepped forward until there was less than a couple of inches between his face, and the boy's chest.

'You asked for your situation to be resolved and we can assure you it will be. Who resolves it is neither a defining factor, nor any of your concern.' Sean sternly looked up into David's eyes.

The boy stepped backwards, out of discomfort.

'Have the boys entered the school yet?' asked Jermaine

'N-no, I went in and they're not in their usual place,' answered David, a softer tone of voice than he'd had before.

'Best thing you can do is keep your distance. We don't want you to scare them away. Just stay out of sight, and if we need you, we'll call you.' Sean turned to face Jermaine, acting as if David no longer existed.

'Ok, thank you.' David scuttled away from Jermaine and Sean, with a look of fear and relief in his eyes.

Sean looked at David from the corner of his eyes, then returned his attention to Jermaine, 'Who'll take lead?'

'Don't know, flip a coin?' replied Jermaine. He didn't mind either way.

Sean pulled out a ten pence piece and flipped it. 'Heads,' he called out. He caught the coin, and then looked down at it. 'Guess you're taking lead on this one Jermaine. I'll go and stand over there by the tree. At least that way, we can approach them from both sides when they come. Stop them from running away.'

Jermaine nodded in agreement, 'Whoever sees them first, whistle to alert the other.'

'No problem.'

Still looking at each and every face that walked past him, Jermaine waited for the bullies to arrive. A few minutes passed, when Jermaine caught sight of a group of five boys, walking towards the school. From his distance, he couldn't see their faces clearly, but the way the other children cleared a path for them, hinted that they were the targets.

In order to alert Sean, Jermaine pursed his lips to whistle, but Sean had seemed to have noticed the group himself. Sean nodded and backed up, so that the tree covered him from sight of the boys.

Taking a deep breath, Jermaine walked towards the bullies, looking for the leader of the group. Once he was within a few feet of the group, he stopped. He planted his feet, so he was ready to act. He had tactically placed himself on a direct collision course with the leader. Seeing the boys, how frail and weak they looked, removed any feelings of worry Jermaine may have previously had.

'Oi, move out of my way my-yute,' demanded the bully. He was at least a quarter of a metre taller than the other boys.

Without the slightest hint of fear, Jermaine looked up at the boy, straight into his eyes, and simply responded, 'No.'

All the boys, apart from the leader, started laughing. One of them turned to the leader, and said, 'You got told fam. He straight up said "No", like he's your dad bruv.'

The group then continued laughing harder than before.

The leader looked around at his group, and began to get enraged. He dropped his rucksack, reaching a hand out, attempting to grab Jermaine. Jermaine stepped to the side, avoiding the grasp, and grabbed a hold of the bully's hand. He then took hold of the boy's index finger and began pulling it back, along with his entire arm, behind his back.

As if the music had stopped in a game of musical statues, all of the children around stopped moving, and silence descended upon the school entrance. The looks on the faces of the children spoke a thousand words. They looked at Jermaine, holding the bully, in complete astonishment.

The leader bent backwards, his entire body following the direction of his hand. Jermaine then elbowed the boy in his stomach, and the bully released a gut-wrenching squeal of pain, as he fell to his knees. At that moment, Sean approached from behind the group and kicked one of the boys in the back of the knee, making him drop to the floor. He then grabbed the boy by the chin, with his left hand, and then used his right hand to punch him in his back.

The three other boys looked at their two friends on the floor, then back at Sean and Jermaine. Both of them looked the boys directly in their eyes, Sean periodically punching his hostage in the back, and Jermaine slowly bending the leaders finger further back, causing him to release another squeal in pain.

'Run away,' said Jermaine, with a cold, heartless look in his eyes.

The three remaining boys ran into the school as quickly as they could.

Jermaine returned his attention to the leader of the group.

'Please, you're going to break my finger!' pleaded the leader, tears forming in his eyes.

'Do you know who we are?' asked Jermaine.

'No, I don't. Just a couple of psychos!'

Jermaine pulled the finger back further. The boy squealed in pain.

'Do you know who we are?' Jermaine asked again.

The leader of the bullies looked at Jermaine, then down at his tie, then back up at his face. He turned his head and looked at Sean in the same way. His face turned as white as a sheet.

'No way, you guys are too young to be one of them.'

'Good, so you do know. Your days of picking on the weak are over. If we catch wind of you doing anything, which can be deemed as bullying, even in the slightest sense of the word, we'll be back. Consider this as a warning,' declared Jermaine, bending the boys finger back even further, just enough not to break it, but enough to cause the maximum amount of pain, 'We have eyes and ears everywhere, remember that.' He let the boy go, who scurried off across the ground on his knees, cradling his hand.

Sean released his victim, who fell to his stomach, and subsequently began dragging himself along the floor.

Jermaine and Sean looked around at the faces staring at them, some in horror and fear, but the majority, completely filled with admiration. They both zipped up their coats, and began to briskly walk away. Once out of sight of the children from Park High,

Jermaine looked at Sean, who had the largest smile on his face that Jermaine had ever seen. The smile seemed to be contagious, as it began to spread across Jermaine's face. Sean raised his hand, his smile still consuming most of his face. Looking at Sean's hand, Jermaine decided not to fight the urge, and high fived it. The two then started running back to school, in order to avoid being any later than they already were.

*

The clock outside the school office read 09:10. Jermaine and Sean walked through the front doors and shuffled past the desk, half expecting to be asked why they were both so late, but the office manager acted as if she'd not seen them. They both continued walking down the hall, with nobody saying anything to them. They eventually came to a junction, nodded at each other, then went their separate ways, to their different lessons.

As Jermaine walked into his maths class, his teacher raised her head as she noticed him enter, but for some reason pretended not to. She then went back to her lesson. For the first time, Jermaine truly felt like he was a part of the Bully Hunters.

14

Debrief

As the lesson progressed, Jermaine couldn't relax. He felt his heart still beating from the thrill of the hunt. He couldn't keep his hands steady. He looked at his palms, and clenched his fists. He felt so powerful; in control of everything around him. They had all seemed so weak to him. He knew that he could have taken on all five of those boys on his own. He felt completely unstoppable.

The bell for the start of break rang, and Jermaine gathered his books, threw them in his bag and rushed to the bike shed. The journey there felt longer than it ever had. He couldn't wait to give a detailed account of the event to the rest of the Hunters.

He arrived at the shed, and stopped to compose himself. He turned the corner, noticing the sixth formers all sat around the picnic table, or the steps situated outside the port-a-cabin.

'So, how did it go? Where's Sean?' questioned Jared.

'Went fine, Sean should be here any minute. We both got back without any issues,' responded Jermaine, bursting to explain what had happened in detail.

'What did I miss?' asked Sean, turning the corner. He dropped his bag down on the floor, next to the picnic table, as if it was just dead weight, slowing him down.

'We were just about to debrief. So, tell us everything,' Jared invited, as he placed a half of a Snickers Duo into his mouth.

The two boys began explaining everything that happened. The excitement in their voices was reminiscent of a child telling his friends about a birthday party that he had just thrown the day before. They finished each other's sentences, gave demonstrations, and even threw in the odd sound effect for good measure.

Once the story had been relayed to the group, Jermaine and Sean looked at the Hunters. They all sat in complete silence and seemed to be trying to avoid eye contact. The silence was eventually broken by an outburst of laughter from Camille.

Like a yawn, an outbreak of laughter spread across the remainder of the group. The only member still sitting with a straight face was Chris. Slowly, a smile began to creep into the corners of his mouth, but looked as if it were subdued by his cheeks, then beaten back into a scowl.

'I'm sorry, you guys look so pleased with yourselves, I couldn't hold it in,' stated Camille, walking past Sean and Jermaine, whilst wiping a tear away from her eyes.

'Yeah, hilarious,' mumbled Jermaine, quite irritated that they had all been looking at him as if he was a joke.

'Don't take it so personal guys, we were all the same way after our first hunts, we just had nobody to look at us filled with excitement when we were younger. It was quite a show, the sound effects did tip it into humorous though,' said Jared.

The bell for third period rang, and the sixth formers all stood up, walked past Jermaine and Sean tapping them on the shoulder, still chuckling.

'Well, I had an amazing time,' said Sean, still bubbling with excitement. The laughter hadn't seemed to throw him, or change his mood, which Jermaine did slightly admire, 'Anyway, we better get to our lessons. Don't want to be late again,' continued Sean.

'A quick point before you both leave,' started Chris, who was still sat on the step, 'I want you both to remember this feeling, I know you must have felt powerful, as if you ruled the world and nothing could harm you. Hold on to that when you face these bullies.'

Chris stood up and walked past the two boys, 'Keep in mind that those feelings you felt, and probably are still feeling, are the same thing that the bullies must feel when they're beating on a weak child. They must feel that they are powerful. They must believe that nothing can harm them. Think what you would do to keep hold of that power.'

Chris turned and faced the two boys, 'There's a saying about a mouse being cornered, and fighting back to defend itself, but that force is nothing compared to a lion fighting to defend its position as the alpha male of a pack.'

With that, Chris walked from behind the shed.

Jermaine and Sean stood there thinking. They had both felt strong. They hadn't ever considered why someone would bully somebody else until that moment. The feeling of power they felt was a high, like nothing they'd ever experienced before.

Jermaine and Sean walked out from behind the shed and into the playground.

'I guess I'll see you here at lunchtime for training,' said Sean.

Jermaine agreed.

15

Withdrawal

Jermaine awoke in his bed and looked over to the clock. It was six in the morning. He had still not been able to get out of his usual routine, even though it had been nearly a week since he'd had to wake up to go to school. Outside was dark, which didn't make Jermaine feel any better about being up so early.

The sound of the birds chirping and the neighbours scraping the ice off their windscreens occupied Jermaine's hearing. He lay in bed and stared at the ceiling. Since the holiday had begun, he'd felt empty, as if there were something missing. He turned his head and looked at his school uniform hung on the door of his wardrobe, as if it were patiently awaiting him to take it off the hanger. Funnily, that was all Jermaine could consider doing.

The thought of putting the uniform on and making his journey into school occupied every morning. There was a momentary heart palpitation within Jermaine's chest as he considered it. Lethargically, he got out of bed and fell to the ground into a plank position. He managed to do sixty-four push-ups before he began to feel tired, then switched over onto his back and began his crunches.

A few moments later, he stood up and walked downstairs. He went into the living room, pushed the door closed behind him, and sat on the couch. If he wasn't awake before, the sensation of the cold leather on his bare arms and legs ensured he now was. The hum from the television powering up was louder than usual. Instinctively, Jermaine pressed the numbers 601, changing the channel to Cartoon Network. As he sat back, his eye caught the white Christmas tree in the corner, near the window. He turned his head to look at the tree and began scanning the room, taking in all the decorations around him.

A strange feeling came over him, which he couldn't truly put into words. He turned his attention back towards the television, which was now showing Christmas adverts, pushing toys onto children, in a hope that they would pester their parents enough to ensure a purchase for the biggest shopping day of the year. The same feeling flushed through Jermaine again. He felt an overwhelming need to change the channel. He reached for the remote control, but whichever channel he switched to, there were adverts for products of some kind, clawing for their product to be the Christmas gift of choice.

Filled with disappointment, he turned off the television and sat back, his head leaning back onto the sofa, staring towards the ceiling. Above his head, Jermaine could see a piece of tinsel stuck to the wall with double sided tape. The tinsel looked as if it were holding onto the tape with all its might, but was losing the battle.

Suddenly, it dawned on him; it was Christmas that was bothering him. He had never noticed it before but he felt as if he were seeing the holiday for the first time. It felt...wrong.

The whispering voice of Jermaine's mother called out, 'Jermaine, is that you down there?'

'Yeah mum, it's just me.'

Jermaine heard his mother walk down the stairs. She pushed open the door to the front room.

'Jermaine... is everything ok?' she enquired.

'Yeah, I'm fine,' he replied. His mother had never approached him with her concerns. It made Jermaine feel quite uncomfortable.

'You just, you don't seem yourself ever since the holiday started. Well, you've seemed distant for a while now. If there were something wrong, you would tell me wouldn't you?'

Jermaine looked at his mother and saw the worry in her eyes. She had never been an emotional person, so he gathered that it must have been difficult for her to approach him in such a manner.

'Of course mum. I'm fine though. School is just...' Jermaine contemplated how he should word it, 'more demanding than I anticipated, that's all.'

Jermaine's mother looked at him for a moment, a smile eventually revealing itself on her face. 'Ok,' she said. She stood up, and gave Jermaine a kiss on the forehead.

'I'm going to make some breakfast, you want some?'

Jermaine sat still, in a state of shock. He couldn't remember the last time his mother had kissed him. This show of affection was something he was not particularly prepared for.

'Jermaine?'

'Y...yes mum?'

'Breakfast?'

Jermaine composed himself. 'Yes please, thank you.'

*

The Christmas holidays seemed to pass too slowly for Jermaine. He normally willed and wished them to take as long as possible; he once heard positive thinking can change your reality...it never did. This year was different. Each day felt like a millennium.

Christmas day came around without the usual excitement Jermaine was accustomed to feeling. The entire family went to his uncle's house, as they did every year. Presents were given to Jermaine, as per usual, although opening them had seemed to lose its enjoyment. He ate a single plate of food; he couldn't bring himself to eat his usual two full plates. He also skipped his normal two helpings of Jamaican rum cake, which his uncle was famous for, amongst the family.

Looking around the room whilst the family played bus stop, he noted the happiness on everyone's faces. The day must have still held the same magic that it always did, he just felt numb to it.

Regardless of how hard he tried, the feeling of glee just would not fill him. He eventually realised that nothing he did seemed to excite him. Video games had lost their intrigue. Television seemed more irritating than entertaining. The only thing that made him feel the slightest bit excited was when he thought of going back to school and hunting some more bullies. Remembering the look on the faces of those he had dealt with made his heart race and blood boil.

Jermaine attempted to recreate the feeling he felt when dealing with the bullies, as well as break the monotony of sitting around doing nothing, by working out as much as he could. He spent the remainder of his holiday training as much as his body would allow. He would train until he was barely able to stand on his feet. Even this didn't have the desired effect.

As time drew to the last weekend of the holidays, Jermaine began to feel desperate to get back to school, wishing he could just sleep until it was Monday. As if he were stood beside him, Jermaine heard the voice of Chris saying, *"Think what you would do to keep hold of that power."*

Spring Term

16

Strength

Monday finally arrived. Jermaine's entire essence filled with excitement. Putting on his school uniform felt better than anything he'd felt during the holiday. He considered that this was more than likely the way soldiers must have felt when they put on their suits of armour in the days of knights and kings. Adjusting his green and black tie, he looked at himself in the mirror and smiled.

Once he arrived at school, Jermaine felt like he was home. As he walked through the doors, he noticed a smell. He had never smelt the scent previously, but now he couldn't ignore it. It was a mixture of freshly cut sawdust and carpet. It overwhelmed his nostrils. He inhaled a deep breath and basked in the aroma.

He walked through the school and headed straight for the wall by the boys gym. As he expected, Sean was already there waiting. This was the first time Jermaine had been happy to see another kid after a prolonged period of time.

'Hey Jermaine!' exclaimed Sean, reciprocating the excitement that Jermaine was feeling, despite his attempts to hide it. Regardless of his efforts, a large smile forced its way onto his face.

The two boys exchanged a masculine embrace, right hands clasped together along with left hands wrapped around the others back, patting in a friendly gesture.

'You had a good Christmas?' Sean enquired, a smile enveloping his face.

Jermaine's smile dissolved and changed to a look of disappointment. 'No, not really. Something just felt a little...weird. Missing. I don't know.'

Sean's expression turned to one of relief, 'Oh, good.'

Jermaine looked confused, which led Sean to raise his hands in protest, 'No! Not good that you didn't have a good Christmas, I just had the same experience but thought it was just me.'

'Oh,' the two boys began to chuckle.

'Hey guys, good holidays I hope,' uttered a voice from behind the boys. They both turned to see Craig standing behind them.

'Oh, hey. Good thanks, what about you?' answered Jermaine.

'Yeah, good, good. I had a lot to look into. Did you guys hear about a fight that took place outside Park High just before the holidays? It was apparently two boys wearing our school colours that put the hurting on,' Craig explained, looking both of the boys straight in their faces, periodically switching his attention between them, 'from what people are saying, the two boys looked a little like the two of you. Weird right?'

'Yeah weird, anyway, I better get to class, have to see my form teacher about something.' Sean said, directing his speech predominantly at Jermaine.

Jermaine felt as if this was an excuse for Sean to make a quick escape from the uncomfortable conversation. Sean hopped down off the wall and began walking towards his form class in the science block.

After he watched Sean walk away, Jermaine turned his attention back to Craig, who was staring at him with a slight smirk on his face. Jermaine then jumped down from the wall, and placed his bag on his back.

'I'd better get going myself. Don't want to be late for registration on the first day back.'

Craig smiled, 'True, wouldn't be a good start would it?'

'I'll see you around,' Jermaine began to walk away.

'Yea, see you around. Oh, I nearly forgot to say, there was something else quite strange that I heard happened before the holiday,' began Craig, 'some meeting between a group of kids...some rather large people were supposedly in attendance. Could be something for you to look into?' insinuated Craig, still fishing for a sign that he was correct about Jermaine's connection with the Hunters.

'Not my job. I'm just trying to make it through secondary like everyone else,'

As he walked away, Jermaine thought about Craig. He wondered how he always received his information. He also decided that he probably wasn't part of the Hunters, as Sean had treated him with just as much dismissal as Jermaine did himself. There had also been no sign of a connection over the past months. Of course, there was always the possibility that he and Sean were in the dark of Craig's true position. Jermaine shrugged the thoughts off, as he couldn't find a concise answer, and went to registration.

*

At the end of the day, Jermaine made his way to the field. He had received a note from Camille that had been hand delivered to him by a random child in the school. The message read;

'Training grounds, after school. Don't be late. Camille.'

The same mixed feeling of anxiety and excitement reared its ugly head again. The feeling consumed Jermaine as he drew closer to the training grounds entrance. He had been looking forward to getting some real training in all holiday. He gathered that he would begin his strength training now, but didn't know what to expect from Camille.

As Jermaine drew closer to the entrance, he noticed Sean walking towards him from the distance. Sean seemed to also be making his way to the same location.

'Camille?' asked Jermaine.

'Yeah. I think we're starting our strength training. Must have proved ourselves on that last mission.'

'Good. I've been itching to get back into it,' Jermaine admitted.

'Yeah, me too, just not sure if I'm up for this so soon after all that feasting I did over the holiday,' Sean grimaced.

The two boys walked through the bush, replacing the branches that kept the entrance to the location a secret from the masses. As they both strolled onto the training grounds, they saw the figure of Camille sat on the steps. Jermaine began to pick up his pace once he made out the frustrated look on her face. Sean followed suit.

Once the two boys were within ten feet of Camille, she stood up and closed the gap.

'Have a nice break from it all? Good Christmas? Loads of presents and stuff?' questioned Camille.

Jermaine begrudgingly replied, 'Yeah, it was o.....'

'Good,' Camille interrupted, dismissing his answer, 'well, as you've had such a blissful little respite, I think it's time for us to get right down to work.'

Unbeknownst to Camille, this was the best news she could have given the two boys. Jermaine began to feel his foot shaking and his hands became impossible to keep still.

'So far, you've been working on your stamina and discipline. Now, we're going to move onto strength training,' Camille declared, 'strength can change the tide of a battle. The correct use of power can dictate the victor in an altercation.'

Camille turned around and started walking inside the training building. She waved her hand in a gesture for them to follow her. Once inside, she walked into the centre of one of the mats.

'We will be conducting plyometric workouts to condition your muscles to be capable of more explosive actions.'

Camille sat back into a squat position, 'This is called a squat push-up.' She fell forward onto her palms, keeping her legs bent. She then bent her arms, lowering her body down to the floor until her nose was no more than a couple millimetres from the mat. She then pushed off the ground using her arms, returning to a squat position.

Camille stayed in the squat position, 'And this is called a squat turn.' Camille then jumped up in the air, turning one hundred and eighty degrees, then landed back into a squat. She then repeated the squat push-up, followed by another squat turn so that she was facing the boys again.

Jermaine and Sean looked on at Camille without too much concern.

'That rotation is classed as one. We'll start today's workout with one hundred of those,' Camille said with a tinge of happiness in her voice. Jermaine and Sean's relaxed expressions instantly changed to looks of horror and slight disbelief. Jermaine noticed that Camille's face seemed to gleam as theirs became more sullen.

'Remember my challenge to move me off the mat? Well, that will be slightly modified here. Until you're able to shift me, you will not move on to combat training, so you'd better get started at building up that strength of yours,' Camille threatened, 'so what are you waiting for? Let's begin.'

The two boys walked over to the side of the room and removed their shoes.

'She's enjoying the thought of our pain,' Jermaine whispered to Sean.

'Yeah, I noticed. A true sadist,' Sean placed his shoes together, with his socks inside them. He held his stomach, exhaling deeply. Jermaine smiled at this display of discomfort, happy that he never indulged too much over the break.

The boys then approached a mat each, assumed a squat position and once Camille said start, they began.

17

Elise Walker

After the workout, Jermaine and Sean ambled towards their bus stop to make their way home. After the 'squat push-up and turn' rotations, Camille made them do a set of further gruelling workouts such as spider jumps, V push-ups and hurdle sprints. The boys watched her smile grow more menacing as their discomfort increased.

The boys lacked any energy once they arrived at the bus stop. They both leaned against the glass of the bus stop, then slid down to a seated position, leaving a smudge mark from the sweat on their backs.

Jermaine sat and stared at the floor between his legs. Although he felt like he was a walking apparition, just clinging onto life, he also felt more alive than he had felt for the past two weeks. Neither boy said a word to each other, mainly due to the fatigue they felt; they just waited in silence.

A few moments passed before Sean's bus turned the corner. Sean looked up and began his attempt to stand. After a couple of seconds of willing himself to stand more than anything else, Sean made it to his feet. He looked down at Jermaine who was also making an attempt to stand. Once both boys had found their feet, they looked at one another listlessly. The bus pulled up at the bus stop as Sean made an attempt at a goodbye gesture with his hands, but gave up, deciding to give a half-hearted nod instead, which was reciprocated by Jermaine.

Once Sean had boarded his bus, Jermaine leant against the bus stop again, this time deciding to stay on his feet as the ascension from a seated position was too much work to repeat.

'You look tired,' chimed a silky voice from behind Jermaine. He turned to see Elise stood behind him, a cheeky smile on her face. Jermaine dug deep and used his last reserves of energy to stand up straight. Suddenly, he became aware of how much he had been sweating and how bad he must have smelt.

'It's gone past five-thirty; a bit late to be heading home isn't it? You look like you've been running a marathon,' she probed.

'Yeah, I was just doing a little...exercise with a friend,' Jermaine replied, thinking how odd that must have sounded after the words left his mouth.

Elise raised an eyebrow, 'Ok.'

'Why are you here so late?'

Elise raised the case in her hand, 'Music lessons. You're not the only one who does extra-curricular activities,' she stated in a playful manner.

'Oh, which instrument do you play?' Jermaine asked, trying to avoid standing too close to Elise, in case she caught a slight whiff of his body odour.

'It's a flute. My parents wanted me to take up an instrument when I was in primary, and this happened to be the lightest and easiest to walk around with, so I went with it. Didn't expect to truly fall in love with it though.'

As Elise finished speaking, she noticed a few people at the bus stop beginning to walk towards the curb, which turned her attention to the approaching bus.

'Well, this is me,' she said, turning back to face Jermaine.

'Oh, that's me too,' responded Jermaine, pleasantly surprised that he would get a chance to speak with Elise further.

The two boarded the bus, walked upstairs and ventured to the rear seats. As the bus drove its route, Jermaine and Elise continued to speak about: interests, likes, dislikes, school, specific teachers; anything they could talk about, they spoke about. Jermaine felt so comfortable speaking with Elise, his previous concerns regarding his scent slowly dissipated into nothing but a small, insignificant thought in the back of his mind.

Jermaine had experienced female company in the past, but none as in tune with his way of thinking as Elise was. It felt as if he were speaking to a friend he had grown up with, but never had the chance to speak to before.

After, what felt like no more than a few minutes to Jermaine, Elise reached up and pressed the bell, 'This is my stop. I thought *I* lived further than anyone else in the school. Where are you jumping off?' Elise asked as she stood up out of her seat. Glancing out of the window, Jermaine realised that he had actually missed his stop by quite a significant distance. He had been so enthralled by his conversation that he had completely lost awareness of where he was.

Felling slightly embarrassed by this fact, Jermaine turned back to Elise and said, 'Not too far from here.'

Elise raised an eyebrow and smiled, 'Ok, well, have a good evening. See you around,' and then made her way down the stairs and off the bus. As the bus began to pull away from the bus stop, Jermaine instantly reached up and pressed the button. Once off the bus, he crossed the road and caught the next bus heading back in the direction he had come from.

18

Next Generation

As the weeks passed, Jermaine and Sean continued their strength training with Camille. Their days followed a less exciting process than they did before the Christmas holidays. The boys wondered why they were not given the green light to accompany any hunts. They saw the sixth formers leaving the school, and then returning, from what they assumed were hunts, but they were never requested to join.

Their days began to resemble those of average boys of the same age. They went to school, went to lessons, hung out during break and lunch. The only thing that made them feel different was the fact that they had their gruelling sessions with Camille after school.

When both boys had trained together, it was always challenging, but bearable. In contrast, training with Camille seemed to be established purely to try to force them to quit as quickly as possible. Breaks were sparse and short. Exercises were frequent and long. On a few occasions, Jermaine felt as if he would have been sick if he didn't stop, so he stopped, which led to a barking session in his ear from Camille.

Their training had extended beyond the initial circuits, and also included a more refined and physically demanding list of activities. Camille made the boys pull rolled up training mats, stuffed with weights, which had been strapped to their backs. They were sent to run boxing drills, holding kettle bells in each hand. Jermaine's least favourite workout was the least active; the boys were required to stand with their arms outstretched, holding a weight in each hand. If their arms fell below a ninety-degree angle, they had to do a fifty press-ups, and then continue. Camille called this the scarecrow. It was her favourite.

Although both boys despised the training regime, they had noticed that they were becoming stronger. The initial workout routine now felt like Camille was cutting them some slack. Other than this factor, for Jermaine, a saving grace was that he was able to get the bus home with Elise on Mondays and Wednesdays, when she had her flute lessons.

Both Jermaine and Elise never officially stated that they would meet on those days, but they would wait for each other at the bus stop, if one of them were running late. Jermaine had begun to get closer to Elise. She had mentioned a brother once, but never seemed to want to talk about him. Jermaine thought this was kind of strange, although never pressed her on the subject. The two had also begun to start meeting more frequently in the mornings. Jermaine looked forward to the time he spent with her, more than nearly anything in his day.

The monotony of the daily routine finally changed one day, when Sean and Jermaine were summoned to the bike shed for a meeting with the rest of the Hunters. Since the holiday, Jermaine and Sean had seen Camille every evening for training, Jared periodically to change the book assignments, and the twins in passing throughout the school. Jermaine had only seen Chris from afar, as he was walking through the school one day, but didn't manage to say anything to him as he was with a teacher at the time. From his distance, Jermaine couldn't make out which teacher it was.

Some part of Jermaine felt excited that he would see the group all together again. However strange their relationship was, he had started to see them as his friends.

The Year 7 boys arrived at the bike shed to see the sixth formers already sat at the picnic table, mid-conversation.

'Here we are,' said Alex, looking at the two boys approaching the group.

'Take a seat,' said Maxwell as the twins stood up, making space for Jermaine and Sean.

'Thanks,' Jermaine sat down, still wondering what the meeting could be about.

Chris looked at both Jermaine and Sean, alternating his attention between the two of them.

'Do you understand why we chose you to join our group?' Chris questioned, getting straight to the point.

Both Jermaine and Sean thought deeply before they answered.

'Because we showed potential to be great Hunters?' answered Sean, quite confident with himself and his answer.

'And your answer?' enquired Chris, turning his attention to Jermaine from Sean.

'Because there was no one else,' responded Jermaine, pessimistically.

Chris smiled for a fraction of a second and then his expression returned to the straight laced one he usually donned.

'You are both correct. You were the best of the candidates we saw, but you are both missing a vital aspect of this situation. You haven't considered the fact that we only have one year left at this school. At the end of this year, we will all be leaving for university, or starting our own businesses; continuing our lives past the bully hunting,' explained Chris.

Like a bolt out of the blue, the reality of this fact hit Jermaine. He had the feeling that he already knew this, but just kept lying to himself, as if not giving the thoughts a voice would make them not be true. The first set of friends he ever had, however strange their relationship, would be disbanded so soon. He lowered his head and stared at his hands on the table.

'Now, regardless of the fact that you are both showing promise, it's not feasible that the two of you will be able to maintain the legacy of the Hunters on your own. This situation leaves us with a dilemma which can only be resolved one way.'

'We need more members,' interjected Jermaine, raising his head. His sadness that the sixth formers would be leaving began to turn into rage. He felt that he had been teased with something that he would ultimately lose so soon. He felt stupid for letting his guard down and expecting anything more. This was always the way it went for him.

'Exactly,' replied Chris, pleased with Jermaine's ability to discern the situation so well.

'So, who is it going to be?' Sean asked anxiously.

'Well, that's what this meeting is about,' started Jared, 'we want you two to choose those people.'

Jermaine and Sean both had expressions of surprise plastered on their faces.

'We'll be choosing them? Why?' Jermaine uttered.

'They'll be your team, not ours. We could choose who you will be spending the next six years of your lives fighting beside but it makes more sense that a decision that will impact on you more than us is made by yourselves,' Jared explained.

'How? How are we supposed to choose who would be suitable for the group? We're not even completely clear as to why you chose us.' Jermaine couldn't conceal his anger towards the entire situation. It was overpowering the normal level of fear he felt around Chris. He didn't want to get anyone else; he had just begun to grow used to the idea of being actual *friends* with the sixth formers and Sean.

Chris sat forward and locked eyes with Jermaine, 'You know why we chose you. You may not be able to verbalise it simply, but you know. You can feel it. We are all alike. Different, yes, but more alike than the majority of the school, if not the country,' he declared, his words quelling Jermaine's insubordinate tone.

'To simplify things for you slightly, we do have certain aspects that need to be taken into consideration with your choice,' Jared began to explain, 'you can't choose just any random person within the school, they have to be in your year group. They have to be trustworthy, and they must join the group of their own free will.'

'Other than that, you have carte blanche,' concluded Chris, sitting back, releasing his locked eye contact.

Jermaine stood up. 'Are we finished here?' he asked.

Chris smiled to himself again and looked up at Jermaine, 'We've said what we needed to.'

'Good,' Jermaine snapped as he turned and began to walk away.

'I'd better go after him,' Sean announced, with an awkward smile on his face.

Chris nodded in silence.

*

Halfway across the playground, Sean caught up with Jermaine. Jermaine noticed Sean walking beside him, but never showed any acknowledgement of his presence.

'So, what was that about?' Sean asked after a few minutes of following Jermaine in silence.

'Nothing.' Jermaine retorted, lying to Sean. He didn't know how to verbalise what he was so irritated about without sounding soft, or weak.

'Ok...well, we need to get these new recruits. It's quite exciting if I'm honest. No idea where we're going to begin though.'

Jermaine listened to Sean partially whilst scanning the faces of any Year 7s he could see. He realised that it would take them a long time to vet each kid, then watch him or her to make sure they have the right characteristics. He didn't speak to any of the other Year 7s, apart from...like a runaway train, the answer ploughed into Jermaine's mind without warning.

'I know who the first will be. They'll be able to help us choose the others also,' he declared, whilst rushing into the school building, Sean following quickly behind him.

*

Jermaine and Sean approached a bunch of Year 7 boys and girls. They stopped just on the outskirts of the group.

'Craig, we need to talk,' announced Jermaine, raising his voice loud enough to interrupt the conversations that the group were having.

The children in the group turned to face Jermaine with annoyed expressions, until they noticed who it was. The expressions changed from annoyance to slight fear and reverence. Even though nobody knew that Jermaine and Sean were part of the Bully Hunters for sure, everyone suspected it, which meant that they were not to be messed with.

The group separated, revealing Craig walking towards the boys.

'Hey guys, to what do I owe the pleasure?' Craig asked, sarcastically.

'We need to speak with you in private,' said Jermaine as he walked away from the group, gesturing to Craig that he should follow him.

The boys led Craig away from the playground towards the rear of the humanities block, one of the most secluded parts of the school. As they went towards the dilapidated building, Craig began to feel progressively anxious. Leaving the safety of the playground, he felt like he was heading straight into a lion's den. For the first time since the school year began, Craig wished his brother were there to protect him.

Once the three boys had arrived at their intended destination, Craig clasped his hands together in a praying fashion, 'I haven't told anyone anything, seriously! Please, don't do whatever you were thinking of doing. I won't bug you two about it anymore,' he pleaded, his hands pressed so tightly together his elbows were raised at a ninety degree angle.

'Relax; we're not going to do anything to you. We just want to talk,' said Sean, swallowing the laugh in his throat.

'You were right. We are part of the Hunters,' Jermaine admitted.

This piece of information shocked Craig back to his usual self; dissolving all the fear he had just felt. 'What? You're actually admitting it? Ah man. I wanted it to be a more dramatic reveal, like I see you guys beating on some bullies, catch it on film, blackmail you...'

The unimpressed looks on Jermaine and Sean's faces stopped Craig in his tracks. Suddenly, Craig regretted his words, 'Or like this is fine, perfectly fine.'

'We're telling you now because we need your support. Well, your help,' continued Jermaine.

Craig began to relax once he realised that the boys weren't going to attempt to 'silence' him. His initial thoughts of fear swiftly replaced with intrigue.

'What kind of favour? Do you need someone to be taught a swift lesson in respect or humility? I thought you guys were capable of doing those things yourself,' Craig replied.

'We don't need your physical capabilities, just your brain.'

'What? What about my brain?'

'We need you to help us look for other people who you think could possibly be members of the Hunters. You seem to be the most clued up Year 7 in these matters,' Jermaine explained.

'Am I?' responded Craig, a look of surprise on his face.

'Well, you knew we were a part of the group,' Sean interjected.

'Seriously? Everyone knows who's in the Hunters, and at the same time, nobody knows. It's one of those paradoxes,' Craig answered, 'There won't be a person in this school above Year 8 that doesn't know exactly who is in the group and what they do, but nobody has any proof.'

Sean turned to Jermaine, 'Well, if he can't help us with this, then what's the point in asking him to join?'

Craig heard this but did not fully digest the information initially.

'Yeah, maybe we need someone else to be our intelligence. There are a couple other possible candidates for us to look at.'

'Wait, wait, wait; you're offering me a place with the Hunters?' Craig asked, in complete disbelief.

'Well, we thought you were the best for the role, but obviously we were wrong.' Jermaine tapped Sean on the shoulder and nodded towards the direction they came from, insinuating that they should leave, 'we won't take up any more of your time.'

Craig stopped momentarily and looked at the two boys starting to walk away. He had half expected them both to turn around and start laughing, saying "only joking". After Jermaine and Sean took a few steps, Craig realised they could actually be serious.

'Hold on!' Craig bellowed.

Jermaine and Sean stopped but never turned around.

'I never said I couldn't do it, just meant that I didn't have to use my brain to realise the two of you were in the group.'

'So you can find us some prospective members?' Jermaine questioned over his shoulder.

'Yeah, that's not a problem, I know a few Year 7s that would fit perfectly into the group,' Craig answered, full of enthusiasm.

'Well, there's no time like the present,' Jermaine stated, continuing to walk away.

'So.... is the offer for me to join still open?'

Jermaine and Sean stopped and turned to face Craig.

'If you think you're up to it?' uttered Sean.

'Seriously?' Craig exclaimed, overcome with a rush of adrenaline.

'What do you say, want to hunt bullies with us?' Jermaine asked, as he extended his hand out for Craig to take it. Craig dove forward, bypassed Jermaine's hand, and hugged him instead. After a few seconds, Craig realised what he was doing and released Jermaine.

'Sorry, just never thought this day would come,' Craig said, straightening Jermaine's jacket out.

'We'll take that as a yes then,' chuckled Sean.

19

Recruitment Drive

Jermaine, Sean and Craig spent some time observing a large variety of kids in their school. They watched everything these candidates did. They observed what kinds of friends they had, how they interacted with those friends, where they ate lunch, whether what they ate was healthy, if they played sports and which sports they played; they even considered their punctuality and attendance.

Whether it was the boys being too specific, or whether each possible candidate just didn't meet the necessary requirements, none of the candidates Craig had put forward were good enough matches for the Hunters. Each child had a couple of the requirements, such as strength, determination, intelligence but they each seemed to lack something. Jermaine couldn't explain to Sean and Craig what it was, but he knew there was something that didn't feel right.

*

Two weeks after the search had started, Jermaine and Sean were concluding another gruelling training session with Camille, when Jared arrived at the training grounds. Jared walked into the training building and approached both boys as they were gathering their bags.

'How is the search going? Have you found any members for the group other than Craig?' Jared asked. Both Sean and Jermaine shook their heads in disappointment.

'Well, at least the one choice you did make was a good one. I had actually put him forward as a possibility when you had been chosen. He seemed to be inquisitive enough to be a consideration, just didn't compare to you I guess.'

'You put him forward?' Jermaine tried to hide how chuffed he felt to hear this from Jared by asking the question.

'We each put a person forward as a possibility. He was my choice, you were Chris'.'

'Chris put me forward? He personally chose me?' Jermaine thought to himself.

'So, Chris just makes the decisions?'

'We're not a dictatorship Jermaine. We're equals. Although it may seem like Chris makes all the decisions, that's only because we have faith in him. We all trust his opinion, as he trusts ours. We've been working together for over six years. That wouldn't have lasted if he called all the shots. We all voted, and chose you.'

'Stop swelling his head. Chris also chose Sean, remember that. You're not that special,' Camille shouted out from across the training gym. Sean smiled at this statement.

'Well, Craig was the best person we could think of. He knows more about the group than I do. Also, haven't seen anyone with as much knowledge of what's going on around here as he does. Other than him though, it's not been so straightforward. Just can't seem to find anyone else suitable,' Jermaine explained, wiping the sweat off his face with a towel.

'Just been one problem or another,' Sean added.

'What have been the parameters for your search? Maybe you've been looking incorrectly,' suggested Jared.

'I guess that's possible but I have nothing to go on. How am I supposed to know what to look for?' Jermaine asked, dropping his towel onto his bag and looking at the time on the wall in the training room. He was aware that it was coming close to the usual time he would meet up with Elise.

Jared drew closer to Jermaine, 'I thought you had the ability to observe your surroundings? That was apparently one of the strengths that Chris sold when he put you forward for the group.'

He considered what Jared had meant by this statement. What was he over looking?

'This group was made out of *necessity*, not convenience. Before the group, we were all individuals, then we found a common cause. We all *needed* the group, we didn't know it then but we needed each other. Anyway, I'm sure you'll figure it out. Look forward to seeing who you choose,' Jared stated as he walked towards the door of the room, 'ah, before I forget, you're due a report on 'The Chrysalids' by the end of the week. No excuses.'

Jared's words kept on floating around Jermaine's mind as he walked over to say goodbye to Camille and Sean. As if he had never seen it before, the birthmark on Camille's face stood out more than ever. Abruptly, the realisation of the meaning behind what Jared had said sunk into Jermaine's mind.

'Necessity.... NECESSITY! Of course! Sean, I'll explain to you and Craig tomorrow. I know what we've been missing!' Jermaine exclaimed as he grabbed his things and rushed out the door.

'What was that about? Most lively I've seen him in a while,' Camille mused.

'No idea. Maybe the workouts are finally getting to him,' answered Sean.

*

The next morning Jermaine sat on the wall near the boy's gym waiting for the others to show. After a few minutes of waiting Sean approached and sat on the wall next to him. The two boys greeted each other as Craig began to walk over to them.

'So, we're here. What's going on?' Sean enquired.

'What have we been looking for in the possible candidates so far?' Jermaine fired.

'A mixture of things. I'd say namely strength and intelligence,' Sean replied, not sure where Jermaine was going with this question.

'As well as a desire to help others...and a healthy diet to some extent,' added Craig.

'Ok, so how did we come up with these features as the things we're looking for?' Jermaine asked quickly, as if trying to get to his point as soon as possible.

'Umm, I don't know,' uttered Sean.

Craig stood still for a moment, thinking, then said, 'The other Hunters I guess. We were trying to find people that fit the mould of them.'

'Exactly! We've been trying to find fighters that we believe could replace the sixth formers, but we've been missing a vital aspect. Jared said to me yesterday that they became the Bully Hunters out of necessity. That didn't make sense to me until I looked at Camille.'

Sean and Craig were listening to Jermaine, still waiting for him to clarify his point.

'The birth mark on her face,' Jermaine continued, 'she must

have been left out or possibly bullied for that. Then look at the others, Jared is, well, big, the twins, when I first saw them, I couldn't tell if they were boys or girls and Chris, if you didn't know him, you would think he's the same age as us.'

'So, what you're saying is that they were all bullied?' Sean asked, beginning to grasp what Jermaine was stating.

'Actually, that makes perfect sense,' Craig interjected, 'By what the two of you have told me, you were both recruited because you were either bullied yourself or you stood up to bullies.'

'This is my point. We've been trying to find people we believe can fight, which is important, but as Camille said the first time we saw her, you can teach anyone to fight, what you can't do is put the drive to fight into someone. That needs to be there before.'

'So, we need to find people who are being bullied?' asked Craig.

'Not necessarily. We need people who understand what it's like to be alone. Know what it's like to be treated differently because they aren't like the majority. I wouldn't say it's a hard and fast rule, but it will give us a foundation to search from. We need to find people like us,' Jermaine clarified.

Craig scratched his head, 'So, we need to find...misfits. People who don't fit in with everyone else.'

'I think that's a good place to start,' Jermaine declared, 'Craig, you think you can have a list of possibilities by lunchtime?'

'I'll get on it... Hold on, does that make me a misfit?'

Jermaine and Sean ignored the question. They both hopped down off the wall, 'we'll meet up then.'

The three boys said goodbye to each other and went their separate ways to their form classes.

*

With the groundwork completed by Craig, he, Jermaine and Sean went to see a selection of Year 7 children who fitted the newly established profile they were looking for. There were a mixture of boys and girls, who varied from tall and thin, to short and fat. They varied in race, religious backgrounds, levels of physical capabilities and even certain levels of academic strengths. With all of their differences, the one characteristic that they all shared was that they were outsiders to some degree.

Some had a small number of friends, but always lagged behind in the groups they had established. Others had no friends at all and stayed on their own. Whatever the case was, they all seemed to be odd puzzle pieces that just didn't completely fit in with everyone else.

Unlike the previous set of children observed, many of these choices showed promise to be possible members of the Hunters, but there were two in particular that stood out above the rest.

The first was a young girl named Amita Daliwal. Amita was a small Indian girl, with a long, pitch black plait reaching down to the back of her thighs. Unlike most of the children, she always had her perfect uniform attire on. Her tie was never out of place, her blazer never had so much as a speck of fluff on it, and her shoes shined as if they were polished every day.

The three boys spent a long period of time watching her throughout break and lunch times. They would move on to other possibilities, but would always feel an urge to observe her again, as if there was a draw to her.

Amita would follow a routine of either sitting in the library, studying her math books, or in the gym, practicing her gymnastics. She was extremely talented in both and didn't seem to make any time for anyone, or anything else. The boys had observed her interactions with people, which always led to nothing. She would seem to be sociable, but never went the next step to actually establish any kind of relationships.

This disregard for fellow students led the three boys to dismiss her from the group initially, until one day. Craig and Sean had continued to observe another possible member, but Jermaine couldn't shake the feeling that there was something about this girl. He took it upon himself to follow her to the gym for a final time to see if he could figure out what it was that he could subconsciously see.

Whilst she practiced her gymnastic routine, which she had been conducting since the boys had initially stumbled across her, a group of girls from Year 9 appeared in the gym. Jermaine, intrigued by this change in situation, observed the girls as they began to approach Amita.

Once the girls were in front of her, they began to watch what she was doing in a condescending manner, pointing and sniggering at her as she performed her manoeuvres. Amita finished a series of perfectly executed flips, when she turned and noticed the girls standing there watching her. The group of girls encroached upon Amita's personal space, an air of aggression in their approach.

Through the window, Jermaine couldn't decipher precise words, although he could tell that they were making derogatory statements due to the expression on Amita's face. After a few comments were shared between the girls, the one who seemed to be a leader of the group pushed Amita to the ground. At this moment, Jermaine dashed to the door in order to enter the gym, which was a taboo as it was meant specifically for the female students; this factor did not cross Jermaine's mind at the time however.

When Jermaine had entered the gym, he saw Amita bound up to her feet and clench her fist. She then unclenched and took a step backwards. The group of girls began to close the gap between them and Amita when Jermaine called out, 'Hey Amita.'

The group of girls stopped and turned to see Jermaine. Amita peaked her head around the girls and looked at Jermaine with a confused expression on her face, The Year 9 girls also wore a baffled expression, quickly turning into a look of recognition and fear.

The leader of the girls turned back to face Amita and stuttered, saying, 'Y..y..yeah, so as we were saying, ummm, nice flips and all. Keep it up.' She then looked at her followers, and opened her eyes wide, nodding her head in the direction of the door. As they walked past Jermaine, they all smiled and then walked progressively faster as they cleared his field of vision.

Jermaine then walked up to Amita, pulling a card from his pocket. 'A group of like-minded people would like to meet up with you. We'll let you know when. Hope you can make it.' He then turned away and walked out of the gym.

Amita looked at the card and read aloud, 'BSBH?'

The second candidate turned out to be a boy by the name of Zach Peterman. Sean had taken a liking to this boy for some reason unbeknownst to himself. Zach was one of those understated children, who everyone saw, but nobody took notice of. Jermaine, Sean and Craig noticed that his clothing always looked dirty. He wore trousers that were too small for him, and always seemed to have a stain of some sort on his shirt. The soles of his shoes would seem to stay stuck to the ground, as if they hadn't realised that the rest of the shoe was already rising off the ground.

The three boys watched Zach as he sat alone in the playground with the only thing he was never seen without; an old violin. He would do nothing but sit on a bench and play his music. During break and lunch, the boys observed Zach tuning and practicing.

Whilst watching him, Sean, Jermaine and Craig saw a group of Year 10 boys walk past and stop to listen to his music. These boys then threw change on the ground at Zach's feet and started laughing.

'Here you go, practice for what you'll end up doing with your life,' one of the boys said cruelly.

'Go buy yourself some new shoes,' said another, as the group burst out into fits of laughter.

Zach ignored the boys and continued playing his violin. As the Year 10 boys were getting no response from Zach, one of them grabbed the violin out of his hands. Zach instantly sprang up like a jack in the box and stamped on the boys foot, screaming, 'Give it back! That's my dad's violin, give it back *now*!' tears forming in his eyes.

Sean darted towards the group of boys before Jermaine and Craig had a chance to consider action. One of the Year 10 boys then grabbed Zach by the throat, and held him up against the wall. The one holding the violin examined it and said, 'You want me to break the stupid th...' and then fell backwards in pain. The violin flew out of his hand and landed in the hands of Sean.

The remaining Year 10 boys stared at the boy who held the violin, now sprawled out on the floor, holding his side and writhing in pain. They looked up to see Sean stood there, holding the violin. Slowly, they stepped away from Zach, holding their hands up. Sean looked them in their eyes and said, 'Leave.' Thankful to get away without injury, the Year 10 boys kept their hands up and backed away, as if they were trying to avoid a wild tiger from pouncing on them.

'Tha..thank you,' Zach panted, 'that was my dad's violin, before he...' Zach's voice trailed off into silence.

'My pleasure. I can't stand people who pick on others.'

'I haven't got any way to thank you,' Zach told Sean, grasping his violin close to his chest.

'Here,' Sean said, as he handed Zach a card with the letters BSBH on it, 'come to a meeting when we call for you, and we can call it even.' Sean then walked back towards Jermaine and Craig, who nodded at Zach as they walked away.

20

Decisions

A feeling of elation surrounded Jermaine and Sean. They had found two strong possibilities in Amita and Zach. Whilst sat on the wall outside the boy's gym, the two boys felt quite proud of themselves when Craig bobbed out from around the corner and stood in front of them.

'Guys, I've been thinking. I know we have essentially exhausted our options of future members by looking at essentially every child who fits our criteria, and that you have sort of settled on Zach and Amita, but, well, you have both chosen someone that you think would suit the group, and I was thinking,' Craig began, seemingly struggling to find the way to continue his statement.

'Go on,' instructed Jermaine.

'Well, I was thinking, I have someone in mind for the group that I think would be a perfect match for us. I think she'd fit right in, and would join if we approach her.

'I've been watching her for a while and think it could work.

Now, I know I'm still new and all, but I thought it would be good if...'

'You're as much part of the group as Jermaine and I are Craig.' interrupted Sean.

'Who is the mystery girl?' Jermaine asked, taking a bite out of his jam and peanut butter sandwich.

'Come with me and I'll show you.'

With that, Craig turned and began to walk away. Jermaine and Sean exchanged a glance and then followed him.

*

The boys arrived at the library, which was bustling with a number of children walking in and out, as well as a large number of children sat reading books.

'Over there, by the computer at the back,' Craig informed the boys, as he pointed towards the rear of the library. The boys looked in the direction that Craig pointed in and noticed a girl sat with a copy of *'Fahrenheit 451'* blocking her face. The girl lowered the book to turn the page, enabling Jermaine to notice that she was Elise.

Jermaine's heart jumped at the sight of her.

'Her name is Elise. She's quite a loner. Tends to sit in here and read most lunch breaks, and spends some evenings going to flute lessons. She seems to have this strange air of strength about her, something that tells me she can handle herself, you know? She's also really pretty, which is a bonus.'

This statement frustrated Jermaine. He tried to hide his irritation as much as he could.

'So, what do you think? Should I keep watching her or should I approach her?' Craig asked.

'Well, you say you've already watched her, and you did show us the people we chose, so I assume you know what you're doing. What do you think?' Sean asked, directing his question to Jermaine.

'It's up to you, but I don't think she'll say yes anyway,' Jermaine stated, standing up and walking away. The reason for his frustration wasn't completely clear to himself. It was definitely not clear to Sean and Craig, who watched him walk away, unsure as to what they may have said to upset him.

*

The following day, the boys organised for their prospective members to come to a meeting behind the bike shed. Jermaine, Craig and Sean sat at the picnic table, anxiously waiting for them to arrive. After a few minutes of nail biting tension, Amita arrived and slowly walked around the corner. She sheepishly edged forward and

Jermaine stood up, offering her a seat at the table.

A moment later, Zach arrived and stood at the corner, awaiting an invitation to proceed further, clutching onto his violin. Sean waved his hand towards himself, inviting him in and telling him to take a seat next to Amita. Zach and Amita looked at each other, and Amita gave Zach a slight smile; Zach looked away, a look of discomfort on his face.

The sixth formers were stood against the port-a-cabin as they stared at the two Year 7 children sat at the picnic table. Zach noticed Camille looking at the violin in his hands. Camille blinked and as she opened her eyes, she was now looking straight at him. He instantly averted his gaze and stared straight at the floor. Camille smirked to herself.

After a couple of minutes, Jared leant off the wall, and scrunched up his packet of Wotsits. He strolled over to the three boys, whilst licking his fingers, 'So, is this everyone?'

'Well, there was supposed to be one more person but…I don't know,' Craig stated, sounding disappointed, 'I guess Jermaine was right about Elise in the end.'

'Who was right about me?' came the voice of Elise from behind the boys.

'Oh, Elise. Great. Nothing, actually nothing,' replied Craig, happier now that Elise had arrived.

Elise walked past the boys, looking at Jermaine, scrunching up her face, 'what are you doing here? What have you been telling everyone about me?' she asked with a cheeky smile on her face. She took a seat next to Zach, smiling at him and Amita.

'I didn't say anything about you. I don't know what Craig is talking about,' Jermaine defended himself, feeling slightly embarrassed.

'Do you guys know each other?' Craig asked, confused by this new revelation.

'Yeah, we know each other. So should we begin?' Jermaine responded, trying to change the subject quickly.

All of the sixth formers walked closer to the picnic table and turned to look at Chris for him to begin the meeting. Chris then extended his hand towards Jermaine, indicating that the floor was actually his. Everyone turned their attention to Jermaine, who was taken back by this at first, initially looking at Elise before everyone else.

After taking a few seconds to compose himself, Jermaine straightened his posture. He took his hands out of his pockets and turned his body to fully face the three new possible members. 'Ok, so we've asked the three of you here today to inform you about what we do, and see if you would like to join us. These imposing looking sixth formers are named Jared, Alex, Maxwell, Camille and Chris,' he stated, pointing at each one as he mentioned their names.

Jermaine went on to explain what he knew about the Hunters, how they protected those who couldn't protect themselves. He told the Year 7's that if they were to decide to join, they would be trained physically, as well as mentally. He highlighted the fact that they would be trained to make them more effective fighters so that they can be true protectors of those who can't defend themselves.

'We can't make you join, that is purely your decision and we'll give you some time to think it over…'

'I'm in,' declared Elise before Jermaine could finish, 'School can be kind of boring sometimes so I don't see why not. Can't really stand bullies anyway, so it makes sense all round.'

Jermaine looked at Elise, shocked that she had responded so instantaneously. He looked at Amita, and then Zach, who both looked equally as shocked as he was. He then turned to look at Chris, who currently wore a smile; the biggest smile he had ever seen on his face.

Amita then raised her hand, 'I'm in too,' she said.

'And me,' Zach added.

Stumped as what to say, Jermaine could only mutter the words, 'Good…that's good.'

21

Testing

Chris stood up and walked over to Jermaine. He placed his hand on Jermaine's shoulder and gently squeezed it. 'Follow me for a second,' he whispered into his ear and then continued to walk away from the group.

Jermaine turned and followed behind Chris, wondering what he was going to say to him. Was he going to praise him for his choices, or reprimand him for something that he may have done without knowing it? As Jermaine followed Chris, all the possibilities of the conversation ahead of him ran through his mind. He even considered the fact that he had recruited four people, which made the group one person bigger than the previous set of Hunters. Was that a mistake on his behalf?

After walking around fifteen steps away from the group, Chris turned to face Jermaine. Jermaine stood still and tried to conceal his nervousness by clenching his fists inside his pockets.

'The recruits are going to have to undergo the same process

which you, yourself had to take. They will be tested on their base fighting skills in order for us to ascertain whether they are strong enough to be a part of the Hunters and if they are, what we will have to do in order to get them up to the standard required to be sufficient defenders.

'I asked you over here because I wanted to bring a few things to your attention. Firstly, this group is a democracy, no one person makes the decision that the others blindly follow, but every democratic system still needs a leader, someone to guide the herd in the right direction. I believe that is you. I think, no, I *know* you have the fortitude to ensure this band of future fighters stay on the correct path.

'I never intended to be the figure head for this group but when the time came, I stood up and took charge where it was needed,' Chris explained, looking straight into Jermaine's eyes. Jermaine could feel the passion and love Chris had for the group radiating out of him.

'Secondly, and probably more relevant, you will be responsible for these new recruits. If they fail the tests, I'll hold you responsible. If they make mistakes, those mistakes will fall on your head. Now, I know that you specifically only chose Amita to join the group. Sean and Craig pushed for the other two, so normally, each person would be accountable for their choices, but I'm going to hold you personally accountable.'

Jermaine thought this was unfair to him. He couldn't understand why he was being treated like he should be the most senior member, especially when Sean had been a member before him. He couldn't understand why he would be responsible for two people he didn't even personally vouch for.

Jermaine thought these things, but never uttered a word of concern to Chris; he just nodded and listened.

'Any fault of the recruits will be a poor reflection on you, and a poor reflection on you, will mean a poor reflection on me, which I'm not willing to accept. I have put my judgment up for scrutiny by having so much faith in you. Don't make my faith be unfounded,' Chris concluded, placing his hand on Jermaine's shoulder again, this time squeezing slightly harder than he had previously.

Chris walked back to the group, leaving Jermaine where he was standing. Contemplating the situation, Jermaine stood still for a moment, allowing the news to fully sink in. He accepted that the recruits were a representation of his abilities, regardless of how unfair he felt it was. The thing he found hard to handle was that his actions could possibly negatively represent Chris. This was harder for him to digest.

Eventually, Jermaine turned and walked back towards the group. He already felt the pressure of the new recruits actions weighing heavily on his shoulders. Chris had taken a seat on the steps of the port-a-cabin and watched Jermaine, as he stood still. In his own world, worrying about the consequences that would follow if any of the group failed.

'Ok, so first things first, we will need to test you newcomers. We want you to fight the person next to you and see how well you fair.' As the words left Jared's mouth, the Year 7s turned to look at each other.

'Fight?' Zach asked, his voice slightly shaking.

'How else would we be able to know if you can stand up to a group of bullies? We need to know what you're capable of. Amita, you shall square off against Zach. Craig, you and Elise shall test one another,' Jared explained, looking across all four of their faces.

'So, Amita and Zach, let's begin,' Chris added, watching their expressions suddenly change from a facade of confidence to one of a child who had just been told that it would have to fend for itself. Chris gestured towards the cabin.

Jared was the first to walk into the port-a-cabin, followed by Zach and Amita. Each of the remaining members of the group trailed behind them, entering the small building. As he stepped in, Jermaine realised that he had never actually been inside this building before today. He had no need to. The port-a-cabin was fairly non-descript inside. The walls were a dirty shade of white, and there were blue tables dotted around the room. The tables had been pushed against the walls, leaving a clearing in the centre of the room for the new candidates to conduct their *'tests'*.

Against the back wall was a cabinet, which had a piece of paper taped to it, with the words, *Completed Hunts* written on it.

Jermaine walked over to Jared and leant in towards his ear, 'Why aren't we having the tests at the training grounds like we did when I sparred with Sean?' he enquired.

'We don't want to show everyone that location unless we know that they have what it takes to actually join us,' Jared turned to look at Jermaine, 'we don't have as much faith in everyone that we had in you.'

Jermaine tried to fight it, but couldn't stop himself smiling at this statement.

'Ok, Amita, Zach, you're up first. Step into the centre and show us what you can do. The match isn't over until one of you submits or is physically unable to continue.'

Amita and Zach cautiously stepped into the circle now created by the group. They exchanged glances and looked around the faces of everyone watching them.

'Whenever you're ready,' Camille said, tapping her feet on the floor and glancing at her watch.

Amita was the first to make a decisive move. She began to close the gap between her and Zach, her fists clenched, as if she were prepared to attack. Zach, following the lead of Amita, did the same.

Once both were within reach of each other, Amita threw a punch, which connected with Zach's shoulder, then she threw another that hit Zach square in the mouth. Zach stepped back from the shock of the sudden collision with Amita's knuckles and composed himself.

Zach, seemingly embarrassed by the fact that he had just been punched in the face, raised his hands in a more aggressive manner and began moving in towards Amita. Once close enough, he grabbed hold of her shoulders and tried to throw her to the ground. Amita, having learnt full control of her body through her gymnastic training, threw her left foot back and planted it into the ground, dissipating the force of Zach's attempted throw. She then threw another punch wildly, this time connecting with Zach's stomach.

Zach tumbled to the ground, landing on his bum with a rather loud thud. The twins released a stifled chuckle and lowered their heads, avoiding eye contact with one another, as they knew this would result in an almighty outburst of laughter.

'Ok, stop,' Chris ordered, 'Zach, stand up.'

Zach fumbled to his feet, his head held low in shame. Chris held Zach by the shoulders, resulting in Zach raising his head, looking straight at Chris.

'What are you doing? Why aren't you fighting? If this were a real situation, you would have been beaten beyond anything you can comprehend. Why won't you fight back?' Chris asked this question with concern in his voice. Jermaine had never seen Chris be so gentle before. So caring.

'Sh...she's a girl. My dad told me never to hit girls,' Zach replied, his eyes slightly welling up. Jermaine remembered this happening when he mentioned his dad before Sean had saved him from the Year 10 boys.

Chris turned to Amita, 'Do you have a problem with hitting Zach because he's a boy?' he asked her.

'No, not really,' she replied.

'There you go. She has no issue, so she would win in a real life scenario. Do you not think she is equal to you Zach?'

Zach widened his eyes, 'No, that's not it. Of course she's equal to me!' Zach answered defensively.

'Well then, fight her as if you were fighting a boy. She deserves to be treated as an equal, not some delicate flower you don't want to harm. She's causing you harm and pain with no consideration for your gender,' Chris concluded.

Zach turned to face Amita and raised his fists again, this time he seemed to have more conviction in his movement. Once the two were within reach of each other again, they began to exchange blows. Zach threw punches wildly, hitting Amita in her arms, legs, stomach;

anywhere he could connect, as Amita did the same.

The sparring match went on like this for a short while until Amita stepped to the side, dodging one of Zach's flurries. Zach lost his footing and slipped on the floor, making another large thudding sound. Amita, noticing Zach on the ground, quickly turned and jumped onto Zach's back. She sat facing Zach's feet, pushing her weight into his body to stop him from being able to move. Zach thrashed about, trying to free himself but couldn't move. Amita, thinking of the best way to end the fight, grabbed hold of Zach's left ankle and started pulling it towards her.

Zach released a yelp of pain as Amita stretched his foot further back than it had ever been stretched before.

'Stop! Ow! I give up!' Zach shouted, smacking his hand into the ground.

'Ok, that's enough. Let him go,' Jared ordered. Amita released Zach's foot. Zach turned over and stared at the ceiling of the port-a-cabin, breathing deeply as he held his ankle. Amita outstretched her hand, offering Zach help to stand up. Zach accepted this gesture and stood up, being careful to not put too much pressure on his foot.

'That was more like it Zach,' Chris stated, 'shake hands on a good match. Next, Craig and Elise.'

Zach and Amita shook hands and then ambled to the side of the room to join the rest of the Hunters.

'Where did you learn to do that?' Elise asked Amita once she was stood next to her.

'Gymnastics training. It's a stretch I always found quite painful. Figured someone who isn't used to it would find it excruciating,' Amita responded, with a smile on her face.

Elise and Craig made their way into the middle of the room.

'Same rules apply here for the two of you. Are you both ready?' Jared checked. Both combatants nodded, 'begin.'

Wasting no time, Craig rushed in towards Elise. Elise did not move from her initial position until Craig was a couple of steps from her. Once they were close enough to make contact with each other, Elise raised her hands in defence.

As if learning from Zach's initial mistake, Craig did not hold back. He threw his strongest punches, each connecting with Elise's forearms. Jermaine felt his heart jump with every punch that connected. He had to forcibly stop himself from jumping in front of Elise and punching Craig square in the jaw, in protection of her.

After a rush of punches, Craig stepped back as he could not make any of them connect with anything but solid bone. Elise lowered her arms, and to the surprise of Craig, she looked as calm and composed as she had before the fight had begun. Jermaine noticed Craig's face and felt the same shock he was experiencing. Jermaine then scanned the room and saw that the rest of the hunters also seemed surprised by this revelation. The only person who did not seem effected by this was Chris, who had a blank expression on his face. Jermaine then thought to himself that Chris nearly always had a blank expression on his face, so that never revealed much in actuality.

Craig shook the shock from his mind and began to close the gap between himself and Elise again, this time intending to go for her legs. Elise then began bouncing on her feet and clenched her fists, raising them to her face, but in a more offensive fashion. Seeing her doing this sent further doubts through Craig's mind, causing him to stop his approach as he re-evaluated his next attack.

As if pushed from behind, Elise propelled forward. Craig jumped back and blindly lunged a kick in front of him, hoping to hit Elise as she approached. Suddenly, Craig felt his other leg give way and himself falling to the ground. He landed solidly on his back, wincing from the pain this caused. He then sat forward and saw Elise completing a turn from the sweep kick she had just executed on him.

Elise then scrambled around Craig before he had a chance to stand, throwing her legs over his chest. She then grabbed his arm and pulled it into an arm bar lock, twisting his arm clockwise. Craig struggled as much as he could but every time he moved, it was as if he made the pressure on his shoulder even worse.

He stopped attempting to free himself and instead tried to punch

Elise's leg that was accessible to him. After the second punch he decided not to try that any longer, as Elise began tightening her grip each time she felt his fists connect with her.

'Ahhhh, ok!' Craig yelled as he began tapping the floor. Elise instantly released his arm and stood up.

'Good job Elise. Another submission,' praised Jared.

'Two - nil, to the ladies. I'm beginning to like these new recruits,' Camille stated jokingly.

Elise helped Craig to his feet and the two shook hands. Craig and Elise stepped out of the centre of the room, returning to the rest of the Year 7s.

'Where did *you* learn to do *that*?' Amita asked, echoing the question asked to her.

'Taekwondo and self defence classes,' Elise explained. The two girls smiled and laughed with one another.

The sixth formers looked at each other as Chris gestured for them to go outside. One by one, they filtered through the door, the last being Jared who turned and faced Jermaine, along with the other Year 7s. 'We'll be back in a minute,' he said as he walked through the doorway, closing the door behind him.

Jermaine looked at the faces of the four new recruits and felt proud of them as well as himself. They had all shown fortitude in their performance, coupled with a fighting spirit. As he scanned their faces, he noticed a clear disparity between the girls and boys. Amita and Elise looked as if they were on a high, whereas a look of disappointment polluted Craig and Zach's faces. He remembered how he had felt when he had lost to Sean. There was the obvious difference between his situation and theirs. Sean had already been training with the Hunters, but at the time, he still felt inadequate.

Jermaine decided that he would speak to them in an attempt to cheer them up as the door to the cabin opened, and the sixth formers began to walk back inside.

'We have made a decision. Each of you have shown that you have the passion required for this group, but some lack the training necessary,' Chris started. Zach lowered his head and started sulking, whilst Craig tried to hide the water filling up at the base of his eye. 'Saying that, each of you will need to be trained fully before we can hand the mantle down to you. Training for each of you starts tomorrow after school.'

Zach and Craig looked up and stared at Chris and the other sixth formers. 'We're in?' Craig's voice was strewn with shock.

'Yes, you are part of the Hunters, well, Hunters in training, if you still desire to be,' Chris answered.

'But we lost?' Zach stated, his voice shaking with every beat of his heart.

'But you tried. Failure is only the first step in success. After we have trained you, you will never fail like that again.'

Zach and Craig almost instantly changed the expressions on their faces to ones of joy. The bell rang and shattered the moment of glee the boys felt.

'After school today we shall meet here and explain everything that you need to know. Till then, rest, you've earned it,' Chris concluded and walked out of the cabin. The other sixth formers smiled at the new recruits as they followed behind Chris.

Elise, Amita, Zach and Craig all started to congratulate one another, smiling and feeling elated that they had all been accepted into the Hunters. Jermaine watched them, considering that they had not known about the group less than an hour ago, but now looked like they had just won the lottery. He could relate to their feelings of elation.

'Well, it's kind of strange to say, but I guess we're a team now,' Sean declared, grabbing each of their attentions.

'The new Bully Hunters!' Craig exclaimed, excitedly.

Jermaine turned to face Craig, 'We have a long way to go until we can officially say that. You all haven't even experienced a training session yet. This is just the beginning. There's a lot that you need to learn before you can formally class yourself as a Bully Hunter.'

Craig looked slightly deflated, but nodded his head, 'I guess you're right.'

'Well,' Jermaine began, 'we better all get to class. One of the requirements to be a Hunter is to always be punctual for lessons. Want to start off on the right foot.'

Sean nodded his head in agreement with Jermaine's statement. The new recruits started walking out of the cabin, making their way to their classrooms. At the rear of the group were Jermaine and Elise. Jermaine had been avoiding talking to her since she had arrived, as he didn't know what to say.

As they were walking to their classes, Elise turned to Jermaine and punched him in the shoulder.

'Ow, what was that for?' Jermaine asked, rubbing the place of impact. Elise threw a harder punch then Jermaine had anticipated her to be able to.

'Whatever it is that you told the rest of them about me,' Elise smiled, 'it's funny. Now it makes sense why you always smelt sweaty those evenings.'

Jermaine felt his face become warm. He considered that, if his complexion were lighter, he would have been as red as a tomato.

22

Second Excursion

As the weeks drifted by, Amita, Craig, Zach and Elise grew stronger. Jermaine and Sean spent their afternoons alternating between training with Camille, and supporting the training of the new members. The new recruits were now on their third book from Jared, and Jermaine had noticed an increase in their confidence.

When he watched the new recruits training, Jermaine noticed how estranged they were from the remainder of the group. They seemed innocent, untainted, fresh. He realised that he was not that much more seasoned with the Hunters than they were, but he felt like he had been with the group for as long as he could remember. He reflected on how uncomfortable he had felt with the group originally but, in hindsight, he had actually slotted in with them quite smoothly.

Creeping slowly closer was the end of the school year. Jermaine felt this eventuality looming over his head. Even though he had the new recruits, he was still dreading the day the sixth formers would leave. He had never lost friends before. In all his time moving schools, he never allowed himself to get attached to anyone, so there was no pain when he eventually moved. This time in contrast, he had failed on that front. He was invested. He wanted to be around the Hunters as much as he could. He had even decided that if he had to, he would travel half way across London to stay at St Peter's; he didn't want to lose his friends.

As the sixth formers only had a limited amount of time to train the new comers before they left, Chris had decided that each *"Hunter in training"*, which he liked to call them, would be assigned a sixth former to impart their personal knowledge upon them. Each recruits specific strength and character was taken into account and matched with someone with similar abilities.

Craig had begun to work closer with Jared. Any time Jermaine passed by the bike shed, he would see the two of them sat beside each other, discussing the ins and outs of hunting. Jared showed him how jobs were categorised, how Hunters were picked for specific tasks and how research was conducted. When speaking to Jared about Craig one day, he stated to Jermaine that it was as if Craig had been born for this specific role. He highlighted the fact that Craig had conceived new ideas on how jobs could be arranged and recorded, which would result in a report, revealing which areas were showing higher activity of bullies.

Jermaine had never seen Jared look or sound as excited as he did when he spoke about Craig. It was as if he had been given a new pet to take care of and nurture. The feeling also seemed to be mutual, as Craig could only be found behind the shed when not in class or attending training sessions.

Instantly Camille swooped up Elise. She had decided that she would build her strength from the offset. She explained that she wanted her to always be one step ahead of the boys in the group. This was not a difficulty for her. She seemed to have an innate ability to fight. Everything Camille taught her, she learned in a fraction of the time it took for the boys to learn it.

Jermaine watched Elise complete a strength training circuit that had initially left him gasping for air. Elise, however, completed the circuit with energy to spare. Jermaine hated to admit it to himself, but this fact drove him to work harder. The thought of Elise being stronger than him made him feel strangely frustrated. He wanted to be the one with the ability to protect her...for some reason.

Amita and Zach had been assigned to the twins. Alex and Maxwell decided that they would teach them their honed reconnaissance skills. They escorted them through the school, showing them the skill of being seen, without being noticed; the ability to blend into a group to an extent that they knew you were there but paid no attention to your presence.

Zach, being as quiet as he was, especially found this role easy.

The fact that Zach carried his violin around with him everywhere was an added bonus, according to Alex, as nobody would assume he was spying on them with something like that in his hands.

Zach found blending into the scenery easier than Alex thought he would. The information he managed to gather about random targets set to him was extensive, as if he had personally had a conversation with the people himself. For most of his life, people tended to treat Zach as if he were non-existent. For the first time, this came as a great benefit to him.

Jermaine and Sean also expected to be paired up with someone; Jermaine hoped it would have been Chris, but no one arranged anything for them. They continued their training, which now started to feel repetitive and monotonous.

*

The Easter holidays drew near. Jermaine and Sean sat on the wall by the boy's gym, eating their sandwiches. Spring was in full swing, regenerating plant life and restoring colour to the once bleak landscape of the field. Jermaine stared at the field as a Year 8 football match was taking place. All he could see were the purple, yellow, blue and orange colours of the flowers disappearing before his eyes as the football landed amongst the petals, crushing them, followed by the studs of the players retrieving the ball, causing irreparable damage to the plants.

He thought back to a novel he had read called 'War of the Worlds' and how insignificant the humans were to the Martians. This led him to think about bullies and how they must feel the same way about their victims. He contemplated the way they crush the weak, with no considerations for their feelings.

'So what do you think?' Sean queried, looking at Jermaine for some form of confirmation.

Realising that he had been daydreaming and completely missed the thread of conversation, Jermaine turned his head and looked at Sean, 'Sorry, I wasn't listening. What were you saying?'

'How much of what I said did you miss?'

'I didn't even know you were speaking,' admitted Jermaine honestly.

Sean sighed and was about to start his tale again when a young boy stood in front him and Jermaine, drawing their attention. The boy reached out, handed a note to Jermaine, and left.

Jermaine looked at Sean, a bemused look on his face and opened the note.

The note read, *'Come to the bike shed, A.S.A.P. Jared.'* Jermaine folded the note and pushed it into his pocket.

'Guess we'd better go,' Jermaine suggested.

'Strange, that's what I was just talking about. I was saying that we would probably be joined up with someone to learn their skills soon. This must be it,' Sean jumped down off the wall, scrunched up the foil from his sandwich and threw it in the bin.

'Don't jump to conclusions. It's probably just a meeting regarding book reports or something,' Jermaine said, as he mirrored the same actions as Sean moments earlier, then grabbed his bag, and started walking towards the bike shed.

'Hey,' Sean said as he grabbed his bag, 'you always just walk off. It's kind of rude you know.'

*

The boys arrived at the bike shed to find Jared and Craig sat at the picnic table, piles of paper in front of them. Jared noticed the two boys as they approached the picnic table and stood up.

'You sent a runner for us?' Jermaine asked, wondering to himself what Craig was doing.

'Yeah, we have a job that needs taking care of,' Jared explained.

'Finally, we've been waiting for a mission since Christmas!' Sean declared.

'There haven't been many incidents as of late, which has been quite strange, but also beneficial, considering our little change of guard procedures we've been conducting,' Jared explained. He turned and reached onto the table, picking up a sheet of paper, 'This job has come from a Year 8 student from Heston Secondary in Kilburn, who is apparently being forced into a fight with a Year 11 student from the same school.

'As Alex and Maxwell have been training Zach and Amita, we haven't had time to completely check all the factors of this request. In emergency circumstances like these, where we can't conduct a thorough threat analysis, we would go as a group, but as this sounds simple enough, and I know that you have been itching to get back out there, I figured I'd get the two of you to support me on this hunt.'

A confusing mixture of excitement and disappointment filled Jermaine. He was overjoyed that he'd be going on another hunt, but the fact that they would only be supporting Jared with such an easy hunt made him feel as if he wouldn't get to experience any action anyway.

'This fight has been arranged for 16:30, so I'll meet you both here at the end of the day, should give us more than enough time to get there,' Jared concluded, turning back to Craig, who had seemingly forgotten about the work he had been doing, and had instead been listening to the conversation, 'Craig, let's get this finished before lunch is over.'

Jermaine turned and started to walk away, followed by Sean.

Once the two were clear of the bike shed, Jermaine rolled his eyes and huffed.

The lunch bell rang, creating a wave of children walking towards their lessons.

'Well, I'll see you after school then. Hopefully we can get some action, if Jared doesn't hog it all,' Sean stated as he patted Jermaine on the shoulder and walked away.

'Yeah, let's hope we get some action. See you then man.'

Jermaine stood still for a moment, then looked up into the sky. He exhaled heavily, then headed towards his afternoon lessons.

*

'Jermaine,' said Ms Taylor, awakening him from his daze. Jermaine had spent the majority of his maths lesson staring out of the window, thinking about a variety of things, none to do with the subject he was currently in class to study. It was becoming increasingly difficult for him to concentrate.

'Are you here with us? I get the distinct feeling you haven't been paying attention to anything that's been happening in this class room,'

'Sorry miss, just have a lot on my mind. I apologise,' Jermaine replied, in a self-reproaching manner.

'Maybe we can have a talk after school, if you'd like to?' Ms

Taylor offered.

'Thanks for the offer, but I'm ok. I have somewhere to be,' Jermaine stated.

'Oh,' a strange look of realisation crept onto Ms Taylor's face. It was as if she knew what Jermaine was referring to. 'That's fine, but if you ever just want to talk, let me know.'

The chime of the bell resonated, saving Jermaine from the awkward conversation. Jermaine gave Ms Taylor a slight smile, packed his bag, and left the classroom with the rest of the children.

After going to his form room to register, Jermaine headed to the bike shed to meet up with Sean and Jared.

'Should take us around forty-five minutes to get to the school. Do any of you have a watch? I left my phone at home by accident today.' Jared asked.

'Yeah, three thirty-two,' Sean told him.

'Ok, we better get moving so we don't get there after the fact,' Jared said.

Sean leaned in to Jermaine's ear and whispered excitedly, 'I never considered the fact that we may actually get to see one of the original Hunters in action?'

'Yeah. Would prefer to see myself in action though,' Jermaine replied, nonchalantly.

As the boys walked away from their school, the difference in their sizes would have made any onlookers assume that Jared was a baby sitter, picking up his children.

23

Ruse

Jared, Jermaine and Sean arrived at Heston Secondary, where the fight had allegedly been arranged to take place. The arranged location of this bout was the field, which was situated behind the school, meaning that the boys had to circumvent the entire school building to reach it.

Whilst negotiating around the building, the boys could see into the playground of the school. Jermaine took notice of the fact that the school seemed completely deserted. Although it was 16:25, he had expected to see the odd pupil hanging around, especially as a fight had been arranged to take place. Jermaine decided to wait until he arrived at the field before he jumped to any rash conclusions, as the entire school could have been congregating there.

After a few minutes of walking around the building, the boys arrived at an entrance to the field from a public footpath. The field was just as deserted as the school had been. Jermaine looked at Sean, who seemed to be just as perplexed at this factor. Jermaine then looked to Jared, who was scowling, as he scanned the terrain around him.

The field was a carpet of fragrant flowers, but was overshadowed by an ominous aura. Straight ahead of the boys was a large hill, blocking their view of the school.

'Let's make our way up to that hill. We'll be able to get a better view from there,' Jared stated.

The boys began to walk for a few moments when Jared outstretched his arms, stopping them from walking any further.

'What is it?' Jermaine asked, clenching his fists, whilst looking around erratically, attempting to see what the problem was. Jermaine could feel the adrenaline rushing through his veins. He looked at Jared, who was slowly ushering the two Year 7 boys backwards.

'There's someone coming,' Jared explained, as a group of heads, numbering over a dozen, began to peak over the hill, 'Keep backing up.'

Jermaine noted the nervous tone in Jared's voice, which made him begin to feel anxious. From behind, Sean prodded Jared with a finger and said, 'They're behind us too.'

Jared and Jermaine turned and saw another group of ten children approaching them. Jared stopped and placed a hand on both Jermaine and Sean's shoulders drawing their attention to him.

'There are too many of them,' Jared explained, 'Once I tell you to, I want the two of you to make a run for it.'

'What?' Sean exclaimed.

'No way! We'll stay and fight with you!' Jermaine argued.

'Don't be stupid!' Jared shouted, staring directly into Jermaine's eyes, 'if all three of us get taken down now, who will tell the others what happened here? I don't have my phone on me. There's no other option.'

Jermaine and Sean both nodded reluctantly. The boys turned around to see themselves surrounded by more than twenty children, a mixture of boys and girls. Jermaine scanned the faces and recognised one of the boys as the leader of the bullies he and Sean had dealt with outside Park High.

'Shame, I thought I'd be able to get a few more of you here,' boomed a voice from behind the Hunters, 'Ah well, I guess the three of you will have to do.'

The three Hunters turned around, noticing one boy hulking above the rest.

'James Grainger?' Jared gasped, shock reverberating in his voice, 'You're supposed to be in Scotland?'

'I was. Luckily, I was allowed to return here to take my A Levels. When I got back, you would never believe the tales I heard about a band of *children*, fighting bullies and protecting the little guys. Even more interestingly, I heard that their claim to fame was a bout between the leader of this group, a small boy named Chris, and a large bully, named James.

'Apparently, this 'Chris' chap took down James, all on his own. A real David and Goliath story, if I've ever heard one. Imagine *my* shock upon hearing this tale. Everyone I spoke to knew this story and made jokes about how weak this James was. Can you imagine how *infuriating* that was? My name had been tainted. Soured by the actions of one, pumped-up little git.'

'What are you expecting to accomplish from this?' Jared asked, breathing deeply.

'You, so called *Bully Hunters,* have gone on terrorising people for far too long. It's about time justice is served.'

'Justice? Justice belongs to those who have been wronged,' Jared declared, defiantly. He looked around at all the faces surrounding him, 'each one of you have been the wrong-doers, justice will stay blind to the likes of you!'

The sound of laughter erupted from James. 'I guess our fists will decide that,' he said as he started walking closer to the Hunters. 'I've never seen you two before. New blood I suppose. That's fine, I'll break you just the same.'

Jared stepped in front of Jermaine and Sean, blocking James' view of them. 'You'll have to go through me,' Jared proclaimed as he took a fighting stance.

'Gladly!' James roared as he charged in.

The two boys collided, like two grizzly bears fighting over territory. Jared began throwing punches faster than Jermaine and Sean could keep up with. The speed he moved seemed impossible for his size. He darted from foot to foot, sending blow after blow at James, who kept his hands covering his face.

A semblance of hope seeped into the minds of Jermaine and Sean. James then lowered his guard and began counter attacking. It was a battle of the giants. As each blow landed, it was swiftly followed by a thunderous sound of flesh impacting flesh.

The sight of James and Jared battling mesmerized all of the onlookers. It was a battle like nothing any of them had ever witnessed before. The sounds of grunting, fists connecting with flesh, and feet shuffling on the ground enveloped the surrounding area.

Even though Jared moved a lot faster than James, there was a distinct difference in strength. Jared began to move slower with every punch that connected. With the last burst of energy he had, Jared attempted one more onslaught, when suddenly, James managed to get a grip on Jared's arm and then threw him to the ground, tumbling into some of the kids surrounding them.

A fire blazing in his eyes, James turned to face Sean and Jermaine, 'Your turn,' he said, as he began to approach them. Jared then appeared from behind, wrapping his arms around James throat, stopping him from moving.

'Run!' Jared ordered, as the rest of the bullies, stirred from their enchantment, piled onto him, attempting to free James.

Jermaine began to move forward, intending on helping Jared, when Sean grabbed his arm and pulled him away.

'We need to go, now!' Sean yelled, his voice riddled with panic as he tugged at Jermaine's sleeve. Jermaine lowered his head and turned to leave. The two boys charged through a couple of the bullies that were blocking their path, whilst the majority were distracted.

James watched Jermaine and Sean as they ran, 'Run little boys! Run and tell Chris I'm coming for him!'

24

Nightmare

The sound of shoes smacking against the concrete was the only thing that Jermaine could hear. He looked around every few moments, just to ensure that no one was following them. As he ran, the image of Jared's face as the bullies piled on top of him like a hungry pack of hyenas, stuck in Jermaine's mind, as if it had been seared onto his brain. Jermaine shook his head to dismiss the image, but nothing seemed to help.

After a solid ten minutes of running, the two boys leaned up against a wall and attempted to catch their breath.

'Should...........we.........catch...........a.....bus?!' Sean struggled.

'No........too.........much........traffic,' Jermaine replied, spitting out the excess saliva in his mouth, 'have....to....keep..........on running!'

Sean rested his head against the wall as Jermaine remained bent over. They waited a few moments and then, as if thinking with one mind, they stood up, looked at each other, nodded and began to run again.

*

After a further ten minutes of sprinting at full speed, Jermaine and Sean arrived at St Peter's. They rushed through the school grounds; empty, except for the odd car and a couple kids leaving their extra-curricular lessons or detentions. Both boys hoped that someone would still be at the training grounds.

As they forced their way through the bush, forgetting to replace the branches disguising the entrance, they saw the new recruits still training.

'Who's here?' Jermaine barked, scanning each of their faces.

'Camille, she's in the...' Craig began, interrupted by Jermaine darting past him into the cabin, followed closely by Sean. Once he tore through the door, Jermaine spotted Camille sat at a desk with a book in her hands.

'Camille, it's Jared! We got jumped and he told us to run, so we ran, and James Grainger was there and,' Jermaine blurted in a hysterical fashion.

At the sound of name *James Grainger*, Camille stood up and practically dove over the table, grabbing hold of Jermaine by the scruff of his shirt. 'You left Jared there?' she shouted. She then reached into her pocket and pulled out her phone, 'why didn't he call us? That fat idiot!' Camille pressed her screen and put the phone to her ear. Jermaine could make out the distinct sound of Chris' voice on the other end of the line.

Camille began explaining what she heard from Jermaine to Chris. After a few moments of this, Camille turned back to Jermaine and extended her arm, handing him the phone. Gingerly, Jermaine reached out and took it. As he placed it to his ear, he instantly began to relay the story in just as frantic a manner as he had to Camille.

'Jermaine, stop! Calm down, take a deep breath and start from the beginning,' Chris ordered, his voice icy cold, snapping Jermaine back to his senses. After taking a deep breath, Jermaine began relaying the events of the afternoon as clearly as he could. He explained how it felt strange from the outset, told Chris the conversation he and Jared had, quoting as closely as he could remember, ending with Sean and himself arriving back at the training grounds.

Once Jermaine finished telling Chris his recount of events, the two stayed in silence for a moment, before Chris queried, 'Is that everything?'

'Yes, I'm pretty sure that's everything.'

'Ok, Camille, the twins and I will go and help Jared. Everything will be fine,' Chris explained, 'now pass the phone back....'

'I want to come and help! I'm sorry we left Jared there, but we had to come and make sure you all knew because Jared didn't have his phone. I'm really sorry, but I want to help, I....I have to help!' Jermaine pleaded, tears welling up in his eyes. The vision of Jared being swamped by the bullies contaminated his mind.

'Jermaine, you'll only get in the way. You've done enough. Just go home and we'll take care of it. Now, pass the phone over to Camille please,' Chris ordered calmly.

Jermaine handed the phone over and wiped the water from his eyes, before they became fully formed tears.

Camille spoke to Chris for a few moments before she nodded, saying, 'Ok, I'm on my way,' and placed the phone back into her pocket. Camille then grabbed her coat and, with a scowl on her face, barged past Jermaine and Sean, disappearing out of the port-a-cabin.

Jermaine stood still for a moment, then turned to leave himself. He was confronted with the faces of the new recruits, as they looked at him for some clarification of how they should respond.

'Is there something we can do? Jermaine?' Elise asked, a concerned look on her face.

'Just go home you guys,' Jermaine responded, walking past them, leaving the training grounds behind him. A trail of desolation hung in the air behind him as he walked.

*

Once Jermaine arrived home, he headed straight into his bedroom. The sound of Jared telling him to run consistently echoed inside his skull, drowning out all other sounds he could hear. Jermaine opened the door to his room, walked inside and closed it behind him. He walked over to his bed and collapsed, face first, onto his mattress.

He could feel nothing but emptiness within him. Weakness plagued his mind. He could hear his own voice in his head, ridiculing him for his lack of strength. Jermaine started to feel tears accumulating in his eyes, so he turned his face into his pillow, creating a patch of moisture where his eyes were.

After laying there, face in the pillow for a few seconds, Jermaine turned onto his back and stared at the ceiling. Doubts started to fill his mind. What was he doing? Why had he chosen to join the sixth formers? What could *he* really do about bullies?

Jermaine closed his eyes in an attempt to block out the negative thoughts, and gradually fell asleep.

*

After what felt like seconds, Jermaine opened his eyes, finding himself on a field, covered in the same multi-coloured flowers as the field behind Heston Secondary. He looked around. Bullies surrounded him. Slowly, they began to close in on him, until they were a few inches away, and as one unified force, they all began to beat on him.

Jermaine covered his head, in an attempt to protect himself, but it was useless. He looked past the flurry of attacks and saw his brother through the crowd. Miraculously, all the sound around him muted, leaving him in complete silence as the bullies continued pounding on him. The image of Anton moved closer to Jermaine and crouched to his level.

'I warned you about them, didn't I?' Anton said, as he stood up, turned his back to him, and began to walk away. Jermaine tried to shout out to his brother, but no sounds were coming out of his mouth. He looked to his left, where he saw Chris staring straight at him.

'Look at you, just getting in the way. I should've never allowed you to be one of the group,' Chris stated, before also standing up and walking away. Jermaine closed his eyes again and when he opened them, he was now in a dark room. Behind him, he could hear the sound of crying. He stood up and turned around to see the new recruits, along with Sean, sobbing, tears cascading down their cheeks.

A pair of hands started jolting forward, grabbing them one by one, pulling them back into the darkness surrounding them. First

Amita. Then Zach. Craig. Sean. Jermaine was powerless. He couldn't move from the position he was in. From behind him, he heard a honeyed voice call his name. He turned around to see Elise, stood deathly still, smiling at him. Abruptly, a hand thrust forward, covering her mouth, followed by others, which dragged her into the darkness.

Jermaine tried to shout in protest, but still, no sound would escape from his mouth. He could feel the moisture of his tears streaming down his face. Complete silence surrounded him. After a few moments, he began turning around, looking for some source of light, feeling in front of him. The darkness was so complete now that he couldn't even see his hands in front of his face. Suddenly, a small speck of light appeared in the distance. Jermaine looked at the light, squinting, trying to get a better look at what it was. Shattering the silence, a deafening sound, like a train headed towards him, boomed into Jermaine's ears. The light began to grow, as if it were coming closer to him. Jermaine felt a cold sensation flow over him. Fear gripped every molecule in his body.

He closed his eyes, but could still see the light. It was as if his eyelids had suddenly become transparent. The light was still making it's way towards him, coupled with that terrifying sound. There was nothing he could do. He tried to turn, but was stuck in place. All he could do was watch the menacing light approach him. Just before the light collided with him, everything fell to darkness again. Jermaine's eyelids seemed to be working finally. Cautiously, he opened his eyes, to only be confronted with James' face, wearing a maniacal grin. Jermaine was frozen in fear, nowhere to run or hide. Out of the darkness, a large hand shot out and grabbed a hold of him by his face, pulling him forward.

*

Jermaine jerked upright. He reached up and touched his face, noticing that he was completely drenched in sweat. That had been the first time Jermaine had ever experienced a nightmare that frightening and emotional. He had always seen people react that way in films, but always thought it was an extreme dramatisation.

He looked out of his window, and saw that it was fairly dark outside now. He turned his head to look at his clock, which displayed the time as 05:30 in the morning. The realisation that he had slept through the entire evening fell on Jermaine like a ton of bricks. He calculated that he must have slept for at least twelve hours straight. He couldn't ever remember sleeping that long.

Jermaine sat up on the edge of his bed and attempted to clear his mind. He tried to push out his thoughts of Jared and James, but they wouldn't offer him any respite. Every time James crossed his mind, it felt as if his stomach was trying to escape his body through his mouth.

As he was now awake, Jermaine decided to just prepare himself for school, regardless of the fact that he was running an hour earlier than he usually did. Once he had finished in the shower, he made his way downstairs into the kitchen.

His stomach grumbled as he scanned the cereals he could eat, nothing looked appealing. They all seemed to lack the flair that they usually had. He reached for the box of cornflakes, his go-to cereal whenever he couldn't choose, and poured a portion into a bowl of milk. As he crushed the flakes into the milk, he felt a hand touch his shoulder, which made him jump from fright.

'Hey, relax man, it's just me,' Anton said, his hands raised, attempting to show no threat. Slowly, Anton lowered his hand and placed it on his brother's shoulder again, squeezing gently, 'Are you ok bro? Coz you seem on edge. Mum was worried about you again. She put some food in the fridge for you, in case you woke up.'

'I'm...I'm fine.'

'What's with the stupidly early bedtime? Thought we could have played some Fifa last night. Been a while since we hung out.'

'Nothing, just felt really tired. Had a busy day at school. Wore me out a little, that's all,' Jermaine replied, looking back at his cornflakes, slowly spooning a mouthful into his mouth.

'Fair enough.' Anton took a bowl for himself out of the cupboard.

'Anton, how do you deal with losing a match?'

'You mean a boxing match? That's easy, you dust yourself off, and try again.'

'But, how do you keep the same passion? Doesn't it make you want to just quit?'

Anton placed the bowl down on the kitchen table and looked closely at Jermaine, 'Defeat is the first step to success. Failure makes you see where your weaknesses are, which enables you to strengthen them. I don't think concentrating on the failure is useful, but how you can avoid the failure again. As they say, it's better to try and fail, than to fail to try.'

Jermaine looked at his brother and thought to himself, *'That's the most profound thing I've ever heard him say'.* 'Thanks bro, I appreciate that.'

'Don't mention it. Anytime,' Anton responded, picking back up his bowl and heading over to the cereals.

'Alright, I better go to school. Thanks again man,' Jermaine said, touching Anton on the shoulder as he walked past him.

Jermaine collected his things for school, said goodbye to Anton, and left the house. He realised that he would have to train harder than he had ever trained before. It had become imperative.

25

Fallout

Jermaine walked into school, which now seemed to harbour a darker atmosphere than before. He walked towards the bike shed, trying not to think about Jared, James or anything else that had made him feel anxious. It was proving to be a harder task than anticipated.

As he turned the corner, making his way behind the shed, he could hear the voice of Chris, speaking in a stern voice, 'It's because we have become too relaxed. We have allowed hubris to fill us with *arrogance* and *pride*. A year ago, this would never have happened!'

Jermaine stood deathly still, observing the faces of the sixth formers. He saw that Jared was not amongst them, which made his heart jump. His mind raced with the possibilities of what had happened to him. A few seconds later, Jermaine noticed Sean walk up beside him. The two boys exchanged a slight nod of recognition, before diverting their attention back towards the sixth formers.

Camille noticed both boys standing there, looked directly at them, changing her expression into a grimace, then looked away.

This short glance alerted Chris to their presence. He then turned around and gestured for Jermaine and Sean to come closer.

The two boys meandered towards the sixth formers, avoiding all eye contact; a look of shame covered their faces.

Chris returned his attention to the sixth formers, 'I think it's best if we no longer use our time to train the new recruits. I feel that we have imparted enough knowledge for them to forge their own paths, as we once did. I don't believe we should completely leave them to their own devices however, so, I suggest we allocate the most proficient of them to train the others in our stead,' he stated.

'I think it should be Elise. She's the most competent. She learnt everything I taught her about strength quicker than I could have hoped for, given the short amount of time we've worked together. She's better than anyone I've trained in the past.' If Jermaine had missed the reference to him and Sean in that comment, Camille's glare in their direction would have driven the message home. She then 'cut her eyes' as she averted her gaze from the two Year 7s.

Chris looked at the two boys, then back to the sixth formers. 'Ok, sounds good enough to me,' he replied.

Jermaine looked at Sean, who returned the glance. They could tell that they were both thinking the same thing. They were being kicked out of the group. Why else would they suggest Elise to lead the training instead of them?

'Now, regarding the two of you,' Chris started. The boys waited with bated breath for the inevitable news, 'you have still not completed your task of pushing Camille off the mat, which is more than likely an impossibility, if we're being honest…so you will be moved on to combat training.'

Hearing this information, Jermaine released the breath which he had been holding, 'I'm sorry about Jared, really sorry. We didn't mean to just leave him there,' Jermaine confessed again, 'Is...is he ok?'

'Jermaine and Sean, what happened is not your fault. You did what you could do; the only thing you could do, in that situation,' Chris highlighted, in an attempt to reassure the two boys again. 'If anyone is to blame for what happened, it's us. We should never have let you venture out to a risky hunt like that without adequate training and preparation. That will be rectified.

'You can also stop worrying about Jared, he's fine. A few cuts and bruises, a fractured bone here and there, but he'll live. He's a soldier, he's been trained for this.'

As Chris finished speaking, the new recruits turned the corner and walked over to the rest of the Hunters. Jermaine noticed that the looks on their faces had changed. He recognised these new expressions, as it was the same as the one he saw when he looked in the mirror that morning. It was as if the glossy sheen of what they were doing had been removed. The concept of hunting bullies seemed to have been sullied by the knowledge that they could actually be severely injured on a hunt.

Jermaine scanned the forlorn faces, surprised when he stumbled upon Elise, who looked exactly as she always did. It was as if the situation had not fazed her in the slightest. As a matter of fact, it had seemed to have an adverse effect on her; she had an even more determined look in her eyes.

Chris turned to the Year 7s, 'I know this must have been a shock to you all, and more than likely frightening,' Chris walked closer to the new recruits, 'this line of work is not without danger. There are those out there who wish to destroy everything we have tried to build.'

The bell for registration rang, followed by the sound of bustling feet and voices.

'We can't let this throw us off course. We must stay vigilant. Training as usual. Elise, you'll lead the program. Camille speaks highly of you, and I have faith in her opinion. Continue the after school routines,' Chris turned his head to look at Jermaine and Sean, 'the two of you, you'll be with the twins. After school will be your first session.

'The best advice I can give you is to prepare yourselves. They won't go easy on you. Let yesterdays experience kindle your resolve,'

Chris then turned again, so that he was facing the entire group, 'This was just the beginning. There will be tough times ahead. We need to be prepared. Being caught off guard is not something I want to happen to us twice,' he declared. He then picked up his bag, turned, nodded at the group and then walked out from behind the bike shed, followed by the twins and Camille.

The new recruits, still looking slightly disheartened, followed behind the sixth formers. Jermaine watched them all leave, then began to walk with Sean towards the school building. As he neared the doors to the maths block, he thought to himself, *'It's better to try and fail, than to fail to try.'*

*

As the pupils of St Peter's gathered their things to go home and see their families again, Jermaine and Sean made their way to the training grounds. They had both been thinking about what Chris had said regarding preparing themselves, although they couldn't really envision what the worry could be. Of all the hunters, the twins seemed like the easiest going. They were always playing jokes on each other and were very friendly and welcoming to all the new recruits. They thought a warning would have been more beneficial when they initially started training with Camille.

Jermaine and Sean made their way through the bushes and saw the new recruits beginning their training session with Elise.

'They're around the back.' Elise informed them, standing up from a quadriceps stretch.

Jermaine nodded, 'Thanks.'

He and Sean rounded the training building and saw the twins standing there, playing a game of rock, paper scissors.

'...paper, scissors!' they both said, as they laid out their choice in front of each other. Alex had drawn rock, whilst Maxwell had drawn paper.

'Ah man,' Alex complained. Maxwell smiled, then turned his head to face Jermaine and Sean. The twins separated from one another, each stood in front of a collection of mats.

'So, as I get first pick,' Maxwell gloated, smiling at his brother, 'I think I'll take you,' he said, pointing at Jermaine. 'I've been wanting to have a knock around with you since that day with the Year 10s by the toilet.'

'Fine with me, been looking forward to a little spar with the little guy here. Guess it all worked out,' Alex declared, an inviting smile on his face.

Exchanging glances, Jermaine and Sean shrugged, and walked towards their assigned trainers.

'Take your shoes off,' the twins ordered in unison, then looked at each other, 'jinx!'

Jermaine took off his shoes and stepped onto the group of mats in front of him. Maxwell did the same, followed by Sean and Alex stepping onto their mats. Maxwell walked closer towards Jermaine and adopted a fighting stance. He turned sideways, slightly bent his knees and raised his hands up to his chin. Jermaine raised his hands, settling on the fact that he would have to fight Maxwell. A memory of the twins sparring the first time he came to the grounds flashed into his mind. He had no idea how he would possibly win this match.

As Maxwell closed in, Jermaine looked into his eyes, but Maxwell's gaze was centred completely on Jermaine's body. Once the gap between them had been significantly reduced, and they were within reach of each other, Maxwell stopped approaching but started circling. Jermaine watched Maxwell and realised that he was going to have to make the first move.

He stepped forward, throwing a punch, which connected with nothing but air, although Maxwell seemed to be stood in the exact same place. Jermaine threw another punch, which had the same result. Suddenly, Maxwell charged forward, shooting out a jab, causing Jermaine to react by covering his face. A moment later, Jermaine felt something smash into his stomach, pushing him back onto the mat.

As Jermaine raised his head, he saw Maxwell slowly lowering

his leg. Irritated that he had fallen for such a basic trick, he stood back up, raised his fists again, then began to close in on Maxwell. Once they were within reach of each other, Jermaine ducked, sweeping his feet, in an attempt to trip Maxwell up. Maxwell casually stepped over the sweep kick and threw a back handed slap into the back of Jermaine's head.

Unable to control his emotions, Jermaine jumped up and charged at Maxwell. As if he had anticipated this action, Maxwell stepped to the side, and threw a full force kick into Jermaine's ribs, resulting in Jermaine crumbling into a foetal position on the mat, moaning in pain.

In between the sound of his moans, the pain, and the voice of embarrassment berating him in his head, Jermaine heard the sound of Sean moaning in pain on the adjacent set of mats.

Jermaine looked up and saw Maxwell's outstretched hand in front of him. He reached out, grabbed it and was raised to his feet. The pain in his ribs continued to throb, as if the kicks were continuing to smack into him. Alex and Maxwell led the two boys, still holding themselves where they had been hit, over to the back wall of the port-a-cabin. Jermaine and Sean both leant back, resting themselves on the wall, and slowly lowered themselves down into seated positions.

'So, how do you think that went?' Alex questioned the pair, as they sat on the floor.

'Not.............so good,' Sean answered, still holding his chest.

'Your entire approach to combat needs to change. We've been giving you the foundations throughout the year. To successfully pass your sessions with us, you will need to draw upon your stamina, strength and intelligence. We're not mindless brawlers, we think before we act,' Maxwell explained.

'We're not here to teach you any fancy kicks or aesthetically pleasing movements. We will teach you how to win a fight. We will show you the quickest and most effective way to end a bout,' Alex added.

'First things first, both of your stances need to be changed before we go any further.' Maxwell stepped away from Jermaine and Sean.

'Yeah, those were a joke,' Alex said, sniggering to himself.

'A breeze could have knocked them over.'

'More like a sneeze.'

The twins began to laugh amongst themselves. After a few seconds, they looked back at Jermaine and Sean, who didn't seem too impressed with being teased, and composed themselves.

'Ok. So, stand up for us and we'll explain,' Alex said, stifling his laughter.

As they stood up, Jermaine and Sean were still in a noticeable amount of discomfort.

'Take the same stance you took just now in the sparring match,' Alex asked both boys.

'But you just said our stances were a joke?' Jermaine enquired, slightly still annoyed at the fact that he was laughed at.

'They are, that's why we're going to change them,' Alex stated.

'So why are we taking the same stance that we took a moment ago?' Sean Interjected. The annoyance Jermaine and Sean felt was presenting itself as insubordination.

'Who's leading this training? I highly doubt either of you were this vocal with Camille. I don't think you would still have all of your limbs if you were.' The reprimand from Alex shocked Jermaine and Sean back into reality. Alex had not been as aggressive as Camille, but something told them both that they wouldn't want to see either of the twins actually angry. Both boys fell silent.

'We need you to be comfortable in your stance. It's better to teach you in a stance you feel naturally inclined to adopt, than teach you something completely alien,' Maxwell interposed.

Jermaine and Sean adopted the stances that they taken previously. Alex and Maxwell approached their designated student, made them bend their knees slightly, turning their bodies to the side,

'This will increase your stability, as well as enable you to move backwards and forwards without much adjustment needed. This position will also decrease the area for your opponent to attack, making you a more challenging target to connect with,' Alex said. The twins then reached out and adjusted the position of the pair's hands, either raising them higher or lower.

'What you want here is to have your hands in a position where they are capable of attacking, but also blocking. Unclench your fists too, that way your opponent never knows for sure what you're going to do,' Maxwell explained.

Jermaine and Sean began to get used to their newly adjusted stances. After holding them for a period of time, both boys started to feel the lactic acid building up in their muscles. Jermaine felt himself constantly fighting the urge to stand up straight. He had been used to standing up on his feet for extended periods of time, as well as crouching for an extensive timeframe, but this was an entirely new experience. This position was somewhere between standing and crouching, a painful medium.

The twins had the boys execute many different drills in the same position. They taught them about different attack distances; close quarter and long distance, as well as when to use them. They showed them the skill of fast, bouncing movements. The twins even taught the boys new basic exercises, such as jumping on the spot, then coming right down into as small a ball as possible, then bursting back up again. Jermaine and Sean had never thought that they could find exercises more gruelling than those that Camille subjected them to. They realised fairly quickly that they were wrong.

26

Absolution

After a long two hour session, Jermaine and Sean felt completely exhausted.

'Good job today guys.'

'Yeah, good job.'

The twins had the same inviting expression on their faces that they always had. Jermaine never knew a smile could anger him as much as theirs was at that precise moment. The jovial looks on their faces completely contradicted the pain he was feeling in all of his muscles at the time. For the first time, Jermaine wished to be back training with Camille.

'So....we only have a week of school left and then it's the Easter holidays. As you guys need as much training as possible, Maxwell and I have decided that we'll be meeting up everyday during the holidays,' Alex declared, still donning his sincere smile.

Jermaine and Sean both lowered their heads, and replied, 'Ok,' wearily.

*

For Jermaine, the final week of term was nothing more than painful. Every day after school, he and Sean would meet up with the twins to conduct their combat training. After every session, Jermaine would leave, his body in more pain than he had ever felt before.

Friday arrived, and even though Jermaine was getting a break from school, he didn't feel like he would have much of a holiday. He still had book reports for the Hunters due, his normal homework, training would take place as usual, and the fear that James Grainger was walking around out there, somewhere, kept him on edge.

Whilst walking away from his final training session of the week, he and Sean said their goodbyes, arranging to meet up on the Monday before the training session, in order to make their way there together. Once alone, Jermaine considered the contrast between how he felt during the Christmas holidays and how he felt now. He longed for the ability to have nothing to do. He craved the ignorance to the dangers out there, which could shatter his entire world, in the blink of an eye.

'Don't know what you've got till it's gone,' Jermaine said aloud, to himself.

'What have you lost?' the sound of Elise's voice invaded

Jermaine's ears.

Elise's voice always made Jermaine's hairs stand on end. He would feel instantly nervous, regardless of what he was doing. Although he did not see her half as often as he had previously, Jermaine felt closer to Elise, now that she was part of the group and knew about that side of his life.

'Oh, just freedom. The ability to do as you please whenever you want to, nothing major, I guess. How's the training with the others going?' Jermaine asked, partially interested, partially just making conversation.

'Good, I'm running a tight ship. Training every afternoon, no breaks, just intense workouts.'

'Sounds like you've been spending too much time with Camille,' Jermaine joked. Both he and Elise laughed.

'Maybe. I'm planning on running training through the holidays as well. They need conditioning. From what you and Sean said, they'll have to be much stronger if that James guy decides to bring the fight to us. Speaking of that, have you spoken to Craig lately?' Elise asked Jermaine, a serious look on her face.

'No, haven't seen anyone but Sean and the twins this week. Why?'

'He told me that there's been a major increase in incidents regarding bullies. Apparently Chris and Camille have been out of school more often than in, just to keep things from turning into pure chaos. The only school that seems to have not been effected is here,' Elise explained.

Jermaine thought about James and the other bullies. He felt his hand beginning to tremble, and placed his palm flat against his leg, in an attempt to disguise it.

'Well, it's a good thing that they have you here to train them,' Jermaine stated, swiftly changing the topic of conversation.

'I don't think that they would agree with you on that one.' They both laughed again.

'Good to see you both still in high spirits,' a voice said from behind Jermaine and Elise. They both spun around and in front of them stood Jared. He had his leg and arm in a cast, was covered in bruises, which looked as if they were healing, and had crutches under his arms.

'Jared!' Jermaine exclaimed, a mixture of shock, happiness and embarrassment.

'Jared, we didn't mean to,' Elise began attempting to repair any damage she may have just caused by being so jovial, considering the recent incident with James.

'It's fine. It's sincerely good to hear you guys laughing. I would hate for everyone to be walking around all glum and sullen. Elise, could I have a word with Jermaine please?' Jared asked, instantly turning his full attention to Jermaine, indicating that his request was more of an order. Elise nodded and walked away from the pair. Jared looked at Jermaine, but Jermaine found it difficult to return the gaze.

'Jermaine, I've been hearing that you're beating yourself up about what happened.'

Jermaine didn't say anything. Instead he just kept on looking at the ground.

'Jermaine, it wasn't your fault, it was mine,' Jared said.

These words angered Jermaine, 'Everyone is constantly telling me that it wasn't my fault, that I couldn't have done anything else, but that's a lie, I could have helped. If I weren't so weak, I could have helped you instead of just running away like a coward!' Jermaine shouted, his fists clenched so tight, his nails were nearly piercing his palms, as tears began building up in his eyes, 'I'll never be that weak again. I'll never let my friends get hurt whilst I just run away and save myself!'

Jared reached out and placed a hand on Jermaine's shoulder. Jermaine looked up, directly into Jared's eyes, 'Remember what I told you. You need brains as well as strength. It's honourable for you to not want to leave your friends in danger, that character trait is why you are one of us, but if you had stayed, you would have just been laying in a hospital bed next to me…or worse.'

Although Jermaine knew what Jared said was true, he just

couldn't shake the feeling that he was a coward.

'If you never want to feel like that again, train. Become stronger, faster, smarter. Protect those you care about, but to do that, you first have to move past that day. Don't let that one experience dictate who you are,' Jared advised Jermaine. He removed his hand from Jermaine's shoulder and balanced himself on the crutches again, 'So, on a lighter note, you'll be training with the twins over the holidays?' he asked.

'Yeah, five days a week,' Jermaine answered, wiping the tears from his eyes.

'Good, you'll need to be prepared. A storm is coming. You'll have your chance to protect people soon enough. Anyway, I better get back home, my mum's going to worry sick if she notices that I'm gone,' Jared explained.

'When will you be back?'

'After the holiday; you can show me how strong you've become then,' and with that, Jared turned and hopped away, on his crutches, nodding and smiling at Elise as he passed her.

'You ok?' Elise asked Jermaine after Jared had left, sincere concern in her voice.

'Yeah, I'm fine. Guess we both have a long Easter break ahead of us.'

'I guess we do.'

27

Friendship

The Easter holidays saw the flourishing of spring. Nature had fully awoken, bringing with it numerous creatures. The buzzing of flying insects, coupled with the marching lines of ants was something that Jermaine always looked forward to at this time of year. They made him feel alive, as if he was a part of something *larger*, that something more than just his issues existed.

The first couple of days were full of training sessions with the twins. Jermaine and Sean met up with the twins in a park, not too far away from St Peter's. They met at the same time, in the same location, beginning each session with a twenty-minute jog. Throughout the training sessions, the twins steadily destroyed every thread of fighting training Jermaine had learnt from Anton. They highlighted all of the bad habits he had learnt; his dependency on his fists being the main one.

The twins consistently emphasised that a fight should be completed as soon as possible.

'If a fight can be finished with words before it's begun, that is the most ideal of situations. We train in case that is not an option. If it isn't, the quickest end to a battle is the preferred course of action,' Alex explained to Jermaine and Sean, repeatedly.

The process of wearing an opponent down, which Anton had taught Jermaine, served no purpose, in the eyes of the Hunters. They intended to finish things as quickly as possible.

'With what we do, there is a high possibility that you will be facing multiple opponents. Extending any part of this bout, could result in your defeat,' the twins had explained to the boys.

Throughout the training sessions, Jermaine constantly thought about the situation with James and the other bullies. He applied his newfound knowledge to a situation like that, thinking about what he would do differently with what he now knew, but regardless of the ideas, it would always end in his ultimate demise. He eventually admitted to himself that Jared was right; nothing he could have done would have changed the outcome of that day.

*

Sean and Jermaine concluded their third training session with the twins and began to make their way home. As the pair walked out of the park, they both heard a whistle from behind them. They turned, noticing Elise and the other new recruits walking towards them.

'Do you guys train here too?' Amita asked, adjusting the rucksack on her back.

'Yeah, every day with the twins... so far anyway,' Sean replied.

'I miss hanging around with those guys. They were fun,' Zach added.

'Well, they're not fun to train under, I can tell you that,' Jermaine said, shaking his legs, in an attempt to put some life back into them.

'Well, it's not like we're having a great time either. Some people seem to want to kill us,' Craig said, jerking his head in the direction of Elise as he spoke.

'Hard work results in results,' Elise responded, the same sinister smile on her face that Camille would have worn in that situation. Jermaine noticed this and felt a chill travel down his spine. 'Jermaine, can I talk to you for a second?'

'Yeah, ok,' Jermaine said, shrugging his shoulders.

Elise led Jermaine away from the rest of the group, until they were far enough to ensure their conversation could not be heard.

'I want you to train me,' Elise said, without a moment's hesitation.

'*Train* you?'

'Yes, train me, combat training,' Elise further explained, 'the sixth formers won't do it, and I'm not going to just sit around, waiting for a situation like the one you and Sean found yourselves in, before I know how to defend myself fully.'

Jermaine looked into Elise's eyes and saw the conviction behind her words. 'I don't know Elise, there are steps that you need to take first.'

'Such as? I'm as strong as you or Sean, and I've had prior training to being part of the Hunters,' Elise highlighted, 'If you think I'm exaggerating, test me yourself.'

Jermaine thought about what Elise said. He knew she was speaking the truth. From the testing, he had seen that she was capable. Considering she had been training with Camille consistently, he gathered that she had to be stronger than she looked. He had also never doubted her intelligence.

Jermaine couldn't turn his gaze from Elise's eyes. The passion within them, it was borderline desperation, 'If the sixth formers find out, they won't be happy about it, especially Chris.'

'Jermaine, who is going to be in charge of the group when they leave the school? Aren't we supposed to make our own decisions? This will be our group at the end of the day right?' Elise asked, watching Jermaine lower his head in thought. After a couple of moments, Elise's patience ran thin and she furrowed her brows in irritation, 'Forget it, I'll just keep training myself!' she exclaimed, beginning to walk away.

Jermaine reached out and grabbed her by the arm, 'Fine, but you have to keep this quiet. If we can avoid it getting back to the sixth formers, that would be preferable.'

Elise's eyes widened with glee as she dove into Jermaine, embracing him, whilst saying, 'Thank you! You won't regret it, I promise!'

The rest of the Year 7s observed this, intrigued by what they were discussing.

'She's asking him out, I bet you, and he just said yes,' speculated Sean. Craig had a disappointed look on his face when he heard this suggestion, but nobody noticed it.

'*He* just asked *her* out more likely. She said no, and now they've decided to just be friends,' Amita countered.

'I think she's just asked him if she can borrow his PlayStation for the holidays,' Craig added. The others looked at him, and then they all burst into laughter.

'So, when do we begin? Today?' asked Elise, still smiling profusely.

'Hey, slow down. We'll start tomorrow, but remember, this stays between the two of us. I'll meet you here at nine, gives us a few hours to fill you in on what I've learnt so far. If we do that each day, then I'll always be able to show you what I have learnt the day prior.

Work for you?'

'Perfect,' Elise said, grinning at Jermaine.

Jermaine noticed, for the first time, that Elise had dimples in her face when she had a fully extended smile.

They both made their way back to the rest of the group. Once there, they noticed the smothered laughter from each of them, but both decided to just ignore it.

'So, should we get going then?' Jermaine asked, attempting to move away from the situation, before it blossomed into something it wasn't.

'Yeah, sounds like a plan,' Craig responded, 'hey, actually, I've been thinking, why don't we all go and catch a film, go bowling or something? We spend so much time together, but never socialise,' Craig suggested.

'Hey, yeah, that does sounds like fun,' Amita agreed.

'I've never actually been bowling,' Zach admitted.

'Let's do it!' Sean said, excitedly. The group exchanged looks and all nodded in agreement. 'Yeah, Jermaine and Elise can sit next to each other,' he teased. The group broke out into laughter, until they made eye contact with either Jermaine or Elise, who both looked unimpressed with the joke, 'Or, maybe not.'

'I need to get home and clean up first, but we can plan to meet up in an hour and a half at Park Royal?' Jermaine suggested. The group agreed and started making their way home, a newly established state of happiness surrounding them all.

*

When he arrived home, Jermaine jumped straight into the shower, put on a set of clean clothes, and was ready to leave within thirty minutes. He walked over to a shelf in his room and pulled down his savings jar. Every piece of cash he had ever received for a birthday, Christmas gift, or just as a present from a visiting relative, was stored in the jar. Jermaine never received pocket money, as his mum never had any to give him. His mum also had a habit of asking to borrow his money when times were rough, promising to give it back; she never did. He never resented this though, as he realised that she would sacrifice everything she could have for herself, in order to feed and clothe her children.

Jermaine counted the money he had, which accumulated to seventy-three pounds and eighteen pence. He had previously calculated that he would have well over two hundred and fifty pounds; if it weren't for all the loans he gave to his mother, and also considered that he had nothing that he needed to spend all that money on anyway. This was, in fact, the first time he had ever reached into his jar to spend anything, mainly because he never had any friends to go anywhere with before. He felt excitement bubbling inside him. He now had a friendship group. Jermaine grabbed twenty-five pounds out of his jar, and left the house, a significant spring in his step.

*

All the 'Hunters in training' met up at the entertainment complex, near Park Royal station. Each member turned up at exactly the time they had agreed upon. Their training with the Hunters had made them extremely punctual.

The group decided to watch *The Avengers 2*, later joking that they were sort of like the Avengers themselves; a band of different people, stopping villains from harming the innocent. Once they had finished the film, they headed across to the bowling alley, which also contained a copious amount of arcades inside.

Jermaine challenged the group to a few games at the arcades, before they went bowling, and as he expected, beat them all. His extensive hours of playing games with Anton had finally paid off. After losing a few games to Jermaine, the group all decided that it was time to bowl. This activity enabled them all to turn the tide on him, as he had never held a bowling ball before, nor did he understand how to throw one down a lane.

The group laughed together and enjoyed each other's company, more than they had ever done in the past. For each of them, it was a new experience, but for Jermaine, it was life changing. After rolling his ball into the gutter, for the seventh time, Jermaine turned to see the group in fits of laughter, tears forming at their eyes. At that moment, watching the glee on all their faces, Jermaine decided that he would never let any harm come to any of them, even if it meant his own demise.

The afternoon came to an inevitable end, and each of the group exchanged friendly hugs and other forms of farewells. Most of the group boarded the same train. The majority of their stops were close by, so they soon alighted, leaving Jermaine and Elise as the only ones left. They sat in an awkward silence for a few minutes, not looking at one another.

As Jermaine's stop approached, he stood up, and said goodbye. Elise looked confused, whilst tilting her head to the side.

'I thought you lived further away from school than I did?' she asked him, suspiciously.

Jermaine thought, for a second, trying to find a viable explanation, but nothing sensible came to his mind.

Elise chuckled to herself, 'Were you always staying on the bus to keep me company? Awww, how sweet of you,' she teased. She then stood in front of him, gave him an embrace and whispered into his ear, 'Tomorrow, at ten, I'll see you then,' smiled, and walked back to her seat.

Jermaine exited the train, swamped in embarrassment. He walked towards the stairs, as fast as he could, ensuring not to make any form of eye contact with Elise.

28

Determination

The next day, Jermaine arrived at the park at 08:45. He waited by the gates, where he had agreed to meet Elise, for a few minutes before she turned the corner. The embarrassment from the day prior was still a fresh memory in Jermaine's mind, but he pushed it out, as much as he could.

'Hey,… so, where do we begin?' Elise asked, getting straight to the matter at hand.

'Well, first things first, I need to see what you can do already,' Jermaine explained, 'follow me,' he said, leading Elise into the park.

Once the pair were in the centre of the park, Jermaine stopped and turned to face Elise.

'Ok, attack me,' he instructed.

Elise, hesitated at first, but then solidified her resolve, and stepped in, throwing a crescent kick at Jermaine. He sidestepped, avoiding the attack and pushed Elise, causing her to fall onto her hands.

Seemingly annoyed by this, she jumped up, clenched her fists, and began to move closer to Jermaine, taking more caution with her actions this time. Once she was within range, she threw a kick towards him, following immediately with another. Jermaine stepped back, and began circling Elise, a dismissive look on his face.

'What are you trying to do? That may work in a martial arts class, but here, you're hitting nothing but air,' he declared, as he rushed in and threw Elise to the ground again.

Elise stood up, her expression now showing a strong sense of frustration. She immediately charged at Jermaine, throwing punches and kicks wildly, this time, connecting with him. Jermaine guarded against the onslaught of attacks, then grabbed one of Elise's legs, mid kick, and flipped her onto her back.

'Ok, now you're trying to hit me, but anger isn't the path to winning a fight, fore thought is what you need. You should attempt to end the fight with as little energy expended as possible,' he explained, whilst rubbing his forearms, 'I will say, you're stronger than you look. That's good, you're going to need that strength.'

He reached out his hand, and helped Elise up to her feet, 'I want to start with a basic circuit, get the muscles warmed up and then we'll begin with improving your stance.'

*

After over an hour, Elise sat down on the grass and stretched her legs. She drew deep breaths, regaining her normal breathing pattern. Jermaine looked down at her, astounded by how quickly she seemed to learn what he was teaching her. It was as if she was a sponge, absorbing every drop of the lesson. Jermaine noticed a look of disappointment on Elise's face as she rested, but couldn't understand why she felt that way.

'Hey, you did great. A lot better than I did during my first session,' Jermaine confessed, in an attempt to reassure her.

'It's not good enough, I need to get stronger,' Elise replied, grabbing a hand full of grass.

'Stop being so hard on yourself. You did better than could be expected.'

'Can we try again?' Elise asked, without looking up at Jermaine.

'You need to give your muscles some time to relax. You don't want to over do it. You could just end up injuring yourself. We'll train again tomorrow, what's the rush?' Jermaine enquired.

'I just...I need to be stronger than the bullies...I need to...,' tears began to roll down Elise's face, wetting the soil in front of her.

Jermaine noticed this, and felt at a loss as to what he should do. He fell to his knees and put his hand on her shoulder.

'What's wrong?'

'Nothing, I'm just being silly. Just… just thinking about my brother,' Elise answered, wiping the tears from her face.

'Is he ill or something?' Jermaine asked, puzzled, wondering how anything with her brother could illicit this kind of reaction from her at this specific moment.

'He died a few years ago. I don't really speak about him,' Elise explained.

'Oh, I'm sorry to hear that. I…I didn't mean to pry,' Jermaine said, feeling uncomfortable and stupid for being so intrusive.

'No, it's fine. I like thinking about him. My family tends to avoid bringing him up, so I rarely get to speak about him. He…,' Elise wiped her nose with her sleeve, 'he committed suicide seven years ago, because he was being bullied by some kids at his school. Nobody knew he was so depressed. He just started being really distant, and one day, my mum found him in the bathroom with an empty bottle of pills in his hand. A few months later I started to take up Taekwondo. I promised that nobody would ever be able to hurt me like that.

'This is why I was so willing to join the Hunters. If they had been around when my brother was getting bullied, maybe they could have saved him. If I can help even one person from bullying, I'll train until my legs fall off!' Elise professed, smacking her fist into the grass.

Elise looked up at Jermaine, her face wet from the tears. As he looked into her eyes, he could see her determination. She had taken her pain and transformed it into an unbreakable resolve.

Elise wiped her face with the other sleeve of her t-shirt, 'Since then, I just found it easier to keep myself to myself. Books became my escape from it all, and everyone just seemed to leave me alone…until you started speaking to me that is,' she concluded, new tears rolling down her face.

'Oh…' Jermaine didn't know what else to say. He rummaged around in his brain for a more emotional response, 'I'm sure he would be proud of you now, if he saw what you're doing in his honour.'

A smile grew on Elise's face. 'Thank you, that means a lot. Wow, I've never told anyone that before.'

'Hey, what are you two doing here?' Sean called out from a few metres away, surprising Jermaine and Elise. Elise wiped her face quickly, removing any evidence that she had been crying.

Jermaine turned to see Sean walking towards them, followed by the twins.

'Oh, errr, we just met up for a jog. Get some early exercise in,' Jermaine lied, attempting to cover up his unauthorised training of Elise.

'But you look dry, where as Elise looks like she's been running a marathon,' Sean highlighted, contorting his face into a perplexed expression. Alex and Maxwell both raised an eyebrow at the same time.

'Yeah, I had a stich, so I stopped, but Elise continued. Anyway, are you guys ready?' Jermaine asked, changing the subject as quickly as he could.

'I better get going. Supposed to be meeting up with the others for training,' Elise stood up, 'thanks for the company, was much more fun jogging with someone, than on my own. Maybe we can do it again sometime. See you guys around,' she said, briskly walking away.

The look of confusion, which Sean wore didn't falter. It held strong, slowly changing into a look at suspicion.

'So, let's get started then.' Getting to his feet, Jermaine ignored the suspicious looks that Sean and the twins were giving him.

'Run your warm-ups,' Maxwell instructed the boys, beginning the training session.

*

The next morning, Jermaine stood at the gate to the park, awaiting Elise. After a couple of moments, he noticed Elise turn the corner. A second later, he also noticed Amita, Zach, and finally

Craig, following behind her.

'Elise, what are they doing here?' Jermaine asked, slightly irritated.

'They wouldn't let it go. They guessed that I was training with you and said that they wanted in. I couldn't stop them,' Elise explained.

'We deserve to be trained too,' said Zach.

'Yeah, we don't want to be useless when things start to get serious,' Amita added.

'Jermaine, something serious is coming, and we need to be able to fight. We didn't agree to join the Hunters, only to sit around and watch everyone else fight. We want in,' Craig affirmed.

'Yeah,' agreed Zach and Amita.

'Looks like we're going to have to train them all,' Sean said, walking out from inside the park.

'Sean! What are you doing here?' Jermaine questioned, feeling like someone was playing a joke on him.

'I thought there was something funny yesterday, and put two and two together. You could get into serious trouble if the sixth formers find out about this…and what kind of friend would I be if I didn't get into trouble alongside you?' Sean smiled, walking up beside Jermaine, 'So, are we starting with stances?'

Jermaine sighed and shook his head, 'Sean, you take Amita and

Zach. I'll work with Elise and Craig. Follow me,' he said, walking into the park.

*

For the remainder of the holidays, Jermaine and Sean passed on the knowledge that they were taught by Alex and Maxwell to the new recruits. The fear that they would get caught slowly began to fall into the back of their minds. The progress that they were making was all that concerned them.

Training the new recruits seemed to also have a beneficial side effect for Jermaine and Sean, as it helped them consolidate what they were learning in their own lessons, enabling them to progress faster each day.

On the last Friday, before school began again, Jermaine looked at his fellow Year 7 Hunters. He thought to himself, *'They look like the Hunters, small Hunters, but Hunters none the less.'*

Summer Term

29

Mass Bullying

The feeling of returning to school was like returning home from a holiday that went on a few days too long. The first two days felt as if the holidays had never taken place. The only difference was that Jared had returned, now using only a single crutch, rather than the two he had before the break, and that Jermaine and Sean were now staying after school for an additional hour, in order to train the new recruits.

The Wednesday morning, of the first week back, whilst walking up to the gates, Jermaine noticed that there were more children than usual staring at him. Whenever he returned the gaze, the children would look away and whisper amongst themselves. Jermaine thought about the reasons behind this, but dismissed it as just another one of the consequences that came with being one of the Hunters.

Throughout his first two lessons, Jermaine realised that the strange looks continued. Whenever he would look up, at least one of the other students would be looking at him, then would look away, and begin whispering something to the person sat next to them.

After an hour of this, Jermaine began to get concerned...and increasingly frustrated.

'What are you looking at? Is there something on my face?' Jermaine blurted out, in his Maths lesson. The students stopped whispering and instantly lowered all of their heads.

'Mr Pearson, step outside right now!' ordered Ms Taylor, a look of disgust on her face. Jermaine placed his pencil on his desk, stood up and walked outside the door.

Ms Taylor followed behind him, closing the door behind her. The rest of the class stood up out of their seats, leaning, to see what was happening.

'What do you think you're doing, shouting out like that in my classroom? I would never expect something like that from the likes of you... Is everything ok?' she asked, looking back into the classroom. All the students dropped back into their seats, and resumed working, as if they had been doing that the whole time.

'Is something, or...someone bothering you?' Ms Taylor asked. Jermaine thought this was a strange assumption for her to come to. He also couldn't help but see the humour in the question, but fought to quell a smile from appearing on his face. He knew that a smile would be greatly misconstrued at that precise moment.

'No miss, nothing like that.'

'Ok....good. There have been reports of a lot of that happening over the past month. We've been told to be vigilant with it. If anything like that does happen, I want you to tell me right away. I know you're one of the quiet ones in the year group.'

'I will miss. I'm just a bit tired. I'm sorry miss, it won't happen again,' Jermaine apologised.

'Ok, make sure it doesn't. Go back in and take your seat. No more outbursts.'

Jermaine walked back to his seat, and sat down. None of the children dared look at him again for the remainder of that lesson.

*

Jermaine decided to head straight for the bike shed at break. There was something strange going on and he knew he would find the answers there.

As he drew near to the shed, Jermaine noticed a large queue of children, it lead from behind the shed, out into the playground. From the other side of the playground, he saw the rest of the new recruits also heading towards the bike shed. Once he caught up with them, he discovered that they had also been receiving strange looks since the morning.

'It feels like I'm some kind of strange celebrity,' Craig said, 'it's cool, but also disturbing…I don't like it.'

'What's with the queue?' Jermaine asked, hoping that somebody had some more insight to the situation than he did.

'No idea. I was about to ask you the same question,' Elise responded.

Jermaine, along with the others, walked towards the mass of children, realising that they were wearing a myriad of different school uniforms. Some of the colours Jermaine had never seen. There were children from schools all over the borough.

Jermaine pushed his way passed the queue, which turned into more of a crowd once it got closer to the port-a-cabin. Jermaine saw the sixth formers standing around. At the picnic table, Chris sat with his hands steeped in front of his face, as he listened to the rabble of the mob in front of him.

'They're terrorizing the whole school. It's been worse these last two days than it's ever been. Some sixth formers are even saying that it's worse than before the Bully Hunters existed!' shouted a disgruntled Year 10, from the front of the crowd.

'They stopped me from going into school today, and they told me that I would regret it if I told a teacher,' a Year 8 girl declared.

'Everyone has been saying that you were all defeated at Heston a few weeks ago. "They're saying that the Hunters don't hunt anymore…is that true?' a Year 9 boy asked, followed by a chorus of agreement and speculations in the crowd.

'Is this why they were all staring at me? Were they all shocked to actually see me alive?' Jermaine pondered.

Chris lowered his hands and stood up. The crowd immediately fell into silence. He walked forward, causing all the children to make a passage for him. Once in the centre, he stopped.

'Everyone, I want to reassure you that we are still here to help you. We have heard your problems and will resolve the issues you have. All of you, form an orderly line and give the name of your school and the person causing you any issues, and we will deal with it,' Chris stated. He then looked back at the Hunters, 'Jared, can you stay here with Craig and Amita? Take the information that we require. Alex, Maxwell, Camille, follow me please.'

Chris walked through the crowd, until he was next to Jermaine. He motioned with his head for Jermaine to follow him as he walked passed.

Jermaine, Sean, Zach and Elise, followed behind Chris and the sixth formers, stopping at the benches outside the DT rooms. The spitters abruptly dispersed once they saw Chris approaching.

'Hunters, it seems like it's begun, as I had anticipated it would. The bullies seem to have taken the ambush as a green light for them to do as they please. James' appearance has galvanized them, much more than I thought it would have,' Chris explained.

'Well, I've been waiting to put some hurting on a few bullies. We should show them all just how active we still are.' Camille suggested, holding out her clenched fist.

'I agree, but we have to take into consideration the scale here. These children have come from all over the borough. We would have to split up in order to resolve all of these situations. We would also be heading in blind, just as Jared, Jermaine and Sean did. After what happened then, I don't want to put anymore of you in danger like that again.'

'Well, we can't sit here and do nothing. We have to act,' Alex said.

'Plus, we will be more careful now, as we know that there could be a trap waiting for us,' Maxwell added.

'Let's go hunting.' The look in Camille's eyes as she said those words reverberated through each of the Hunters stood there. Jermaine felt it; a desire to hurt some bullies. The thrill he felt from just the idea alone surprised him.

Chris looked as if he was contemplating the hardest decision of his life.

'Ok. Luckily for us, Jermaine and Sean have been secretly combat training the new recruits, which means they can at least provide back up,' Chris stated, to Jermaine's horror. As he said those words, Jermaine's heart skipped a beat, and he physically felt himself jerk. 'So, we will split off into groups. Camille, I want you to go with Zach, Amita and Elise, Alex and Maxwell, you take Craig and Sean. Jermaine, you'll be with me.'

'Why are you just taking him? He wasn't any protection when Jared got jumped!' Camille protested, highlighting that she had not moved on from that situation yet.

'Camille, I've made my decision. I know what I'm doing. You don't have to follow my plan, but I would strongly suggest you do. Now, Alex, Maxwell and Camille, ensure you have your phones on you, and make sure you call for back-up if you encounter anything that you can't handle.'

A moment later, the bell rang, serving as a reminder that the Hunters were still students in school.

'Hunters, we will meet near the training grounds at lunch. Prepare yourselves,' Chris advised the group, as he walked back towards the bike shed.

'Make sure that you're all ready and on time. You...' Camille said, standing uncomfortably close to Jermaine, 'You make sure that you stick by Chris, no matter what, do you hear me?' The usual intensity Camille displayed was multiplied by a factor of ten. Her words came with an unspoken threat behind them; if Jermaine ever abandoned Chris, he wouldn't live to tell about it. Camille then followed behind Chris.

'I wouldn't want to be you if something happens to Chris,' Alex said, as he walked away, holding out his hand, for his brother to give him a low-five, which he did.

'Better hope he doesn't even get a splinter, I'd say,' Maxwell added, following behind his brother. As he walked away, Maxwell started acting as if he were Alex's bodyguard, standing between him and any other students in the playground at the time. The twins then began laughing uncontrollably with each other.

Jermaine stood there, sincerely scared by the words Camille had just said to him.

'Don't worry about her Jermaine. She's more smoke than fire,' Elise said, trying to comfort him.

'Smoke kills more people then fire does,' Jermaine replied.

'Either way, you'll be with Chris, nothing will happen to him, or you, for that matter. Anyway, I have History, and Mr Gaines hates it when anyone is late.' Elise walked away, leaving Sean and Jermaine standing there.

'Let's go,' Sean said, tapping Jermaine on the shoulder. The two boys walked away from the benches, heading towards their lessons.

*

Jermaine felt the nervousness building up inside him throughout Art. Surprisingly, Camille's threat wasn't the thing that was concerning him. The true fear came from the idea of being alone with Chris. Even though he'd had conversations with Chris, spent time around him and knew him, probably as well as he knew any of the sixth formers, Chris still scared him.

Jermaine thought about Chris throughout his lesson. Mrs Hodges followed her usual lesson plan of 'Do what you want', as she felt that too many constraints would stifle the creativity of the children, so Jermaine began drawing without direction. Unintentionally, Jermaine had drawn an impression of Chris' eyes into his art book.

Even looking at his own picture made Jermaine feel uneasy. The sound of the bell shattered the chaotic atmosphere that Mrs Hodges had established in the classroom. Jermaine reluctantly stood, collected his things, and started making his way to the training grounds.

30

Clearing The Board

Jermaine was the last to arrive at the training grounds. The Hunters, old and new, were stood around in their groups, each of them looked ready to begin the biggest hunt they had been on that year.

Chris stood on top of the picnic table, 'Hunters, brothers, sisters…we have to leave here with the knowledge that one of us could be walking into a trap. It pains me to have to take a risk as large as this again, but we also need to show these bullies that we are still a force to be reckoned with. If we don't act today, they will think they can do as they please again, that we are not capable. That cannot happen.

'We will do what we train to do. I have faith in every, single one of you. If you believe in yourselves, even an ounce as much as I believe in you, you can do nothing else but succeed.

'As I said earlier, be vigilant. If something is wrong, or you feel that there is a situation that requires more people than you have with you, call in reinforcements.'

Chris walked to the sixth former in each group, and handed them a folder, 'These contain the names of the schools you will be required to visit, as well as the names of the targets. Luckily, we have dealt with many of these bullies in the past, at some time or the other, so their profiles have been included. They seem to be mainly small time bullies, nothing major, according to the information we have anyway. There are some that we have never had the privilege of hunting, so be cautious.

'We have been separated into regions, to keep things as practical as possible. Realise that we could all be having multiple confrontations, so pace yourselves. Today, we clear the board.' Chris finished his pep talk, emboldening the Hunters, 'Jared, we will need you to arrange a cover for all of us, for the remainder of the day.'

'No problem Chris, I'll get on it as soon as you leave,' Jared ensured Chris.

'To the rest of you, good hunting. We'll meet back here once we have all completed our tasks,' Chris concluded, walking over to Jermaine, 'let's go.'

*

Jermaine travelled with Chris to the first school on their list, which was relatively close by. During the journey, neither of them exchanged any words. Jermaine could sense a strange, thick atmosphere around them, a feeling of anxiety and tension. For the entirety of the journey, Chris seemed to be lost in thought. Jermaine felt as if he would be intruding on Chris' thoughts, if he spoke.

Attempting to fathom what Chris could be so enveloped by, Jermaine watched him as they walked. After only a few seconds, he had established a multitude of possibilities, one being whether everyone else would be safe. He considered the responsibility Chris must have been feeling for the situation they were all in. Even though there was no official leader of the Hunters, Chris had already stated that he took that role on himself.

Jermaine remembered the nightmare he had, how he'd felt responsible for each of the new recruits. The realisation that Chris, more than likely, felt the exact same way about *all* the Hunters humbled Jermaine. Regardless of his possible fears, Chris stood strong, and he made the hard decisions.

The two boys arrived at their first location. Chris retrieved the folder, which he had placed into his rucksack. He glanced at the first sheet inside, then closed it, and returned it to his bag.

'This way. They're apparently waiting for children in the alley over there,' Chris informed Jermaine, pointing across the road, 'Just your basic lunch money operation. Alex and Maxwell have dealt with them in the past. They're small time. Won't take us more than a couple of minutes. I'll take point,' Chris said, indicating that he would lead the way.

As the two Hunters entered the alley, they both saw a group of four boys, all wearing the same school uniform, standing around, talking to each other, cigarettes in each of their hands. Jermaine guessed the boys to be in Year 9 or 10 from the size of them, but realised that it didn't really matter. A bully was a bully. Once Chris had started walking down the alley, the group of boys turned to face him.

'What are you two doing in our alley?' the boy closest to Chris asked.

'I think they want to give us their money,' the boy next to him added.

'Well, the only polite thing to do would be to take it, wouldn't it? Get over here, now!' another of the boys ordered. Chris, seemingly following the instructions, walked closer to the group of boys.

Once Chris was in front of the boy closest to him, he stopped, staring straight into his eyes. Every single one of the four boys were taller than Chris, looking down at him, surprised by his lack of fear.

'I think this one's a 'special' one guys,' the boy in front of Chris said, 'not all there, not that it matters. Give me the money you have on you, unless you want to get a bloody nose.

You.....know....what....a......bloody.....nose.....Is.....right?' the boy spoke each word slowly, as if Chris could barely grasp the basics of language.

Chris stood still, showing no reaction on his face, apart from the odd, infrequent blink of his eyes.

'Didn't you hear me? Give me your money, you stupid idiot.'

The boy reached out, towards Chris' pockets, and then let out a scream of pain. Chris stood still, his hand now gripped, tightly around the bully's wrist. Chris tilted his hand forward, bending the bully's wrist backwards, into a painful position.

'OWWW! Guys, help me!' the boy cried out.

Chris looked up at the remaining three bullies, one of which was now charging towards him. Jermaine observed Chris plant one foot on the ground in front of him, and shuffle his other foot backwards, slightly.

As the bully arrived in front of Chris, he pushed him, which had absolutely no effect to Chris' position. It looked to Jermaine, as if the bully had tried to push over a brick wall. It was as if he had fastened himself onto the ground.

Surprised by the lack of effectiveness, the bully threw a punch, which Chris grabbed mid swing. Chris then began crushing the boy's fist in his hand. The bully let out a shriek of pain.

'Who are you?' another of the boys asked, resorting to words, after his friend's actions had proved to be so ineffective, 'What do you want?'

Chris pushed the two boys he was holding forward, causing them to roll on the floor, for a couple of seconds.

'I am the fist that will hurt you. The will that shall break you,' Chris said, in a calm, calculative voice.

'What's this guy on about?', the bully who had attempted to reach into Chris' pocket queried. He stood up, holding his wrist, trying to soothe the discomfort.

'I'm only going to give you a single warning. If I ever hear about you troubling any of the students from this school, I will be forced to come down on you all with full force.'

The boy that attempted to punch Chris stood up. He began rubbing his fist, wincing from the pain. After a moment, he clenched his fists again, and started rushing towards Chris, until he was stopped by one of his friends. The friend spoke quietly to the boy, but Jermaine was able to over hear the words, *'scar'* and *'Hunters'*. The friend then pointed to Jermaine's tie.

The blood noticeably drained from the boys face. He lowered his fists and took a few steps backwards.

'You can't be him. Y…you guys are f…finished. Grainger dealt with all of you!' the boy stammered.

Jermaine stepped forward and asked, 'Do you believe what you are told, or what you see? Want to put it to the test?'

The boys began to back up, shaking their heads, 'We're sorry. We'll give the money back, alright,' the lead boy said, still backing away.

'We won't come back here, we promise,' another pleaded.

'Get out of here,' Chris ordered.

The boys turned, then ran out of the other end of the alleyway, like cats being chased by a pack of dogs.

'That's one down. It's going to be a long afternoon. You can take the next one,' Chris said, walking out of the alley.

*

Jermaine and Chris headed from school to school. They managed to resolve every situation by just being there. The legend of Chris and 'The Hunters', coupled with the sight of Chris, seemed to be enough to reinstall fear back into the bullies.

It was 15:34 once the pair had dealt with the last group of miscreants on their list. They began to make their way back to St Peters.

'That was easier than I thought it would be. Not one of them put up a fight. I thought we would encounter something a little more, challenging,' Jermaine complained.

'So did I,' Chris had a pensive look on his face, as if he were trying to make sense of something.

The boys continued walking back towards St Peter's, another period of silence surrounding them.

*

The boys drew nearer to the school. The streets were now busier than they had been earlier. There were parents around, returning home with their children they had collected.

The siren of a fire engine blared from down the street, increasing to be almost deafening, as it passed by the two boys. Jermaine watched it drive by, wondering where it could be heading.

Suddenly, he bumped into Chris, who had stopped walking. He looked at Chris, who was looking in the sky, staring at a plume of smoke. Jermaine looked up at the cloud of black, tainting the blue and white expanse behind it, and thought that it looked strangely close to where St Peters was. Once he, looked back down, he saw Chris sprinting off into the distance. Jermaine felt a sinking feeling in his stomach.

31

Cleanse By Flame

Jermaine struggled to keep up with Chris, whilst they sprinted back to the school. Chris headed straight to the field, without taking a moment to rest.

Two fire engines were parked directly in front of the training grounds, blocking Jermaine's view of the building. The bush leading to the cabin had been trashed, where the firemen had cut their way through, in order to douse the flames.

The only thing Jermaine could see was a stream of water, from the fire hose, as well as a large cloud of smoke, rising above the trees.

Chris attempted to get closer, but the firemen would not let him pass. All Jermaine could think about was whether the others were trapped somewhere within that blaze.

His heart beat stayed at the same pace, but felt stronger than ever, as if it wanted to escape the captivity of his ribs. A hand touched Jermaine on his shoulder. To his relief, he turned to see Elise standing there.

'We just saw…the smoke and…came running. Is anyone inside?' She asked him, panting, in an attempt to catch her breath.

'I don't know…just arrived myself,' Jermaine found it hard to breathe as his heart beat calmed down.

'Where is he?' Camille asked, fear lighting her eyes.

'He's over there. They're not letting him through,' Jermaine answered.

Camille sprinted off towards Chris, leaving Zach, Amita and Elise, standing beside Jermaine.

A few moments later, Alex, Maxwell, Craig and Sean appeared, equally out of breath. Alex and Maxwell rushed over, and stood beside Chris and Camille. The four sixth formers looked as if they were watching their life's work burn to the ground in front of them.

'Where's Jared?' Jermaine asked nobody in particular, once he had realised that he had not seen him yet.

'I'm right here, don't worry,' Jared said, appearing from behind the group, 'the firemen said that there was no one in the building, luckily.'

Chris, along with the other sixth formers, made his way back to Jermaine and the others.

'Chris, a kid from school brought this to me about ten minutes ago. I thought it was to do with the issues today, until I heard about this,' Jared said, handing a note over to Chris.

After reading the note in his hand, Chris smiled, which eventually grew into a snigger, then a chuckle, and finally a full, blown laugh. Camille reached forward and took the note from him.

'Looks like the temperature is picking up, isn't it? Signed, James Grainger.' Camille crumpled the note into a ball and threw it into on the ground, before spitting on it.

'I'm so stupid. Took the bait like an amateur,' Chris declared, still laughing to himself.

'They just wanted us out of the way, that's what today was about. It was all just a farce,' Jermaine twigged.

'I've had enough. We take the fight to them. We hit them with everything we have,' Camille suggested, the fury she felt emitting off of her like heat.

'First of all, we need to know where they are,' Jared pointed out.

'I think I may know something about that,' Craig said, to the amazement of the group.

'What do you know? Why are we only hearing about this now?' Camille approached Craig; her hands held out in a threatening manner.

'I didn't think about it until just now, but, a few months ago, just after the Christmas holidays, I heard about a group meeting in a school. It sounded suspicious at the time, but I wasn't a part of the group back then, so I just pushed it to one side,' Craig said, in his defence. Jermaine remembered Craig mentioning something about this. He felt stupid for ignoring it.

Chris turned to Alex and Maxwell, 'Check this out. See if there's anything that can help us find James. Any meetings, invitations to meetings; anything out of the ordinary. Use whatever force necessary.'

'Will do,' they both said at the same time, instantly leaving to begin their investigations.

'I'll stick around and see what we can salvage, once the firemen have left,' Jared offered.

Camille looked at the remnants of smoke in the air, 'Scum! I'll join you. See what we can find.'

'We'll help you with that too, won't we guys?' Elise stated

'Definitely, whatever we can do to help,' Sean agreed

'Ok,' Chris said, as he started to walk away, 'When you're all done, make sure you get some rest tonight. Training will begin again tomorrow. We need to be in top form for when we locate James and his enthusiasts. I have someone to see; we'll be needing new equipment.'

Once Chris left, the firemen slowly began packing up, removing their equipment.

'Let's see what we have left,' Jared said, as he began to make his way towards, what was once, the training ground.

Jermaine and the others followed behind him, all feeling crestfallen.

*

The remainder of the week seemed to go as slowly as it could. It was as if the burning of the training grounds had filled the air with a thick substance that caused everything to be more difficult and longer to achieve. It felt like every activity Jermaine did was taking place inside a swimming pool. Just walking alone felt taxing.

Jermaine felt this effect each day, but still went to school, went to his lessons and continued his combat training with the new recruits after school.

His training sessions with the twins had been cancelled, due to their absence, as they searched for information pertaining to James and his cohort.

Yet again, Chris had disappeared. Craig informed the other Year 7 Hunters that whispers of Chris conducting solo hunts had been spreading throughout the borough. The rumours varied. One stated that he was seen fighting an entire football team that week, purely because they had been teasing a rival player over a recent loss. Another stated that he picked a fight with a group of kids because they had been associated with bullies in some way. There were even whispers of him fighting a group of adults who were laughing at a child who tripped over.

Jermaine, along with the other recruits, thought this was not so implausible that it couldn't be true, but that it most likely wasn't true.

Jermaine saw the twins around the school every so often, although they always seemed too busy to talk. Sporadically, Jermaine would cross paths with Camille, who would ask him the same question, every single time:

'Why aren't you training?' she would probe, her face contorted in a way that sent chills down Jermaine's spine. If it were within her power, he knew that she would put him into a perpetual cycle of lessons and training; no breaks for food, sleep or anything else.

Every day seemed torturous for Jermaine. He spent the days waiting for the news that they would be attacking the bullies, and his evenings spent tossing and turning. The nightmares had returned.

They were different than before, but the same every night. Jermaine would see himself, stood in front of the training grounds, surrounded by bullies. They were all different shapes and sizes, but they all had the face of James Grainger. The rest of the Bully Hunters were scattered around the immediate vicinity, each of them unconscious.

Jermaine would then see a Molotov cocktail fly over his head and land inside the training building, setting it on fire. One by one, the unconscious Hunters would be sucked into the flames, followed by a large set of hands, which would pull Jermaine into the burning building.

Every night, Jermaine woke up, his covers drenched from the sweat seeping out of his pores. He made a decision that he wouldn't tell anyone about his dreams, especially his fellow Hunters. The Year 7s seemed to look to Jermaine as their point of reference on how they should feel, so he felt that his confession of fear would serve no purpose but to weaken their resolve.

*

Over a week had passed since the burning of the training grounds, and Jermaine arrived at the school, to be greeted by Jared at the gate.

'Morning Jermaine,' Jared sounded off, more life in his voice than Jermaine had heard in the past two weeks, 'Chris has called everyone to the training grounds. The twins believe that they have found where James is holding his next meeting; it's happening today. It's time…time to get even,' a sinister look illuminated Jared's eyes.

Jermaine nodded and began to make his way to the training grounds. Although his subconscious mind was in fear of the situation, he knew that his conscious self was only concerned with one thing...vengeance, bringing the fight back to James, once and for all.

*

Walking through the broken bush; no longer needing to move anything to clear his way, as the firemen had trampled a clear path, Jermaine saw all of the Hunters stood around, talking to one another. He made his way closer.

Jermaine had not been to the building since the day of the fire. Everything looked different now. The walls had dried and there was no ash in the air, just the wreckage of what was once the place where Jermaine had learned to protect himself, as well as others.

Jermaine noted the barren windows, covered with soot. The burn marks rising up to the roof, where the flames had been slashing against the walls of the building. The smell of ash polluted the air around the burnt husk.

His attention was then drawn to the pile of unsalvageable equipment, which had been piled up by the firemen and doused in water. The Hunters were only able to save a few odd items; the ones that wouldn't burn. They had found some weights, the odd training mat, which luckily, never caught light, but nothing else worth taking.

The training building was no more.

'Something that took years to build has been destroyed, in a matter of minutes,' Chris explained, as he walked into the centre of the group, 'let this image stick with you forever. Let it invigorate you, if your resolve as to why we do what we do ever falters.

'Look at it! The hands of those who value nothing but pain and destruction have tainted our building. They only know how to hurt, breaking things that are not theirs, so that they can feel like they are greater than others.'

The group of Hunters released a murmur of agreement. Chris walked over to a pile of burnt rubble and kicked it.

'What they fail to understand is that these are just material things. We do not gain strength from items we own, but from within one another and ourselves. We look to each other for vigour.

'I know that some, if not all of you, wish to find these bullies to give them a taste of their own brand of justice, but I implore you, don't follow me today out of a sense of veneration, anger, or hatred. Follow me today to show these brutes that the fists of the weak can smash the power of the strong, if there is purpose and valour behind it!' Chris thundered, raising his fist in the air.

Jermaine, along with the rest of the Hunters, raised their hands, cheering, like a band of Viking warriors, preparing to go into battle. Jermaine felt as if the air around him was filled with electricity.

As the roar of the Hunters died down, Alex stepped forward, 'Thanks to the information given to us by Craig, we discovered that the bullies have been meeting in an unused room, at Preton High School. Information has led us to believe that they will be having a meeting today, at the end of school. As these meetings are apparently quite sporadic, it makes sense for us to strike now, before they do something that could lead to innocents being harmed,' Alex explained.

'Today is the day. We will show these brutes the strength we possess. This could be a dangerous battle, so I will not force anyone to join me, but if you do, know that I will personally do everything in my power, to ensure that we return victorious.

'Whoever wishes to fight, we leave from here at the beginning of break. Until then,' Chris concluded.

With that, the Hunters began to make their way back into the school, heading to their lessons. Once they were back inside the school grounds, Jermaine rushed up to Elise, grabbing her by the arm.

'Are you going to go to the hunt?' he asked her.

'Of course, why wouldn't I? I assume you're going, aren't you?' Elise replied, baffled by the odd question.

'Yeah, I'm definitely going; I just…I just don't want to see anything happen to you. James is not your basic bully. He's something worse, something more menacing.'

Elise smiled, 'Why don't you want to see anything happen to me?' she asked, tilting her head to one side, which Jermaine noticed, made her hair fall from her shoulders and hang down towards the ground.

A sharp feeling of embarrassment washed over Jermaine, 'Umm, I wouldn't want to see anything happen to any of the Hunters. I'll see you at lunch,' he said, quickly walking towards his lesson.

32

Feud's End

The bell for lunch rang, followed by the usual hum of children standing up and beginning conversations they had been preparing to have throughout their lessons.

Jermaine crossed paths with Sean, who was also making his way to the training grounds. As they walked, they met up with Zach, Amita, Craig and Elise. They all arrived together as one unit, ready for whatever dangers faced them.

The sixth formers were already at the grounds when they arrived, and began clapping when they saw that all of the Year 7s had arrived. Even Chris was smiling.

'It may have been presumptuous of me, but I arranged cover for each of you already, so you won't be marked as absent,' Jared said, 'I wish I could join you all, but I would just slow you down, so, please give James a few smacks from me, would you?' Jared asked.

The group agreed, then left to Preton High.

*

It took the group just over thirty minutes; at the steady walking pace they were traveling, to make it to Preton High. They had taken back roads to avoid any unwanted police attention. A group of kids on the street during school hours would definitely look suspicious. As they neared the gates, Jermaine began to feel strangely warm. It was as if his blood was heating him up from inside. Sweat began to pour down his forehead, accumulating at the collar of his shirt.

'Let's make our way to the rear of the school. There should be a more secluded access point there,' Chris instructed the group.

The Hunters proceeded to circle the school, until they arrived at a small grass covered clearing, surrounded by trees.

Chris crouched down, signalling for the Hunters to huddle together, 'There's a gate over there. We can get inside over that. Alex, Camille, you stay here with the Year 7s. Jermaine, Maxwell, I want the two of you to follow me.'

'But you don't know how many of them could be in there,' Alex disputed.

'I don't intend to fight them within the school. I want to lead them out here. If we're all inside, it could ruin the plan. Find a good hiding place amongst those trees, and wait for us to come back. We'll be fine. Jermaine, Maxwell, on me,' Chris stood up, and then began to move towards the gate.

Maxwell and Jermaine scurried along behind him, keeping as low a profile as they could. Jermaine glanced back and saw the rest of the Hunters disappear amongst the trees.

Once they reached the gate, Chris looked inside the school, to see if he could see anything suspicious. Whilst he was waiting, Jermaine felt his hand begin to tremor with fear. He attempted to hide it from Chris and Maxwell, by covering it with his other hand; nonetheless, the next thing he heard was Chris' voice saying, 'Fear is the greatest of all destroyers. If you fear defeat, you have already been defeated. Believe in yourself. You are stronger than you think.'

Chris then moved forward, scaling the gate in three motions, landing almost silently on the other side. Maxwell placed a hand on Jermaine's shoulder, smiled at him, and then followed behind Chris.

The fence reached double the height of Jermaine. He looked at it, clenched his fist, exhaled heavily, and then scaled the gate with more ease than he expected, landing beside the two sixth formers, making a marginally louder amount of noise, once his feet met the ground. Looking back at the gate, Jermaine didn't know how he managed to get over it so easily. *'All those workouts must be paying off.'* he thought.

Chris then turned to face Maxwell, 'Show us where the room is.'

Maxwell nodded, and led the boys through the building.

*

The three Hunters made their way through the school, ducking into shadows, whenever they heard the sound of someone in the halls. Eventually, they came across an inconspicuous wooded door, where Maxwell stopped. He looked around one final time, and then turned to face Chris and Jermaine.

'This must be it,' Maxwell declared.

Chris nodded, reached for the handle, twisted it, then carefully pushed it open. Inside, the room was dark. A smell of damp lingered in the air. As their eyes gradually adjusted to the darkness, they could make out that there were a group of tables, all arranged in a hexagon in the centre of the room. Chris walked up to the first table in front of him, reached inside his pocket, and produced a belt, which he then wrapped into a perfect circle. He placed the belt on the table, then, he reached inside his other pocket. This time, he produced a hand full of sand. He poured the sand on the table, creating a small mound, next to the belt.

Finally, he reached into his back pocket, pulling out a sheet of paper, along with a pen. He started writing a note. Once finished, he put the note onto the table, placing a corner under the belt, to stop it from being accidently blown away.

Jermaine looked at the note, which read, *'The clearing behind the school, 16:00. We finish this.'*

'Let's get back to the others," Chris said turning around.

*

Jermaine, and the two sixth formers, arrived back at the clearing. In the distance, Jermaine noticed Elise, who had stood up and started waving, in an attempt to show them where they were hidden.

The three Hunters made their way over to the others. They had positioned themselves behind an old fallen tree, where they could see the clearing and the school gate clearly, but would be hard to spot amongst all the foliage.

'Now, we wait,' Chris said, as he sat down, 'If we found the right place, James will have to come here. His pride won't allow him to do anything else.'

*

An hour had passed. The Hunters periodically stood up and stretched their legs, attempting to avoid their muscles from relaxing too much.

School had ended half an hour ago, and now the sound of the

students from Preton High had reduced down to near silence, indicating that most of them had begun making their way home.

Chris stood against a tree, watching the clearing for any form of movement, when he suddenly clicked his fingers. All of the Hunters turned to look at the clearing.

'I'm here Chris. I loved your message, brought back memories of good times. So, don't be scared, come out. We've already shown that you can be touched. This fallacy of invulnerability that you have tried so hard to establish has been shattered. Everyone knows that you are nothing more than just a group of kids, like all of us. Made of nothing more than flesh and bone. We've destroyed your precious building too. I did take pleasure in doing that? Did you get my note?

'All that is left to do now, is break you, once and for all. As you, yourself said, it's time that we finish this!' James hollered, his voice reverberating through the trees.

'He's enormous,' Zach whispered. The Hunters watched as James and his band of followers filtered into the clearing.

'There's so many of them, more than double the amount of us,' Amita sighed.

'Perfect, the more people I can beat, the merrier,' Camille stated.

Chris raised his hand towards the group, signalling them to hold their positions.

Each of the Hunters began stretching their arms and legs,

preparing themselves for the signal to attack. Even though there were more bullies than them, the Hunters could tell that the bullies were not as trained. They seemed more like a mob, rather than a trained force. Jermaine did notice that there were a few of the bullies, who were stood closer to James, who had a stronger demeanour about them.

Seconds began to feel like minutes to Jermaine. He watched the group of bullies walking into the centre of the clearing, but Chris still held his hand out, keeping the Hunters where they were.

Chris scanned the area behind the Hunters, the gate, the clearing, and finally the tree line. He abruptly dropped to his knees and turned to the group.

'There's another group of six or more approaching us from the right, within the trees. Year 7s, once we head out to face the main group, you engage them. They won't be expecting that. The rest of you, including you two,' Chris said, as he pointed to Jermaine and Sean, 'follow me. Let's bring it to them.' He stood back up, walked past the tree line, making himself visible to the group of bullies, and proceeded into the clearing. The twins and Camille followed after him instinctively. Sean then followed behind them and Jermaine after him.

Once clear of the trees, Jermaine looked on at the large group that they were approaching. Jermaine counted a total of twenty-one kids, boys and girls, and in the centre of them, stood James, head and shoulders above the rest.

Jermaine's hands began to feel sweaty and his legs started to feel as if they were made of lead. He remembered Chris' words and looked at the backs of the rest of the Hunters. Seeing them all jogging straight into battle, heads held high and fists clenched, reinforced his confidence. Jermaine swallowed the spit that had accumulated in his mouth, then started to jog along behind them.

As the Hunters began to close in on the bullies, Chris raised his hand, then, started to spin it around in a circle, signalling for them to surround the group, which seemed crazy to Jermaine, as there were more bullies than Hunters, but Jermaine complied with the instruction and headed over to the right hand side of the group.

As soon as Chris was within an arms length of one of the bullies, he grabbed the boy, landed two clean punches into his gut, followed with a knee, then threw him to the floor, harder than Jermaine had ever seen someone thrown. The boy bounced on the grass letting out a whelp once he had settled on the ground. All the other bullies turned to face Chris and started backing away at the sight of him, which pushed them backwards into one of the other Hunters. Just then, Jermaine fully comprehended Chris' earlier instruction.

At that point, the rest of the Hunters began attacking from their individual positions. Camille sweep kicked a boy, taking him to the ground and then pushed her foot forcefully into his face. Alex and Maxwell each engaged an attacking bully, taking them down with vicious kicks to their stomachs. The bullies, then keeled over, in what looked like excruciating pain.

Jermaine looked to his right, and saw one of the bullies grab Sean by the collar of his shirt. Sean then grabbed the bully's arm, pulled her towards him, dragging her down to the floor. Sean then twisted the girl's arm, near to the point of breaking it.

Jermaine looked back to Chris who he saw walking towards the bullies, all of them backing away from him. He was making his way to James, who was standing still, wearing a smile on his face. He constantly ran his finger up and down the scar on his cheek.

Jermaine then felt a hand roughly grab his shoulder. He instinctively wrapped his arm around the hand and turned, throwing a consecutive set of punches into the gut of the boy that the hand belonged to. The bully crumbled to the floor as if his spine had suddenly been removed from his body.

Two more bullies, a boy and a girl, were now approaching Jermaine. He immediately adopted a fighting stance and moved towards them.

They both approached, the boy kicking his legs out in front of him. After dodging a few of the attacks, Jermaine managed to grab hold of the boy's foot and pulled it towards himself, forcing the bully to open his legs into a split. The girl then charged towards Jermaine throwing punches frantically, in an attempt to stop him having a chance to attack her. Dodging backwards, Jermaine managed to avoid most of the attacks, but was eventually caught by one of the bully's haymakers, which knocked him to the ground.

The girl then began kicking Jermaine, at which point he grabbed her foot and twisted the girl's ankle. The girl let out a scream as Jermaine rolled out of her range and regained his footing.

Quickly, Jermaine closed the gap between him and the bully, hitting her with a flurry of Palm strikes, knocking her to the ground. The boy, who had now stood back up, recovering from the pain of the splits, looked at his friend on the floor, and then back to Jermaine, who had adopted his fighting stance again.

The boy then ran, muttering, 'Forget this.'

Jermaine turned, scanning the battlefield, to find where the other Hunters were. He saw Sean, who had a streak of blood leading down from his nose to his jaw, standing up off of a bully, who was covering his face. Jermaine noticed two bullies running away from the twins, who were smiling as they chased them. Camille had just thrown a boy, cleanly over her head, and grabbed another who was trying to escape.

From behind him, Jermaine heard the sound of voices, screaming out in pain. He turned, to see a group of bullies fleeing from the tree line. Within the trees, he saw Elise holding a limp bully, by the scruff of their shirt, in her hands. The other Year 7s were all engaging the bullies around them, teaching them lessons in humility.

Jermaine returned his attention to the battlefield, looking for Chris, who he finally saw walking straight towards James. They were within a couple of metres of each other, when Jermaine noticed a boy sneaking up behind Chris, a rock in his hand. Jermaine shouted out to Chris, however, the noise from the countless fights happening around him, muted his voice. He ran forward to try and intervene, but couldn't make it in time. He heard a loud crack, as the rock ricocheted off Chris' skull.

Chris, with blood dripping down his neck, grabbed the boy and threw his knee into his chest, causing him to collapse like a sack of potatoes dropped on the floor. Two other bullies charged at the now weakened Chris, only to be decimated by a flash of punches and kicks, which were so fast, Jermaine never even saw them connect. The only indication they had been hit, was when they both collapsed at Chris' feet.

Jermaine eventually reached Chris, wrapping his arm around him, in order to support him. Chris pushed Jermaine away, and continued to make his way towards James, stumbling as he moved.

'You should take a seat shorty. You look a little woozy,' boomed the voice of James as he began to walk forward.

Jermaine rushed back over to Chris, who again, pushed him away. 'I'll deal with this, go deal with the rest,' Chris stated, trying to regain his composure.

'So you still think you can take me? Even like this? You are very insolent aren't you, insect? That's fine with me. I'll break you in half just the same,' declared James, as he reached out to grab Chris.

Chris sidestepped the extended arm of James, threw a quick set of punches into his side, a heavy kick into his left leg, and then jumped back, creating some distance between himself and the giant in front of him.

James grimaced in pain from the blows. He clenched his fists; pure hatred in his eyes, and started attacking. Due to his head injury, Chris began stumbling, as if he was finding it difficult to maintain his footing. James sprang forward, throwing a set of devastating punches at Chris. By a miracle, Chris managed to block all of the attacks. He lowered his arms, then charged back at James.

As he got closer, he executed a glorious looking spin kick, which looked beautiful and effortless. The kick sank straight into James' gut. James clenched his stomach, then threw a back handed slap outwards, which managed to connect with Chris, sending him reeling back.

Jermaine watched this fight unfolding, saw the streak of blood on Chris' head increase in size. He knew that Chris couldn't last much longer out there with James, without causing himself irreparable damage.

Chris steadied himself, and started strolling towards James, who was now standing up straight again.

'You have spirit Chris, but this is a futile attempt. There is no way you can defeat me!' James taunted.

Chris said nothing in response, but continued walking towards James at a slow and steady pace; he couldn't move any faster. Fuelled by anger, James sprang forward, hands raised above his head. He slammed them down in front of him, but Chris dove to the side, avoiding the destructive blow. He then began throwing everything he had left at James. His fists moved incredibly fast, coupled with an assortment of powerful kicks.

James received these blows, only managing to block a few. As Chris began to lose energy, his attacks slowed down, allowing James to reach out, punch Chris in the face, and grab him by his shirt, lifting him off the ground.

'Chris!' shouted Jermaine without realising it.

Chris hung there, limp, his eyes partially glazed over. He turned his head and looked at Jermaine from the corner of his eyes. He then threw a punch into James' throat, which connected cleanly. James stumbled, releasing Chris, who fell to his knees. He stumbled backwards, clutching his throat, trying to breathe. Jermaine rushed over to Chris, and held him, noting how limp his body felt.

'What are you doing? Go and help the others,' Chris insisted, his eyes closing as he spoke.

'What are *you* doing? Aren't you the one who said that knowing when not to fight is part of being a good fighter? What are you going to prove, going up against him in this state?' Jermaine replied.

'We can't let him leave here undefeated. He'll amass another set of bullies, and bring the fight back to us. One of us needs to beat him alone. If we all jump him, he'll just become a martyr. All the bullies here will tell stories of how it took all of us to take him down. He'll become a symbol, a flag for them to fight behind.'

'So I'll take him,' Jermaine said, looking straight into Chris', half opened eyes, 'I'm not scared. You defeated him before, I'm sure I can too.'

Chris looked at Jermaine. He saw a fire in him and felt a strong sense of pride, 'Go on then, show that oaf what the meek can actually do,' said Chris as he passed out.

33

David & Goliath

Jermaine looked at Chris, laying helpless on the floor.

'Somebody help!'

The volume that the words escaped Jermaine's mouth was unbelievable. All the Hunters turned their attentions from the bullies they were beating on and looked over to Jermaine and Chris on the floor. James was still on one knee, regaining his breath. They rushed over.

'Chris!' Camille exclaimed, falling to her knees. She picked him up, resting his head on her lap, 'I need to take him into the school to see the nurse,' she stated, standing up, 'Sean, help me, please!' Camille pleaded, tears streaming down her face. Sean nodded, and the two of them carried Chris towards the school building.

Jermaine stood up, anger bubbling through his veins. He turned to look at James, who had regained his composure, and saw the twins walking in his direction.

'No, I'll deal with him,' said Jermaine as he walked past them.

He felt like David going up against Goliath. All the fear he had been experiencing previously had just disappeared, replaced with cold anger and purpose. The new recruits joined up with Alex and Maxwell, Elise looking noticeably more worried than the others.

James saw Jermaine approaching him and began to laugh. He started stomping towards Jermaine, and, once he was within reach, swung a huge hook at him, which Jermaine, ducked and evaded, throwing a punch into James' left leg.

James turned and threw a couple more punches, which Jermaine also dodged, stepping to the right again. Jermaine punched James in the leg a further two times. As Jermaine was about to throw another attack, James spun himself around quicker than before and reached out to grab him.

Narrowly, he escaped James' grasp by throwing himself on the floor and rolling to his right.

Jermaine was surprised by the speed at which James moved. He seemed weakened from his initial bout with Chris, but was still extremely dangerous. Jermaine realised that he would have to be more careful when dealing with him. It would only take for James to get hold of him for a second and the fight would be over.

Jermaine jumped up and looked at James. He could hear the voices of the Hunters cheering him on. He could also hear the voices of the bullies, who had run away, but were now returning to see

James deal out some punishment, cheering and chanting for James.

His heart began beating at three times the normal rate. He could feel his neck throbbing from the blood racing through his veins.

James began stepping forward, watching Jermaine, like a lion trying to corner his prey. He had lowered himself and outstretched his arms in order to leave Jermaine no option but to move backwards.

'I've had enough of playing around with you, you disgusting pest. When I get my hands on you, I'm going to crush you like the ant you are!' James bellowed.

James continued to close in. Jermaine looked intently at James' leg, realising that he was avoiding applying his full weight on it. He remembered Chris slamming a kick into the same leg, and realised that the punches he landed must have been actually hurting him.

Jermaine quickly formulated a plan. He began leading James towards his left side, forcing him to apply all his weight onto the leg as he turned. Jermaine then noticed a split second where James flinched as he felt the pain in his leg. Jermaine capitalised on this slight opportunity and threw a full force, front kick at James' leg, making James fall to his knees. Jermaine stepped back just before James' hand reached out to grab him.

The Hunters cheered to see James on his knees again, and the bullies watching lowered their heads in disappointment.

Out of frustration, James punched the ground, leaving a football-sized crater in the dirt. He glared at Jermaine and slowly stood up.

'You're strong for such a little boy. I'm actually impressed, but enough is enough.'

James began to apply pressure to his left leg, as if he were forcing himself to feel the pain.

'You think a little discomfort in my leg is going to be your saving grace do you? Come at me again boy, show all these onlookers how weak the Bully Hunters truly are!'

Jermaine looked back at the Hunters watching him. He then looked at James and began making his approach. He tried stepping around to James' right side again but this time, James didn't seem bothered by any pain. It was as if the battle had started from the beginning again. He seemed renewed somehow.

Suddenly, Jermaine thought about the statement that Chris made earlier. He looked at the giant in front of him, and realised that he was still acting in fear. His reluctance to being hit by James was making the fight close to impossible. He was so scared of what a punch from James would do to him, that he wasn't fighting to his highest potential.

The realisation that he would have to face James head on began to dawn on Jermaine. The possibility that James would catch him was higher this way, but his chance of success also increased.

He considered that James was faster than anticipated, but he was sure he could move faster. He then thought back to all his time training with the Hunters. He had felt punches like he could never have expected to withstand, and lived to tell the tale. He decided to do something, which could turn out to be the best, or worst decision of his life thus far.

Jermaine made his way towards James. James lowered his stance, outstretched his hands, preparing to reach out to his side's to stop Jermaine circling around him again, like a goalie trying to stop a penalty kick. James then realised that Jermaine was in fact charging straight towards him.

Jermaine held his guard up whilst closing the gap between himself and James. James then threw a punch, which connected this time, pushing Jermaine back a few steps.

'Got ya!' said James. He then took a step forward and threw another punch, which also connected. James then threw his arm back for a third punch when he felt an explosion of punches connect with his stomach.

James stepped back, surprised by the punches he had just felt.

After feeling the force of James' fists, the fear had subsided within Jermaine. His arms were in a large amount of pain...but he was still in the fight. James was bigger and meaner than most people, but he was still just as human.

James looked around him at the faces of the bullies. He then looked back at Jermaine, who stood at less than half his height, but proved to be more troublesome than anticipated.

James began to have a moment of deja-vu. It was as if the same thing that happened six years ago was repeating itself again. The thought of possibly losing to yet another small Hunter was unbearable.

Jermaine looked at James and started making his way towards him, now filled with confidence that he could possibly beat him. As he got closer, he started to edge forward slowly. He knew that there was a second between punches where James left himself open to attack now. He also knew that he could only withstand a few of James' attacks before it severely impacted his ability to fight.

As Jermaine reached within punching distance, as expected, James began to throw punches, more varied with vicious intent behind them. Jermaine was able to dodge a few of them, but received the odd blow, which he was beginning to struggle to defend against. Whenever the opportunity arose, Jermaine threw an opportunistic punch, or kick, at James' body.

Jermaine ducked and weaved away from the flurry of punches, now seriously beginning to feel the pain building up in his arms. He noticed James was moving in a slightly more laboured manner, and although he gave the impression that he was feeling no pain, he had actually been gradually losing energy; Jermaine's attacks had been slowly chipping away at his stamina. Luckily, Jermaine had not completely forgotten what Anton had taught him about wearing your opponent down.

He also realised that, even though James had been avoiding drawing attention to his left leg, he was actually reluctant to put too much pressure on it. James was now keeping his stature low, heavily guarding his legs.

Jermaine continued weaving in between punches, his arms on the brink of exhaustion and legs now beginning to feel fatigued. Raising his arms felt like he was holding two large shopping bags in each hand.

He sidestepped away from a monstrous uppercut thrown by James, feeling the wind from the punch brush past his face, as it disturbed the air around him. As he stepped in to throw a counter attack, Jermaine's leg almost completely collapsed under his weight.

James, noticing an opportunity, threw his arms around Jermaine, managing to get a hold of him.

The Hunters, who were still watching the fight intensely, gasped as James connected the fingers of his two hands around Jermaine's body.

Jermaine, now in a state of panic, wriggled, attempting to get free of the grab. In the next moment, he felt himself lift off the ground as James' hold tighten around his lower back.

'It was only a matter of time. I'm going to crush every last ounce of breath out of you,' whispered James into Jermaine's ear as he squeezed him, tighter and tighter.

Fear and pain began to consume Jermaine as the hold tightened. He thought of the Hunters, who he could hear calling out to him. He thought of Chris, bleeding on the floor and the bullies cheering James on, as he was about to end the fight. The thought that James beating him would invigorate the other bullies, and that they may then be able to beat the Hunters, overwhelmed his mind.

Alex and Maxwell looked at each other, and then began to take a step forward to aid Jermaine. The bullies, now with a newly found confidence, started regrouping, and began to move forward in James' defence.

Jermaine could do nothing but concentrate on the pain in his back, when suddenly an image of James' leg came to his mind. It was completely unguarded now.

He couldn't move his upper body, and felt as if he would never be able to feel his legs ever again if he didn't hurry. He raised his left leg, turned his foot to the side and threw his leg diagonally downwards, straight into James' left knee.

James let out a yelp of pain, which sounded like a bear roaring. Everyone stopped moving as Jermaine raised his leg again and again, slamming it with all his might into James' knee.

After six successful connections, James released Jermaine, limping backwards in pain.

Jermaine landed on his bum and felt light headed. He looked up and saw James bracing his knee with both his hands.

He knew this would be his only chance to end the fight, so Jermaine drew in four deep breaths, pulled himself upright, and charged into James.

Once he was less than a metre away from James, he threw another punch into the side of James left knee, pushing his leg outwards from his body. James released a cry of pain, which was stopped as Jermaine threw a follow-up uppercut into his jaw, causing him to stagger backwards. James then fell to his right knee, bringing him to the same height as Jermaine.

Immediately, Jermaine released an onslaught of punches, concluding with a spinning backhand. James looked dazed as Jermaine grabbed his head and threw his knee into his face, sending James falling backwards to the ground.

Absolute silence followed the deafening thump of James falling to the ground.

Jermaine stood in front of James, barely enough energy to stand. He looked up and saw the remaining bullies, shock littering their faces.

The words, 'Who's next?' slithered through his lips, accompanied with a look of malice in his eyes.

The bullies backed away slowly, then, once a few feet away, started running, leaving James unconscious on the floor.

Once all the bullies had gone, Jermaine's legs finally gave in and he fell to his hands and knees. The Hunters rushed to his side and helped him to his feet.

'Jermaine, you did it! You beat him. You were amazing! I was so worried,' Elise said, wrapping her arms around him. Jermaine fell limp in her arms, passing out from exhaustion.

'We need to get him out of here. He'll be fine,' Alex stated, picking Jermaine up.

'What are we going to do about these guys?' Craig asked Maxwell, referring to the bodies of the bullies strewn around the clearing.

'Leave them. We'll let the school know that there are some kids, who seemed to have beaten each other up out here,' Maxwell responded.

The group then left the area, a slew of injured and unconscious bullies in their wake.

*

From the direction of the school, the boy with the small glasses strolled into the clearing. He walked past all the bodies laid out on the floor, moaning in pain, stepping over the bullies, showing no concern for them.

He eventually arrived at James, who was still out cold. He adjusted his glasses, reached into his pocket, and took out a notepad, which had a list of names on it. He scrolled through the list, and crossed James' name out.

'Disappointing James. Good thing we don't put all our eggs into one basket eh?' he said, turning around, leaving James unconscious on the floor.

34

Handover

After a few minutes, Jermaine awoke to find himself slung over Alex's shoulder, in a fireman carry. He tapped Alex on the back. Realising that Jermaine had regained consciousness, Alex placed him on his feet. The Hunters surrounded Jermaine, checking to see if he was fine. He dismissed all their concerns, stating that he just needed to go home, to get some sleep.

The group then insisted on following him home, ignoring his attempts to deter them. After six o'clock, he arrived at his house. He walked up to the door, turned, and said goodbye to the Hunters. Elise, looking worried, gave him a hug, before turning to leave.

Jermaine closed his front door behind him, and leant against it. He felt bruised and aching all over, but proud of himself. As he walked in, he heard the sound of his mum in the kitchen.

'Jermaine, is that you?' she called out.

'Yeah mum,' Jermaine replied.

'Come get some food bwoi, your dinner ready.'

Jermaine looked at his clothes. He was covered in dirt; his jumper had been ripped where one of the bullies had grabbed him, and he felt that he looked like death warmed up. He knew that his mum would worry if she saw him in that state. 'I'm just going to go upstairs to change. Be back down in a minute.'

He reached his bedroom, stripped his clothes off, and put on a t-shirt. He noticed that his forearms were nearly purple from the bruises left behind from James' punches, so he decided to put on a long sleeve top instead.

Jermaine headed back downstairs, smelling the aroma from the food. He entered the kitchen, grabbed his plate, placed it on a tray and walked into the living room.

Once sat down with his family, he devoured his dinner without taking any breaths in between. His brother and sisters watched him consume the food like a vacuum cleaner. He hadn't realised just how hungry he was until he swallowed his first fork full.

Feeling like he had eaten too quickly, Jermaine slowly stood up, kissed his mum on the check, out of gratitude for the meal, and said he would go upstairs to have a shower.

When he walked into his room, he sat on his bed to rest his legs. The walk up the stairs had put a strain on his body like it never had before. The desire to lay his head down for a second overcame him.

What had felt like only a minute later, he awoke feeling the rays from the sun on his face. He turned his head to look at his clock. The time read 07:15. He had fallen asleep the moment his head touched the bed. A bed sheet had been wrapped around him, and pillow placed under his head. He didn't remember experiencing any of it. Putting two and two together, he figured that his mum must have come to check on him.

Trying to sit up, he felt his entire body scream out in agony. The pain from the fight with James had truly set in. The walk to the bathroom that morning felt like a pilgrimage. Every step took more self-discipline and determination then he was aware he had.

In the shower, he found it nearly impossible to lift his arm, as his shoulders had seized up. He was covered in bruises. His legs felt like they didn't belong to him. Lifting them more than three inches off the ground seemed like an impossible task.

After the most agonising morning of his life, Jermaine left the house to make his way to school.

*

Behind the bike shed, Jermaine saw Jared sat at the picnic table, reading a book.

As he got closer, Jared looked up over his book and smiled. He stood up, reached out and placed a hand on Jermaine's arm, removing it when he saw Jermaine's face contort from the pain.

'Oh, sorry Mr Hunter? How are we feeling?' enquired Jared.

'Pain,' Jermaine replied, 'I haven't felt this tired since…well, ever.'

'I'm not surprised. That's to be expected after you, single-handedly, take down the biggest bully anyone has ever seen.'

'Well, Chris did soften him up for me first. It doesn't seem quite real to be honest. It feels like a dream, as if I'll wake up any moment,' Jermaine said, 'come to think of it, what happened to James, The last thing I saw, he was laying on his back in the grass.'

'Well, word is, his parents packed his things together and are sending him back to Scotland. I guess they think it's too dangerous for him down here in London,' Jared explained.

'Good riddance,' Jermaine began slowly rotating his shoulder backwards. Like a bolt from the blue, Chris' face flashed into his mind. 'Have you heard anything about Chris? Is he ok?' His concern was clearly detectable through the tone of his voice.

'I'm fine,' Chris said, stood behind Jermaine.

Jermaine turned to see Chris, a gauze patch taped to his head.

'How are you? How is your head? Shouldn't you be in the hospital or something?' Jermaine asked, surprised to see Chris back at school so quickly.

'It's fine. A few stiches, but no concussion. I don't do hospitals, so I got out of there as soon as possible. I heard what happened with James. I'm sorry that you had to deal with that situation.'

'It's fine, I felt that I needed to beat him, or at least try,' Jermaine explained.

'Well, you made a statement with your actions. You seem to be the topic of conversation everywhere. I managed to beat James when we were both the same age, you on the other hand, managed to defeat the most infamous bully, six years your senior. If what I did made me well known and feared…you are going to become legendary.

'You've surpassed all of my greatest expectations for you Jermaine. You should be immensely proud of yourself,' Chris smiled at Jermaine. For the first time, Jermaine saw Chris as more than just the head of the Hunters. He felt like he was his equal…his friend.

'Jermaine, I want you to follow me, I think it's time that you meet someone."

Jermaine nodded, said goodbye to Jared and followed behind Chris.

As the two walked through the school, Chris didn't say a word. Curiosity started to grow within Jermaine. Who could he be taking him to meet? Why was he the only one meeting the mystery person?

*

The two boys arrived outside the humanities block. Chris stopped walking and turned to face Jermaine.

'As you know, at the end of this year, the other sixth formers and I, will be leaving here to go to University, meaning that the Hunters will need another person to be their frontrunner. As I said before, I want that person to be you.

'I can't force you to take on that responsibility, but I know you can do it. Since I saw you protect Sean, I knew you had what the Hunters need to continue. After yesterday, I'm sure that there couldn't be a better candidate for the position. You showed a lack of concern for your own safety, in order to defeat the foe that was in front of you. That dedication and drive is what a great leader needs.'

'I….I don't know what to say…thank you for believing in me, but why are we here?'

'Follow me.'

The two boys walked over to the door of Jermaine's geography classroom. Chris knocked the door, followed by a voice saying 'come in', and opened it. They saw Mr Balding sat at his desk, marking books.

'Good morning sir' said Chris, pulling up a chair towards the desk. Chris signalled for Jermaine to do the same, which he did.

The two boys sat in front of the desk and Mr Balding closed the book he was working on, then looked up over his glasses.

'So, word is you've been busy.' stated Mr Balding, looking at Jermaine.

Jermaine looked at him, then back to Chris, then at the teacher again. It then clicked to him.

'You're the founder of the Bike Shed Bully Hunters? I heard about you. Craig mentioned something about a rumour that a teacher started the Hunters. So it's true?' questioned Jermaine, with complete surprise on his face.

Jermaine closely inspected the teacher and it all started to make perfect sense. He was small and frail. He looked as if he were probably bullied when he was at school. Who else would start a group that intends to turn the tide on bullies?

'I thought it was essential that the two of you had an official introduction as you may be taking over,' explained Chris, 'Mr Balding is the reason we can exist in this school. He looks out for us.'

'How does he *"look out"* for us?'

Mr Balding leaned forward, he steeped his hands in front of his face, and placed his chin on them, 'Absences, which have been cleared by me, will no longer exist. I have worked out an arrangement to ensure that the faculty will leave you to your own devices, and, any tools or equipment you need to conduct your work more effectively, I will arrange, but that's all dependent on you and your team meeting some basic requirements.

'Firstly, lateness is not tolerated, unless you have a hunt, which requires you to be out of school, in which case, someone will always have to inform me.

'Secondly, grades will have to be maintained. If I notice any of the group falling behind in schoolwork, they will no longer be permitted to leave for any hunts, period.

'Finally, all teachers, at all times, will be shown the up most respect. If I catch wind of any of your team failing to meet these expectations, I'll pull the plug on their special privileges.'

'Did you get all that?' asked Chris, a look of complete seriousness on his face.

'Yeah, that's fine. It seems quite reasonable,' responded Jermaine.

'Good, I look forward to working with you Mr Pearson' said Mr Balding as he stretched out his hand. Jermaine reached out and shook it. Chris then stood up.

'Are you ready for your exams Chris?' asked Mr Balding, turning his attention to Chris.

'As much as I can be. Last minute revision is the order of the day,' replied Chris. This was the first time Jermaine had actually realised that Chris was a student of the school. He'd always known it, but his maturity seemed to overshadow the reality.

'Good, remember, I expect big things from you Chris.'

'Yes sir, I hope to not disappoint,' Chris tapped Jermaine on the shoulder.

Jermaine stood up and looked at Mr Balding.

'I'll see you in class on Monday Jermaine,' said the teacher, as he lowered his head and continued with his marking.

Jermaine and Chris walked outside of the classroom.

'He's a good man. Gave us purpose when we were lost. If you follow the rules and keep to your part of the arrangement, he'll keep to his,' Chris explained. Jermaine nodded to show his understanding. 'I've asked everyone to meet at the training grounds. I assume that they'll all be there waiting to see you especially,' Chris remarked, walking towards it, Jermaine following behind him.

*

After a few minutes, Chris and Jermaine arrived at the training grounds. The rest of the Hunters were already stood there, speaking with each other. Once they noticed Jermaine, each of them began congratulating him on his victory over James, patting him on his back, then apologising after they noticed his look of pain.

Chris walked over to the steps of the scorched building, stood on them and said, in a loud and clear voice, 'Everyone, I don't want to cast a shadow over a reason to rejoice, but, I feel that this needs to be said. I want you all to recognise that this is not the end of all our troubles. James was not the only bully out there that can cause us a problem. I don't want the Hunters to become complacent again.

'Training and continued vigilance is the only thing that will ensure that the Hunters are a constant force to be reckoned with.'

'But where are we going to train? This building is gone. We need somewhere that we can train together,' Sean stated.

'You're right,' Chris said, 'that's why you're going to repair it yourselves. The benefactor of the group has arranged for you to have all the things you need to get the building back to the way it was. No, even better than it was. The building is still sound. New windows and a new roof will be installed by the end of the day, along with paints, brushes and whatever else you may need, then it's down to you all to repaint and decorate it, however it suits you, as it will be yours from now on.'

'You guys aren't going to help us?' Zach asked, surprised.

'We have a lot of cramming to do,' Chris answered, followed by a chorus of depressed sounds coming from the sixth formers, 'Our exams are coming up, and with recent events, we haven't had much time to prepare ourselves. Either way, it will do you all good taking full ownership of the building. Jermaine, you know who to see if you need more supplies.

'This building will be like the phoenix, rising from the ashes. It will take hard work from all of you, but I'm sure that if you put in the effort, you will see the results.'

The group heard the bell for registration ring.

'We leave it in your hands.'

With that, the sixth formers left the training grounds and made their way to their form classes.

The Year 7s turned to Jermaine, who looked back at them, unsure what he should say.

'Ok guys…I guess we meet here after school and get started.'.

35

Sports Day

Over the following weeks, whenever they had completed their training, Jermaine and the other Year 7s spent every break, lunch, and the odd evening, repairing the damage to the training grounds. Whenever they needed more materials, Jermaine would inform Mr Balding, and they would be there within a day. Jermaine wasn't sure how much teachers were paid, but was surprised that Mr Balding could seem to afford all the things he asked for, without batting an eyelid. He realised that there must be a lot more to the teacher than he knew.

Throughout the weeks, the sixth formers would appear sporadically, helping out where they could, but we're hardly seen. Jermaine understood that this was how it would be from now on, just him and the Year 7s. It felt strange and scary, but exciting, all at the same time.

The Year 7s kept an appearance behind the bike shed, in case anyone needed their help. They didn't receive any requests as news of Jermaine's fight with James had spread throughout London, changing as it went along. Some stories consisted of Jermaine defeating all the bullies on his own and knocking James out with a single blow, others had Jermaine defeating an entire school, which was full of bullies and James simply begging for forgiveness before Jermaine even raised a hand.

Regardless of the story, bullies, city wide, had seemed to be less active.

Jermaine also noticed that children just seemed to move out of his way. It was as if the power, which Chris had wielded, had now been passed on to him.

*

The school year was drawing to a close. All of the pupils at St. Peter's were no longer thinking about academics. Instead, their full attention had been diverted towards sports. Jermaine saw more children on the field than he had never seen there before. Some were just enjoying the rays of the sun whilst it lasted, which was never very long in London. Others however, were training.

Sports day was drawing near, the day that everyone showed what they were worth. No matter what group you belonged to, if you had any ability in physical activities, this was the time for you to shine. Jermaine had never really been interested in taking part in sports days in primary school. He didn't see the point. His mum never turned up to support him, and he could never win anything anyway. This year seemed different to him though.

He woke up in the morning, put on his only pair of jogging bottoms, along with the matching jumper, and made his way to school. Whether it was because of the amount of children taking part, the way the day was taken so seriously at St Peter's, the fact that he had been training all year, and felt in the best shape of his life...or a desire to impress someone, Jermaine decided that he would give every activity his all.

'Someone looks ready to show off,' Jermaine heard from beside him. He turned to see Camille stood there, dressed in a tracksuit outfit.

'What do you mean? Everyone is wearing something like this?' Jermaine replied, slightly embarrassed. He had intended to show off...Just a little.

'I'm just messing with you. Geez, you Year 7s have no sense of humour. So where's the rest of your motley crew?'

'Don't know, you're the first person I've seen. Well, the first Hunter I've seen.'

'I know what you meant. Well, have fun. This is always my favourite time of year. I get to use my training for something else than pounding on the face of a bully. Getting loads of Gold Medals is always a pleasure. See you around. Don't go easy on anyone. You've put the training in, you deserve to win something.' Camille said, as she walked away, waving her hand over her head at Jermaine.

Jermaine admitted to himself that he had no intentions of going easy on anyone. He wanted to win. He wanted to finally be a winner at something, not just that odd boy, standing in the corner, watching someone else get recognition for their skills.

He reached into his pocket, pulled out a sheet of paper and unfolded it. He looked at the timetable for what his first activity was.

'Javelin, you're with me,' Sean said, walking up beside Jermaine, 'My class is going after yours.'

'Hey man, you alright? Just looking at when the track and field activities begin.'

'They're not till later, after lunch. I'm excited about those myself. The amount of running we've been doing lately, we're going to destroy it!' Sean declared, a mischievous glint in his eyes. Jermaine could see that Sean was thinking exactly the same thing he was. He wanted to dominate.

The two boys headed over to Javelin together. They took their turns, but didn't do as well as they thought they would have done. They had the strength, but not the technique. Although Jermaine managed to bury a quarter of his first Javelin into the ground, directly in front of him, he managed to finish in fourth position. Sean beat him, coming in third place in his class, and clearing Jermaine's distance by a couple of metres. Jermaine did find it funny that the javelin was actually taller than Sean was.

As they headed to their other activities, they met up with the other new Hunters. Each of them seemed excited about a different activity, and all came with their own stories of success. As a group, they watched the other year groups participate in their sports. The main attractions however, were the sixth form sports. The other Hunters seemed to revel in the joy of using their training to succeed. The twins were amazing at Long Jump, nearly clearing the entire sand pit, without breaking a sweat. High Jump also seemed to have been created purely for the likes of them. Their long legs proved to be a distinct advantage in those sports. Camille excelled at all the strength sports. When she competed in Shot Put and Javelin, crowds formed. Everyone was amazed by the strength that she exerted with such a small frame. Jared didn't seem to have much of an interest in any of the sports. 'I'd rather read a book,' he said, as he sat under a tree, eating a bag of Wotsits.

Jermaine and the new Hunters never saw Chris during the start of the day. When asked where he was, the twins answered, 'He's probably preparing himself for the races. He takes them really seriously. Something about it that he's always loved. You'll probably see him later.'

Even though James had been defeated, and the threat of bullies had subsided to almost nil, Jermaine felt a strange feeling throughout the day. There were a few instances when he felt like someone was watching him. He couldn't put his finger on it, but some form of ominous energy seemed to be surrounding him. From the look of happiness on everyone else's faces, it appeared that nobody else had noticed it.

*

The day was drawing to a close. Jermaine felt that the school must have realised that the biggest draw for the crowds were the races, as they left them all until last. Jermaine hadn't done terribly well throughout the day, but he knew he would definitely succeed in the races. He'd trained his body to run. His stamina and strength training had built his legs up to a point that running felt more natural than walking did now.

The Year 7s were the first to race. Each class had a race alone, to determine who the fastest were. As the Hunters were all in different form classes, they all won their individual races with ease. Jermaine knew that his real challenge would come from the final race, where he would have to face off against Sean, Craig, Zach, and any other boys who had qualified.

It was time for the 100m sprint. All the boys took their positions in their lanes. Jermaine removed his jumper, revealing a vest underneath. His body had been sculpted by his training over the Year, resulting in a physique that even Anton would have been proud of.

The boys crouched down, waiting for the sound of the pistol to tell them to run. Jermaine looked around, taking note of his fellow hunters, all crouched down beside him. They all exchanged wishes of good luck before the race began, but he knew that it was every man for himself once that pistol fired.

BANG!

Jermaine exploded from his starting position. Every muscle in his body released a burst of energy, absorbing every piece of oxygen it could, in order to push himself further and further. Faster and faster. Jermaine tried to block out the other racers, but in the corner of his eyes, he saw someone creeping just ahead of him. Although he didn't mind Sean beating him in Javelin, he was not going to allow another of the Hunters to beat him here. Jermaine lowered his head and pushed his muscles harder than he had ever done before. He could feel his heart smashing against his ribs. It felt as if his legs were tearing at the ground, every time they connected with it. Each second took an eternity, but slowly, nobody was in his peripheral field of view…then he saw something that sent a chill down his spine. There was a boy, wearing small glasses, holding, what looked like a notepad in his hand. There was nothing visually significant about this boy, but Jermaine felt something strange when he saw him…something scared him.

Jermaine slowed for an instant, and out of nowhere, Zach tore ahead, passing the finish line just in front of him. Jermaine slowed himself to a stop, turned around, and started walking through the crowd. Something told him that he had to find that boy. He had to know who he was. After a minute of searching, Jermaine accepted that the boy had gone. The feeling that he was being watched also left him. 'Who was that?' he thought to himself.

'You alright?' Elise asked, finally catching up to Jermaine.

'Yeah, I'm fine, just thought I saw someone. Must have been nothing,' he replied, turning to face Elise.

'Well, good race, you came second. Zach seems to be popular now. Everyone thinks he's Usain Bolt!'

'Yeah, I'll get him next year. He'd better enjoy it whilst he can,' Jermaine joked, trying to dismiss the mystery boy from his mind.

'Hey, looks like you got a little fan club,' Elise pointed out, nodding her head in the direction of a few Year 7 girls, who seemed to be staring at Jermaine. 'Guess all that training has paid off for something else eh?'

Jermaine felt uncomfortable, and flattered, all at the same time.

'Let's go congratulate Zach,' he said, trying to swiftly move away from the girls watching him.

*

The Year 7 female race came, and Elise took first place, which everyone expected. Amita came second, closely behind her. The gap between them and the other girls in the year group was immense. It took a few seconds for the next runner to cross the line after Amita, making the two Hunters feel extremely proud of themselves.

The last race of the day was the sixth form 100m sprint. Jermaine and the other new Hunters stood around, looking for Chris. They eventually saw him approach his lane. He had taken off his t-shirt, revealing a multitude of muscles, scars, and marks. His body resembled that of a soldier, who had been in more battles than years he had lived. Every mark seemed to have its own story. Some form of 'tale' behind it. Chris' face was deadly serious. It resembled the expression he wore when he was walking towards James in the clearing.

Chris stared at the finish line, never averting his gaze from his goal. The twins walked over to the Year 7s and stood next to them, joined by Jared and Camille.

'What's with all the scars?' Craig asked Jared, 'and why aren't any of you racing along with him?'

'None of us are fast enough to get into this race. Just so you know, Chris isn't the only physically capable sixth former at the sprint. There are a couple of really good runners in there with him. Plus, I wouldn't want to get in the way of Chris and his goal. He'll devour you.' Jared then looked down at Craig, 'The scars are from hunts. Sometimes they go without a hitch, but others, they can get messy. Something for you all to remember.'

Chris adopted his starting position, and waited for the pistol.

BANG!

He moved like a machine. Each muscle in his back contorted as he ran. No motion was wasted. He looked on top of his form. Even though Chris was sprinting exceedingly fast, the other runners were keeping in good pace with him. The Year 7s then understood what Jared meant earlier. Only Chris could have any chance of succeeding in this race.

Although it was a close call, Chris tore past the finish line first, steam literally rising off his head. He walked back to his start position, collected his top, and walked over to the rest of the Hunters. To Jermaine's shook, the sixth formers didn't congratulate Chris. It was as if he hadn't run at all, they just talked like nothing happened. The Year 7s may have not understood it, but they followed the example, and went on as normal.

*

The awards ceremony began, and each activity had at least one Hunter on the podium, except the sixth former sprint. Chris wasn't there. The medals were handed out as if Chris had not won. At the back of the crowd, Jermaine saw Chris standing, overlooking the proceedings, and decided that he wanted some answers.

'Hey,' Jermaine said nervously to Camille, 'Why isn't Chris up there getting his medal? He won. He should be recognised for that.'

Camille looked at Jermaine, then smiled. 'He didn't run that race for a medal. I don't even think he was racing the other runners. I think he was racing himself. He ran this race in Year 7 and won. He took the medal, and just gave it away. Never explained himself. That's just Chris. He never wants recognition, just the challenge. That's what makes him the way he is.'

Jermaine contemplated this, and slowly began to understand. At that moment, something Jermaine thought to be impossible happened; his respect for Chris increased.

36

Changing Of The Guard

Eventually, the training grounds were completed. All the old equipment had been replaced with new ones, and the walls had a new vibrant green colour on them. Jermaine figured this would act as a further form of camouflage...and he just liked the colour. The Year 7s had installed some new speed bags, fighting mannequins, along with bars for pull ups and upside down sit ups. Jermaine looked forward to training in there with his group of friends. The building felt more like theirs than it had before. More like home.

*

The final day of the year arrived, and the Hunters gathered at the new training grounds after school.

'You have all worked incredibly hard to rebuild this building and make it even greater than it was before,' declared Chris, 'the bullies can try to destroy what we have, but we rebuild. We rebuild stronger and better than before.

'This was a second home for us Hunters for the past six years, and now we're passing it on to a new set of defenders; Protectors of the weak.

'I want you all to remember that the Bully Hunters aren't just a group, we aren't just kids, we are a thought, a message to any who attempt to prey on those who can't protect themselves. We let them know that justice is swift... and can be extremely painful.'

The group cheered at his final word. The atmosphere was charged with energy.

'Today is the final day for us sixth formers. We leave the name of the Hunters with you all, the next generation of protectors. Take pride in the fact that we couldn't hope for a better group to continue our legacy.'

The Hunters applauded and Chris stepped down. He walked up to Jermaine and whispered in his ear, 'say your first words as the leader of the group.'

Jermaine looked around and saw all eyes were on him. He walked up to the front and stood on the step.

'Hunters... no, friends, I never wanted to join any groups before, mainly because I didn't feel I fitted in with people. I learned to like my own company, as it was all I had, but I'm proud to say that I believe we have all found somewhere we can call home.

'To the sixth formers, no matter where you go, I know I will always regard you as one of us. This is and forever will be your home.'

The new Hunters all clapped and cheered in agreement.

'To my new fellow Hunters, we will continue to be a beacon of hope for those who need us, and a clenched fist to those who force us to use it.'

The Hunters cheered as Jermaine stepped down. They patted him on the back as he walked past, smiles on all of their faces.

*

The Hunters left the training grounds, making their way to the front of the school.

The sixth formers stood still, looking at the building, as the new Hunters watched them.

'Well, that's the end of an era. I'm going to miss this place,' Jared explained, his voice wobbling, as if he were about to cry.

'Stop being a big girl!' Camille teased, as she punched Jared on the arm.

The Hunters said goodbye to each other, wishing each a good summer, planning to meet up with each other in a few days.

Jermaine noticed Chris standing alone, looking at the building.

He walked over to him, 'It's all yours now. Take care of it.' Chris extended his hand, which Jermaine took, and shook. He then pulled Jermaine in and embraced him. After a moment, he let go, smiled at Jermaine, and then began to walk away with the other sixth formers.

The new hunters walked over to Jermaine and stood beside him, watching the sixth formers leave. They all then noticed Camille reach out and hold onto Chris' hand.

'Why is she holding his hand?' Craig asked, his voice sounding extremely perplexed.

'What do you mean? They're dating,' Elise stated.

Jermaine, Zach, Sean and Craig looked at one another, the same shocked expression on all their faces.

'How did you know?' Sean asked.

'Girls talk,' Amita said.

'You knew too?' Jermaine asked.

'You know what, it makes a few things make more sense actually,' Zach said.

'Boys, eh?' Elise said to Amita, and the two of them laughed.

'Everyone, we'll need to meet up during the holidays to train. We need to make sure that we're prepared for whatever comes next year. We won't have the sixth formers to help us out anymore, it'll be all on us,' Jermaine stated.

The group agreed, and arranged to meet up in a week on the field to begin their new regime. They each said their goodbyes. Jermaine walked behind them, a feeling of pride and happiness overwhelming him.

*

Jermaine stood at the bus stop with Elise.

'Is it just me, or does it feel weird that we're actually the Bike Shed Bully Hunters now?' Elise asked Jermaine, a smile on her face.

'It is strange. I don't think it's truly sunk in yet.'

The two stood at the bus stop, and could see a 92 bus at the traffic lights down the road.

'This is me today. Have to go to my grandparents tonight. So, what do you think about Camille and Chris? Do you think two Hunters dating works?'

'I don't know. It didn't seem to affect them, so I guess it can work. Why do you ask anyway? Did you want to ask one of the guys out or something?' Jermaine asked, secretly hoping Elise would say no.

Elise laughed, as the bus pulled up, 'No, I was asking for your sake. It's quite obvious that you like me. Anyway, I'll see you next week,' Elise grinned, waving to Jermaine, chuckling to herself.

Jermaine stood at the bus stop, utterly stunned. He thought for a moment. He then looked at his reflection in the bus stop window and admitted to himself, 'Maybe I do.'

Epilogue

The boy with small glasses walked out from beside St Peter's. He placed a phone to his ear, and waited.

'Hello sir. Yes sir, they've left, it's just the New Bloods now. I know sir, James was a disappointment, but he did manage to allow us to gain some insight into these new Hunters. With that information, dealing with them shouldn't be as difficult as before.

'I do have something in mind. Yes sir, it should prove to be quite effective. Don't worry sir, the Hunters will not last very long. Things will return to the way they should be.

'Thank you sir. Definitely. I will keep you informed. Goodbye sir.'

He lowered the phone from his ear, placed it inside his pocket, adjusted his glasses, and walked away from St Peter's.

The End

Keep an eye out for the second book in the series;

BIKE SHED

BULLY HUNTERS:

BLACK SHEEP

COMING SOON